Clear Light of Day

Copyright Stephen Jones 2017 (all rights reserved)

This book is fiction however many of the places referred to, do exist; characters are not based on any one person and any similarity is coincidental. The procedures described in the SHU of Corymbia Prison, mirror those of Special Handling Units in maximum security prisons in Western Australia.

The names of Australian Naval personnel and vessels have been changed to protect the security of those working in the Australian Defence Force. The capabilities and specification of the patrol boats are accurate, as are the details concerning the 'private contractor's equipment' and vessels used.

This is **book four** in the **'Maximum Security' series**.

I would like to dedicate this book to those who encouraged me; who read my other books in this series, who gave me constructive criticism; those who stood by me despite being unsure about my endeavours.

Chapter One

David sat at the breakfast bar chewing thoughtfully on a mouthful of cereal, he had a new mobile phone in front of him on the stone bench top surface. Next to it was the old phone, and he had just loaded 'Smart Switch' onto both devices and was in the process of transferring the data from the old phone to the new one.

A message appeared on the display informing him that in twenty minutes his new phone would effectively be 'cloned' and would look and operate like his old phone. He had been putting off this task since buying the new phone a few days earlier. Fifteen minutes later the operation was completed using the home Wi-Fi network and David slipped the SIM card from the old phone into the new one and booted it up. He continued playing with it, trying to work out how to mute the sound when Natalie waddled into the kitchen.

"Hi babe." he said, "Sorry did I disturb you when I got up?"

Natalie was eight and a half months pregnant, she was not sleeping well and was feeling irritable and uninformed. It had only been a couple of weeks since she had taken maternity leave and Matt Roberts had stepped up into her position as Superintendent of Corymbia maximum security prison. Matt was doing as he had been told and was keeping Natalie firmly 'out of the loop'. She understood and appreciated it really, but she had never had to rest so much in her life and it was frustrating her far more than she thought it would. First, as the bump got bigger, she had to abandon her uniform, and then the department had ordered her not to enter the prison itself, as they wanted to protect her from any danger the inmates might pose. It was odd as the opposite was probably the case. She had a remarkable calming effect on most inmates; who seemed to become compliant immediately when they saw her and gave the impression they were in awe of her. Now she was on leave and when the baby came, David would take paternity leave as well.

Just a couple of months previously they had been jet-setting around the world for her brother Frank's wedding in Kenya and in another month he and his wife Endana would be visiting them and their new nephew.

Part of her frustration was that her leave would not just be 'a maternity break,' and then a return to work. The plan, which was firming up nicely, was that they would both then take a whole year of unpaid leave. David had been offered a job by Frank's friend Billy, which would mean travelling back and forth between East Africa and Western Australia, whilst overseeing business for Billy. Frank was going to work alongside David on a part time basis. They were all very excited about the prospect of this new chapter in their lives. Natalie secretly believed; that they probably wouldn't return to work in the prison again. She knew this was the right move for now, but also wasn't sure how she would feel in the future. It was a wise thing that they could 'test the waters' first, and a year out would give them more clarity about the future. 'You only have grace for the present', she kept reminding herself.

"No, I was awake when you got up" she said holding her tummy. "This young man seems to want to play Aussie rules football in the early hours of the morning, and if he grows up to be anything like last night he'll be on a winning team for sure." She smiled at David. After nearly two years of marriage, he was still the focus of her affections. She knew every inch of his features and the expressions his face made, she often thought she could read his mind when she saw them. Then there was the way his smile created dimples in only one cheek, the little tuft of hair next to the thin scar line, where the hair would no longer grow; she paused and took a deep breath. Every time she saw the scar she was reminded of the shot ringing out and seeing David lying in a pool of blood. She refocused and saw his clear, bright blue eyes that lit up her day staring back at her. She knew he felt the same way and was just as excited about their baby, who would soon be with them.

"I was just thinking about my leaving drinks this afternoon; you sure you'll be ok if I stay a couple of hours later?" he asked looking concerned. She felt the large expansion she was carrying, still all front and centre; keeping her figure looking trim from the back.

"Yes, no worries" she said smiling. "I know he's 'dropped,' but I'm not going to give birth just yet. There's a couple more weeks to go before there is any risk of that."

David had to plan his leaving party early due to staff leave arrangements and everyone wanting to be there.

"Ok, I'll be back by five thirty" he said, and walked over to the sink to wash up the dishes.

"Leave them for me" Natalie said, "I'm going 'mental' here, for things to do."

David kissed her; it was long and lingering. A kiss that promised more but that would have to wait. "Love you babe" he said.

"Love you too" said Natalie after him.

David walked into the garage and opened the door with his remote control. He lifted his helmet off the bike's gear lever, and his jacket off the backrest. He pulled the jacket on, and now anyone looking could see the patches he'd sown to the back. 'Prayer, the ultimate wireless connection'; 'Remember when bikes were dangerous and sex was safe?' and 'Loud pipes save lives!' Balled in the helmet were his gloves, he took them out and placed them with the helmet on the rear back rest and reached down to the registration plate. The number plate was mounted to a Grifter storage box. A 7x4x2 inch box made of durable polypropylene, it was almost invisible behind the registration plate. It was a discreet, lockable, weather-resistant storage compartment perfect for storing items like a mobile phone or your registration and insurance documents or some small tools. It was so secure and unnoticeable he knew people who put cash and keys in them. Working in the prison, he also knew inmates that had concealed drugs in them, or left the box open to lower the plate, so that it couldn't be seen by cameras or Police speed traps.

David took his mobile phone and switched the Bluetooth on, and then returned it to his pocket. He placed the helmet on his head and activated the Sena SMH10 communicator on the left side of the helmet. It spoke softly to him in a woman's voice, "Hello" and moments later, "You are now connected to a Bluetooth device".

David liked his gadgets and the motorcycle had a security device attached to it that allowed him to merely be in the proximity of the bike, and its alarms would automatically deactivate. He didn't even need a key to start the bike, that too was part of the technology. Some of his friends had teased him about his love of technology, "What if it breaks down?" someone at church had said to him when he was explaining the system to them. David had memorised the pass key though, and which controls to tap in sequence to override the electronic security system, so he wouldn't be inconvenienced in any event.

He sat astride the 2016 model Harley-Davidson Softail

Breakout. A bike that he had saved several years for, and he just enjoyed the moment. Harley-Davidson certainly had a reputation for incorporating modern technology with classic design elements from the past, and this was perfect for David.

Everything on the bike was either chromed or painted black, with the black accents on the lower fork legs and mufflers giving the bike a little flavour of yesteryear. Little bullet lights keeping the rear end looking clean. The lights were all-in-one, with the tail light, brake light and turn signal all contained within. True, they were small and had several jobs to perform, but with the LED lights it got the job done easily. Harley had taken this air cooled, twin cam Softail, and separated it from the family at birth; they took the frame and gave the steering head a 35-degree rake, more than any other Softail had. This stretched the overall length of the bike to over 96 inches, this with a 67 inch wheelbase, made it the longest Softail that Harley built. But honestly, nobody would notice the bling once they beheld the massive 240/40 R18 rear tyre. The long wheelbase and big rear tyre made the bike handle a little 'differently' in the corners, but what it lacked in the corners it made up for in the straights!

The length of the bike and the low seat height made it look long, low and mean! David didn't think anyone who had any sense would mess with this bike. Many of the 'Bikies' or Outlaw Motorcycle Gangs (OMCG); some of whom were housed in Corymbia Prison rode 'Harleys' and they were known to be most unforgiving, even if David was! The bike had cost David four months' salary in total, and he loved it. The reason it had taken so long to save for the bike, was that David recognised that there were more important priorities for his money; and he operated a rule of 'obligations, needs and lastly wants'. He supported several charities, and gave through his church to many projects that literally made life better, for others so much less fortunate than himself.

This had been playing on his mind recently and he wondered if he should let the bike go. He wouldn't be able to ride it so much if he was out of the country anyway. Natalie would give birth soon and although she would never say so, David was sure that she would be more concerned for him as a father, on a large powerful bike. Natalie hadn't been able to ride for a while due to the baby, and when the little fellow arrived, it would be an impractical toy. He had been mulling it over in his mind, and he was sure that he would be able to get a good price for it. He decided to chat to Helen at the Harley shop in a couple of weeks, when it was due for a service.

David turned the ignition knob, pushed the starter and the bike fired up with a bang followed by a deep throbbing rumble. He did what he always did and prayed for safety on the road, not because he ever 'tempted an accident' by driving badly, but because of the other idiots on the road. He revved the engine as he pulled away, thinking 'at least they will hear me coming'.

Chapter Two

David arrived at the prison and after parking his bike in the usual spot, he stored his Swiss Army knife and USB data drive in his gloves, pushing them into the helmet which he then rested on the bike's gear lever.

He walked towards the imposing gate house, which was set into the high embankment, on top of which were two razor sharp fences which ran around the whole prison site. The service road between them was patrolled by armed TRG officers in vans. Below, in the gate house, staff arriving passed through the double bulletproof doors and walked through the lobby, past the 'Cashier's office' to the scanners where they showed their photo identification, and then placed everything in their possession on the trays; in much the same way as 'airport security' lines passengers up, and makes them pass through security checkpoints. The difference being that there were many more items that were not allowed into the prison, even for personal use by staff. No: mobile phones, laptops, USB thumb drives, alcohol, drugs, or spare clothing to name just a few of the items on the lists displayed at the gate - along with the notices about the penalties that disobedience to the rules carried.

The staff stepped through a metal detector one at a time, which had a habit of 'randomly' lighting the blue light, and any person that happened to had to submit to a full body rub down search.

This morning the alarm and blue light seemed to be 'going off' on every other person, and the gate house staff whose job it was to screen, search and interview those entering, had tired of this and were waving staff through the gate, saying, "It's broken." The Gate staff also employed 'sniffer dogs' in an 'airlock' section between another set of bulletproof glass doors, effectively trapping staff in this area. They knew this would expose any drugs being brought in, and so were not concerned too much with the random blue light this morning. Maintenance would fix the light soon enough, the metal detector was still working.

Many of the staff, when they had begun to work at Corymbia Prison thought that this process was too rigorous but after a short while it became normal. Visitors attending Corymbia were segregated and identified, then interviewed and given a biometric tests to prove their identity with an eye / iris scan and finger printing, or both They passed through a separate metal detector, body scan and pat down search before entering another 'airlock', and finally being allowed into the prisoner visit area.

The 'day staff', which included Vocational Skills Officers, Administration staff and Educators, like David, found themselves waiting in front of more bulletproof glass through which the West Sally Port was visible, and the inspection pits and mirrors which were installed to fully view any vehicle that passed though.

David couldn't help glancing at the repaired glass, where a bullet had ricochet and hit him. He started to reach up to touch the scar on his head but deliberately stopped himself, as he had many times over the past few months and thought, 'I must break this habit or I will forever be bound by the trauma of the memory.' He was no longer having nightmares about being hit by the stray bullet, which was a result of an officer shooting himself, when stopped from entering the prison. It still featured from time to time in dreams though.

Another door opened automatically, operated by the TRG officers, and staff were able to access the personal alarms.

Every alarm was unique to an individual and correlated with the number on the keys, which only they could draw. Constant surveillance of both visitors and staff was observed by the TRG officers during this process, and occasionally they were known to make ID challenges even on staff that they knew. This had become even more so since Natalie had got back from her mission to the Congo, where she had used her knowledge of security procedures to break her brother out of a prison. She had help of course, in fact it had been David's idea in the first place. Upon her return; as Superintendent she had tightened up security in her prison, and closed the loop holes in procedure that had enabled them to recover Frank so easily from Goma's prison.

Once inside the prison, officers attended the morning debrief and confirmed their daily duty schedule before going to relieve the night staff, who had unlocked and allowed the inmates to take breakfast in the 'day rooms' on each wing of the units. The medical staff had been dispatched and were doing the rounds to each unit and dispensing 'early meds' and issuing lists to attend the Infirmary later.

The muster count was then phoned in from each unit and confirmed against the central tallies; lists were then drawn up, from 'scheduled appointments' to the daily required workers. The lists were checked against alerts on each prisoner to ensure safe conduct during the movement, and the 'protected prisoners' in Unit 6 were lined up to be escorted to their work places and education; at that time there was no other movement of any other prisoners taking place, such was the sensitivity of their status.

David walked through the lobby collecting a radio at the small booth on the right, before going on into the prison. He missed walking in with Natalie and giving her hand a quick squeeze at this point before parting to enter the prison itself, and then making his way past the chapel and the Psych's programme department to Education.

Upon reaching the Education department, he opened the large gate with one of his keys and then locked it behind him. He then unlocked and opened the door to the Control area. From this position the whole prison could be observed. He placed his name tag next to his office number on the board and then exited and locked the control room door again. He was first in this morning, and there were no prisoners in the area yet; in fact, there didn't seem to any staff in the area either. He thought it was odd, but they may well have taken an extra five minutes in the tea room, so he decided not to be concerned yet.

He made his way across the garden to his office and unlocked his office door and went inside. He saw the answerphone message light flashing and wondered if someone was calling in sick. He left the door slightly open knowing that whoever was in next would probably pop in to say 'hello', and he wasn't disappointed; as soon he saw the petite figure of Meredith Jones, with her straightened black hair, brushed into a stylish swirl. Meredith was in her late twenties, and had taken on David's teaching load when he became the manager of the Education Centre.

"Hi Meredith" he called out. Meredith looked up and seeing the door slightly ajar she pushed it open and stepped into David's office.

"Hi Boss" she said, mimicking the way a prisoner might address the manager. She smiled displaying a wide set of white teeth and David grinned back.

"You've settled in well," he said.

"Right at home" she fired back, settling into this morning's banter. "Going to do a full search of the computer network this morning" she said, "I found some rather unsavoury pictures on one of the inmate accounts yesterday. I'm not sure where they came from but I think we need to find out."

David took in the information and then asked, "Called security yet?"

"Not yet, I want to know where they have come from first. They may be part of the Wikipedia off-line download, that 'computer support' put on last week."

Meredith replied, "We don't want to embarrass ourselves now, do we?"

David thanked her and asked her to keep him informed, knowing that security preferred to know sooner rather than later in these matters. He thought though that she was right in protecting the centre, and if it was a 'self-inflicted' problem, then they could uninstall the offending software.

Soon the full complement of staff were in and the work of the day began. Prisoners were escorted to Education, searched and sent to classes where the tutors ran their lessons in a 'no nonsense' fashion. David ate lunch with his staff, but as they had become accustom to him disappearing to have lunch with Natalie, the conversation seemed guarded around him.

"Lighten up guys" He said, "I know I'm the boss and all, but I'm not the Superintendent." The staff smiled at the irony and relaxed.

"Sorry David" said Tracey. "It's just that it's funny. We don't see a lot of you, then we see lots of you, and we know in a couple of weeks you will be away for ages." Her eyes had filled with tears, and David tried to move the conversation along and smooth over the emotions that he felt as well.

Finally, at the end of the day, the inmates were counted out of the Education Centre and escorted back to their units. All the staff left together and made their way past the Outcare building and Visitor's Centre, towards the bike shed. David opened the Grifter box and retrieved his phone and wallet, placing them in his jacket pocket.

"Nice bike" said Meredith as David got on. "Want to buy it?" said David, "I'll give you a good price" he added. Meredith laughed and held her arms out by way of saying what all could see. Her legs would not be able to reach the ground if she sat astride the big bike.

"See you there" said David as he started the bike and swung it out of the shed.

The leaving party had been arranged at the 'Hole in One' golf club near the prison, and so David didn't bother to switch on his Sena SMH10 communicator. He pulled into the Golf club carpark three minutes later and parked the bike, near the function centre where the staff would meet. It was a secure location with a mechanical bar-gate, so David left his helmet on the gear lever and hung his jacket on the backrest as he did in the prison carpark.

Selwyn and Charlotte were already waiting for him as he walked in, "What can I get you?" Selwyn shouted from the bar. Charlotte stood at a table nearby and met David with a big hug.

"Light beer" called David over Charlotte's shoulder.

"How's Natalie?" Charlotte asked.

"Doing very well" said David, "Just feels a bit big and uncomfortable all the time. No patter of tiny feet for you yet?" She looked at him with an expression that left David feeling he'd been reproved. 'Security personnel must be taught that look,' he thought.

The remaining staff arrived soon after and treated David to a few more drinks and called on him to say a few words, which he did whilst trying to keep the mood light. He reminded them that he would still be around for another couple of weeks, so this wasn't 'goodbye' despite the fact that he would be away for a while.

The party continued with members of staff expressing their appreciation for David and then eventually people started to leave. Selwyn and Charlotte being the first; wishing David well and asking him to convey their love to Natalie.

Soon there were just a few folks left and David said as he got up to leave, that he would see them after the weekend and wished them all well. He walked towards the function room exit, thinking about the number of drinks he'd had, and the number he'd refused. Counting alcohol units and calculating that he was probably safe to ride.

Chapter three

Natalie was getting worried. It was now six thirty pm and David wasn't home. 'He said he'd be back an hour ago' she thought. She had been through the 'I don't want to fuss' thoughts, and then had tried to call him to say, 'it was fine if he wanted to stay later.' The phone was off though and her call went straight through to an answer-phone. Now she was feeling a bit cross and upset and was thinking that she might let David know about it, in no uncertain terms, when he got home.

She had just started to pace again, when she heard a car pull up onto the driveway. She breathed out heavily and thought, 'he's had to get a lift home, the lightweight.'

She walked towards the front door and could see someone standing there, so she paused expecting David to open the door himself, but he didn't. Then the doorbell rang. She marched to the door, now her frustration was building. She pulled open the door and was about to give David a piece of her mind, when she saw two policemen standing before her.

Suddenly time seemed to slow down; she saw a 'look' pass between the officers and immediately knew something was wrong. She felt confused by what she saw, and felt a pang of fear hit her deep in the pit of her stomach.

She could hear one of them speaking now, "Mrs Natalie James?" The question just hung in the air.

"Yes" she heard herself say.

"May we come in please?" The second officer was now saying.

Natalie looked at them and said "No!" The Police officers looked at each other again and said, "Please may we come in? We have to inform you of some tragic news... "

Natalie felt faint, she didn't know why; she hadn't been told what the news was. She thought, 'It could be anything couldn't it?' but really, she knew by the look on these police officers faces that someone had died, and David wasn't home as he should have been.

One of the officers took the initiative and steadied Natalie and just walked her back into the house. The other followed and after they had sat Natalie on the settee, they said, "Mrs James, I'm so sorry to have to inform you that your husband has been involved in a motorcycle accident." He took a breath and Natalie interrupted him, "Is David alright?" she asked, knowing in her heart he wasn't.

She felt a wave of nausea and pain fill her as she heard the officer say, "No, I'm sorry Mrs James, he died at the scene."

The second officer placed some items on the table in front of Natalie, and she looked at them. They were so familiar to her. David's wallet and phone, undamaged, just sitting there on the table as if he'd placed them there himself. She felt tears welling up and she pushed them down again. She had to control this, there would be time for grief later. The first officer was saying something, she tried to listen, but there seemed to be a time lag, in what she was hearing.

"Mrs James, we need you to make a formal identification of the body." Then he said, "It doesn't have to be now, but you will have to as next of kin, some-time soon, certainly in the next few days."

The second officer was asking if there was anyone he could call for her, so she wouldn't be alone. Natalie thought for a moment. She thought Jack would know what to do, but she heard herself say, "Charlotte Hooper." She felt like she was in some dream, or on a remote-control ride and things were just happening that she could no longer control. Her choice of person to help her at this moment even, seemed to be pre-chosen for her.

The police made the call after getting Charlotte's number and explained the situation to her.

"She's coming right over now" said the police officer, as he passed her the phone, "she wants to talk to you."

Charlotte was in shock and was blinking back the tears as she said, "I only saw him an hour or so ago. He was fine then."

The officers made Natalie a cup of tea, and stayed with her whilst she drank it. Natalie was clearly not doing well and the grief was starting to flow past her filters of professionalism. She stood and started to walk towards the bathroom, saying, "I'm fine, I just need to go to the toilet." She got half way across the room when she realised she wasn't fine and she turned back to the police officers who were now on their feet staring.

"Call an ambulance" she said, "My waters have broken." Then everything went black and she crumpled to the floor.

Natalie woke in the ambulance with paramedics around her. The police were nowhere to be seen. The paramedic by her side said, "It's ok; the baby's ok and you are ok. You are on your way to Fiona Stanley Hospital. The cops said your friend had been informed and will meet you there."

The Ambulance, with its white, blue and red lights flashing without the siren, brought Natalie swiftly to the hospital where she was processed quickly through the emergency department, before then being transferred to the 'Maternity' unit. Here she was wheeled into a labour suite and attached to various machines and monitors. 'Just lie back and let it all happen' she thought, and then for the first time, she realised that she hadn't felt alone. Sure, a whole lot of emotions were going on, but she was now acutely aware that there was a peaceful presence in the room with her. It wasn't just the soft music and quiet atmosphere, there was someone here with her. It was spiritual. The verse of scripture that had sustained her brother during his recent trial came to mind, *"All things work together for good, to those who love God."* Frank had not known how God could work his problem for good at the time, and Natalie certainly couldn't think that any good could come of this situation. However, there was no doubt that this truth was imposing itself on her situation.

Suddenly the quiet was interrupted with the arrival of Charlotte Hooper. The two, security trained, professional prison officers, became the young girls that they really were and wept in each other's arms.

Soon practicality took over, and along with various nurses and midwives and the labour continued. Natalie found that she was both in a lot of pain and quite high on the 'gas and air' mixture she was breathing, to counter the pain of the contractions. She could see that there was someone pulling Charlotte away from the side of the bed. Then she watched as Charlotte ran out of the room. Natalie couldn't make sense of any of it and then a man who looked like David in a hospital gown came into the room. It looked just like David wearing surgical scrubs. None of the staff paid any attention to him. They seemed to ignore him. Was it possible that David had been allowed by God to return to see her one last time? To see his son born? Could it be, or was it just all in her imagination? The last thing she remembered hearing was, "She is in distress. There is a complication. Natalie, we are going to have to operate and deliver the baby via C section." As she slipped under the anaesthetic she called, "David!" and heard him clearly say, "I'm here babe, I'm here."

When Natalie woke she felt very sore and could see the bump of her tummy had flattened considerably. Charlotte was sitting by the bed in a chair, asleep.

"What time is it?" asked Natalie.

Charlotte woke with a start and leaned forward, "Thank God you're alright" she said, "I don't even pretend to understand what the problem was, but we nearly lost you."

"Yes. I thought so" said Natalie. "I saw David!" She started to cry.

Charlotte held her hand and said, "Yes it's lovely that he made it to the birth. You have no idea how much trouble it was to get him there."

Natalie looked strangely at her friend and said, "You saw him to?"

"Yes" said Charlotte and suddenly realised that Natalie hadn't been told.

"Oh Natalie!" she said, tears suddenly running down her cheeks, "He's ok, he's alive, he really is alive. They wouldn't let him in to the labour suite as he had no ID on him." She choked back tears and took a breath. "And I went to see if it was true, and I had to tell them that I'd have them all arrested if they didn't let him in, and then they did, and then I wasn't allowed to come back, and then you needed a 'C section' and then...." Charlotte laughed with relief and Natalie stared in disbelief and said, "Where is he?"

Chapter Four

David had walked out of the function centre exit and discovered to his horror that his bike was not where he'd left it. He stopped and stared at the empty space. Anger rose in him and he reached for his phone, realising as he did so that he'd left it in his jacket pocket with his wallet. He turned around and walked back into the function centre and met Meredith on her way out. She was reaching into her bag to retrieve her keys and nearly bumped into David.

"Oh!" she exclaimed. Then looking at David's expression, "What's wrong?"

Meredith listened as David told her his bike had been stolen and asked her if he could borrow her mobile phone. David looked at his watch and saw it was five fifteen. He decided he wasn't late so he'd call the police and then Natalie to let her know what had happened. Five minutes later he was still trying to get through to the Police. He thought about calling the emergency number, but as inconvenient as this was, it wasn't an emergency.

"Can you give me a lift please?" he asked Meredith.

"No problem David" she replied, and she walked over to a metallic bronze Toyota 86 which was parked close by.

"Nice" said David, repaying her compliment of earlier. Meredith opened the car with the remote and slid in behind the steering wheel. She then slid the seat closer to the wheel until she was pressed up against it. She looked back at David who had done the exact opposite and pushed the seat back, giving himself more leg room.

She smiled. "Only way to reach the peddles" she said with a shrug.

David gave Meredith directions towards home and then called the Police again. There was still no answer, so he asked Meredith if she wouldn't mind diverting to Armadale Police station, which she was happy to do. When they got to the Police station there was such a queue of people that David said, "Typical Friday night! Leave me here and go on home. I'll be fine." Meredith wasn't sure about leaving David in Armadale, but he persuaded her that he'd get a taxi home if necessary. It was only after Meredith had left that David realised that he didn't have any way to contact Natalie.

He waited in the busy Police station, feeling more and more frustrated. He nearly gave up but he knew the Police would want to know why he'd not reported the theft immediately. It was six thirty by the time he was able to see a civilian Police officer, who wasn't very helpful at all. David was repeatedly asked to show identification, which he patiently explained had been stolen along with his bike. It seemed that nothing could be done without first being identified.

"This is ridiculous" he exclaimed at one point, "How can I give you ID, if I've come to report it stolen!"

"I thought you said it was your bike that was stolen sir?" said the officer.

"Yes, that too" said David.

"Well which is it?" asked the officer.

"Both" said David now on the verge of losing his temper. "Look I need to call my wife, she'll be worried about me. Have you got a phone I can use please?"

The civilian policeman was less than helpful, saying there were pay phones outside which he could use. David tried to explain that he had no money or credit cards; "Or phone or bike" said the unsympathetic police officer. It was now six forty-five and David tried to find a phone that was working, but they were either broken or would only work with a credit card. David thought how ironic it was to have a phone that wouldn't work without some means of payment even if you had to make a reverse charge call. He went back to the Police station and walked to the front of the queue. He was angry now and ignored the shouts, to get to the back of the line.

There were two officers handling enquiries now and so David waited for a female civilian policewoman to finish with her 'customer', and then stepped up and asked her if she could help. She began to tell him to go to the back of the queue, but David explained that he'd been there and done that and went on to tell her about his frustrating end to the day.

"ID please" she said as she got the report form and a pen; she then looked at David's exasperated expression and said, "Sorry, force of habit."

David filled the forms and made his statement, and then the woman gave him her mobile and he called home. The phone rang and rang but was not answered. David looked at his watch, it was now seven - ten, and David was worried. He called Natalie's mobile but that went unanswered as well.

Now he was upset and stuck in Armadale without a way to get home. He was about to call a taxi, when the police woman returned to the counter. She had a tired and concerned expression on her face.

"We've cross checked the registration and found your bike Mr James" she began, and went on, interrupting David's comments about that being a good thing... "It's a real mess and the rider's dead. Huge accident with a 'semi.'"

David took the information in and then thought, 'well that takes care of next week's service and selling it I suppose.' He tried not to think of the dead thief or the broken bike.

"Can you call me a taxi please?" he asked. "We'll do better than that sir" she said, "We'll take you to the hospital where your wife is having a baby. I have someone bringing a car round now. Please just wait outside."

David was confused for a moment, and then it made sense. He wasn't able to contact her. She would have tried to contact him, but of course not been able to. The police officer passed him a copy of the report for the insurance, and said they would send an addendum along confirming the bike had been found, and it's condition.

David left the Police station and jumped into the car that had just pulled up alongside the curb. Thirty minutes later the police car was outside the maternity unit of Fiona Stanley hospital. He got out and the car drove away.

Reaching the secure maternity unit, he pressed the buzzer to be allowed in.

"Please identify yourself" came the disembodied voice.

"David James. You have my wife Natalie in one of your labour suites." The door buzzed and opened when David pushed it. He walked in and up to a desk where a sour faced woman behind it held out a pudgy hand and demanded, "ID please!"

David fought to keep his temper and cover the stress he was feeling. It was no use though, it looked like he was going to have a repeat of the Police station again. Suddenly there was a commotion and he saw several nurses and a doctor run into one of the labour suites. He turned back to the receptionist and said, "If you don't show me where my wife is right now, I will go look for her myself."

The woman narrowed her eyes and then pressed an alarm button. Within half a minute, two large security men were standing by David and one was asking him to leave. David was completely overwhelmed and was now feeling on the verge of taking the matter into his own hands. He recalled the combat training he'd received at the weapons and tactics day, and turned to look at the security guards, with a view to defending himself, suddenly and with force.

Then he heard one of the security men say, "David James? Hey I know you." then he turned to receptionist and said, "Did you even check to see if his wife was here?" The receptionist lowered her eyes and looked embarrassed.

David tried to place the man who had identified him. He thought he might have been a prison officer at some point, yes, he was one of the ODP crew from a year ago. "Tony? Is that you?" said David. "Such a bitch" muttered Tony looking at the receptionist, then, "Yes mate, how's the head?" The other guard now released his grip on David's arm and said to the receptionist, "Which suite?"

The receptionist looked unwilling but gave up the information, and the guard went to check the suite and came back with Charlotte Hooper. Charlotte dissolved into tears at the sight of David and hugged him so tightly as she explained what had happened. David said that he'd not been told any of the details, and added, "No wonder I got a Police escort here." He was glad when Tony took him to the labour suite, but sad that only one of them could be with Natalie. Charlotte said that she would stay at the hospital and wait for the birth. David was then given surgical scrubs and told to go in but stay out of the way.

Chapter Five

"Where is he?" Natalie repeated.

"He took my car and went home to get some things for you, he'll be back any minute. I'm sure," said Charlotte.

Within ten minutes David entered with an overnight bag, which had not been picked up by the ambulance or Police at the house. Tears of relief and joy flowed again.

"I am so sorry," said David.

"You couldn't have known," said Natalie.

"They didn't tell him anything" chipped in Charlotte.

"What a way to begin the weekend" said David, "At least I got my phone and wallet back. I found them on the table in the sitting room. I also identified Meredith's phone number from the calls I made on it and sent her a message thanking her and explaining the events of the evening. I told her that I wouldn't be in on Monday as my paternity leave was going to start then!"

Natalie smiled as she registered the last piece of information. 'They were now a family on holiday' she thought.

"I was glad I'd got my wallet back, as the receptionist actually asked me for ID again on the way in" said David, looking at Charlotte.

"Un-be-lievable!" exclaimed Charlotte. Then to Natalie's puzzled expression, "Never mind, you don't want to know!"

"Have you seen him?" asked Natalie.

"Not properly, they only let me hold him for a moment after they delivered him" said David, "They checked him over and said he was fine."

Charlotte said, "They told me they were bringing him up for a feed soon." Natalie and David looked at Charlotte as she continued, "Well they tried to throw me out a couple of times, that is until I said I was your sister, then they seemed happy to let me know whatever I wanted." She looked guiltily at Natalie.

"Well, you are!" said Natalie, "Sister in arms!" "That's what I figured" said Charlotte.

They laughed and then fell silent.

"Your bike" said Natalie sadly.

David took a breath, "Just a bike" he said unconvincingly. "Still, I was planning to sell it soon, and given the circumstances of today, it's the least of our worries." Natalie smiled at David and squeezed his hand.

It wasn't long before David and Natalie's baby was wheeled in to the room and the nurse handed him to her, "Have you thought of names yet?" asked the nurse. Natalie was thoroughly absorbed as she looked at her son, she thought, 'he's amazing, and I love him even though this is the first time I'm meeting him.' Then suddenly remembering everyone else in the room, she was 'brought back to the present'. She thought for a moment and then said, "We've thought of a few but I think we *have* to settle on..." "Nathan" both she and David said together. The nurse smiled and wrote the name on the baby's ankle ID; adding it to the typed label which read, 'baby James – mother Natalie James': and then left explaining that the breakfast round would take place soon, and that Charlotte and David could get food at the cafe, on the ground floor.

When she had gone, Charlotte said, "Lovely name, but why do you '*have'* to pick that name?"

David explained that they had thought of a few names and considered their meanings. Nathan was one of the oldest names of all the choices they'd agreed on. "It meant 'to give' in Hebrew" he said.

"Wow" said Charlotte, "you've been given a baby, sure." Then she looked at Natalie nursing the baby at her breast and said, "but I can see you've also been given David back. Good choice. It also has a nice ring to it, 'Nathan James.' Now if I have a daughter...." She laughed along with Natalie who said, "Getting 'clucky' now?"

David tried to return the look Charlotte had given him at his leaving party the night before and failed miserably adding to the hilarity and laughter of the girls.

Nathan would now stay in the room with Natalie until she was discharged, and having been washed and changed, he smelled clean and new.

David was in a thoughtful mood and said quietly, "My mum used to say, 'a baby is a long tube, with a loud noise at one end, and absolutely no sense of responsibility at the other." Charlotte laughed and said, "She'll be excited to be a grandmother, won't she." There was silence in the room and Natalie said, "She would have been, I'm sure she would have been."

Charlotte looked awkwardly at David. "Yes, she would have been delighted to see this day." There was no need to say more; it was obvious that she wasn't able to, as she'd died before David had even met Natalie.

"I'm so sorry David" said Charlotte. "It's ok" he replied. "I'm sure she knows... where she is now."

When Natalie's breakfast arrived, Charlotte gave David a lift home and then continued home herself to update her husband Selwyn, who still thought David had died the night before. 'Hopefully he won't have passed that news on' thought Charlotte. David left promising to return soon and to get Natalie's car. He also needed to sort out some things, not least the bike insurance and Police reports.

David had just finished a call to the Swann insurance company and put them in touch with the Police, who were handling the wreck of the bike, and death of the rider who had stolen it. He was reassured that they would pay out the current market value of the bike, and he felt a little more relieved that he wouldn't have to sell it now. He knew it would take some time to get used to, not having the Harley, but the wonderful distraction of having a son would make that much easier.

The door-bell chimed and he got up and walked to the front door. Opening the door, he saw a Policeman looking through a note book. David stared at him. "Natalie James live here?" asked the Policeman.

"Yes. What's this about?" asked David. The Police officer looked him up and down and replied, "and who might you be sir?" David didn't reply but whipped his wallet out and handed the officer his driver's licence, and waited.

The policeman looked at the licence, and David could metaphorically see the wheels turning in the Policeman's mind by looking at the expression on his face. The look of confusion and then puzzlement as he tried to make sense of what he was seeing, and the task he'd been given.

"Umm," began the officer as he seemed to come to a decision..., "Umm I'm here to escort Mrs James to the formal identification of her husband..." He looked at the licence, and then again at David, "who died last night in a motorcycle accident."

David raised his eyebrows and held out his hand for the driver's licence. The police officer looked at it once more, and then at David as he gave it back. "Is this a good time?" he asked.

"Where to start." said David. "Do you actually talk to each other, or check the collated reports on an incident?"

"Pardon, sir" said the Policeman.

"I mean," went on David; "Say a mistake had been made, and you wrongly informed someone of a death, how would you know? How would you rectify that?"

The Policeman shifted uncomfortably, then smiled and said,

"Are you saying sir, that the reports of your death have been grossly exaggerated?" This misquote of Mark Twain infuriated David further.

"This is not in fact, a laughing matter" said David. "For a start; *you should know* that my wife, having been informed of my death was then admitted into hospital to have a baby, yet here you are on our doorstep not twelve hours later. I don't know about you, but even my sketchy memory of 'high school reproduction' would have given me a clue, that women wouldn't be home just yet after such an event. Then there's the matter of the fact that I'm not dead, and no one thought to apologise, or rectify that bit of shocking news." David took another breath and calmed himself a little. "Now. Here you are... and I'm sorry, I don't mean to 'shoot the messenger,' so to speak; but I do mean to suggest that you could communicate better with your peers and maybe work out who did steal, and then die on my bike!"

The Policeman took a breath, and said, "Yes, I can see that you are upset sir. I'm sorry to have bothered you. I will go and check on the matter; as you say, sir." Then he turned and walked away before stopping and added, "Please convey my congratulations to your wife, and I'm glad to see that you are well, sir."

David closed the front door, muttering to himself and vowing to follow up the report at the Police station.

He heard a phone ringing in the house. It wasn't his phone as that was in his hand. It was Natalie's. He located it quickly and answered it, "Natalie's phone." There was silence on the other end for what seemed like a whole minute. It was probably less than a quarter of that time when David repeated, "Natalie's phone" and then, "Hello?"

Jack Pritard recovered himself from hearing a dead man's voice. "David, is that you?" he said uncertainly.

"Don't tell me," said David, "News has reached you of my recent demise?"

"Well I'm pleased it isn't true" said Jack, "But Selwyn called me last night as he thought I should know." David looked down at the phone and could see many missed calls from Jack. "Thanks for calling Natalie." David said, and he went on to explain that upon hearing the false report, Natalie had gone into labour and was currently in the maternity unit.

"Congratulations" said Jack "Wow, what a start to your weekend." Then he paused, "I suppose you will start your leave now and... Wow what a start to the next chapter of your lives."

David ended the call thanking Jack again, and thought, 'Jack was right, it was just like starting again. A new life, a new son, paternity leave and then, a new job.'

Chapter Six

Two weeks earlier: Garcia Dominguez was being been held in the SHU at Corymbia Prison, and he hated it now as much as he had when he arrived nearly a year ago.

The Special Handling Unit or SHU as it was known to staff, was a prison within the prison. The security was so tight it was like an exclusive nightclub. If your name wasn't on the list, then you weren't getting in. That was true for both inmates and staff. The list wasn't even drawn up by prison staff. The Minister and a special panel met regularly to 'vet' staff and consider inmates to be admitted to the SHU.

The SHU was literally beyond the Multi-Purpose Unit which had it's own TLA or 'three letter acronym', and it went beyond in punishment and isolation as well. The SHU like other units had two wings which were identical in terms of architecture. Each side had an exercise area, a sitting area with a kitchen, a classroom; with an art easel, and an old stand alone computer on a desk, but there was no printer. Then, beyond this, there was a line of seven cells.

The cells all had a stainless-steel latrine, with moulded seat, which wouldn't move or detach; a shower area with one tap and faucet built into recesses in the wall, so they could not be removed. The temperature of the water was warm at all times. And there was a bed. There was no TV, no radio, and since an inmate had tried to escape by drawing a shotgun pointing at an officer looking through the observation hatch, there was no table, chairs or writing materials in any cell. This contravened the 'human rights' rules for holding convicted prisoners, so the classroom held some basic drawing and writing materials, some books and some educational software on the computer.

It was a sparse existence. Cameras were installed in each cell; in the hallways and every other room had two cameras. Multiple observation monitors were placed in the staff monitoring areas. They operated twenty four hours a day, seven days a week. All prisoners were observed at all times, no matter what they were doing. It was also against the rights of incarcerated people to record sound with the video, and the inmates knew this. They knew that anything they said could not be recorded and admitted into evidence. What they didn't know was that they could be heard, and the testimony of the monitoring officer was admissible in evidence.

Only two inmates from each side were released at any time, and they had two hours with which to exercise or use the classroom or talk to the other, before being locked back in their respective cells. A different inmate was unlocked at a different time every day, so the pairs of socially interacting prisoners was randomised. There was no contact whatsoever with the prisoners on the other wing.

Domingez knew that Bruce Harris was in the other wing. He had heard the man shouting, even screaming on occasion. He thought the man was going mad. It happened to people locked in places like this. He had still not decided if Bruce had betrayed him though. It was Bruce that arranged for the prisoner called John to ingratiate himself to Domingez. The man had turned out to be 'prison intelligence.' He understood why he was not allowed to have contact with him. The conversation that Domingez had played over and over in his mind, might be the last one that Bruce ever had with anyone, if he discovered he had betrayed him.

Garcia Domingez had tried to impress the others on his wing, but he had no leverage with which to cause fear. The other inmates just walked away from him. He couldn't even predict who would be let out at the same time.

There was the hairy artist man. Art seemed to be the only educational course that could be done in the SHU. Most subjects were banned, others too difficult to deliver in the restricted environment. Computer studies were possible but gaining a qualification fell apart as the work could not be printed, or even stored for assessment. 'Hairy Art' as he nicknamed him, kept to himself and did his work in the classroom. Then there was Alabi Akbar; he called him the terrorist but, in reality, Alabi was in prison for knifing his brother in a family feud. He was an aggressive proselyte, and it was that which had secured him a place in the SHU; all he ever wanted to do was talk about Allah and he made a huge 'song and dance' about being religious. He never shut up about his rights and freedom of religion. Domingez didn't like him, but he had said that he had contacts, and Domingez needed contacts. The other inmate that he had spent any time with was the most unlikely bikie he'd come across. The man was clean shaven, tall, lanky and friendly, the only thing out of the ordinary were the tattoos. Domingez had been told that this man, named Paul, had set another inmate on fire, and was a danger to everyone.

Domingez was also very angry at not being allowed to have 'contact visits' with his lawyer, who was also his girlfriend. He had been able to smuggle all sorts of things into the prison through her. That is when he could touch, kiss and hold her. Now there was just a plate of glass between them; no drugs, no SIM cards and the conversations at visit time were recordable, so no real information; although he had built up a rudimentary code with her for requests for things to be done outside the prison. He was sure that she was uncomfortable with much of it, and he was unsure how much of what he asked for was actioned. He felt as impotent as he was. It was a real fall from the lofty heights he once enjoyed that was for sure.

The only way out of the SHU was to bide his time and be nice to everyone. That was all very well, but he was tired of it already.

The doors to his cell snapped open suddenly and he stood up from the bed. He walked slowly towards 'limited freedom' and heard his name being called with the other inmate he would share a couple of hours with today.

"Domingez! Middleton!" 'That's Paul' he thought as he stepped out of the cell into the hallway. He glanced right and nodded to Middleton, who gave a slight lift of his chin, back in his direction.

Both men walked towards the communal area and made themselves some warm tea. The water never got to any temperature that would scald. "For reasons of security" he'd been told. He sat on a hard, plastic chair and put the unbreakable plastic cup on to the table, which was itself bolted to the floor. "Yo, Garfield." Paul said as he sat opposite.

'It seemed Garcia wasn't the only one to make up nicknames for the inmates' he thought. He didn't like it but there was nothing he could do about it. Nothing that is, that wouldn't attract immediate retribution from Middleton or the guards. "Yo. Paully" he replied.

Middleton had been isolated from the bikie gang he'd been a part of. The 'grass' whom he'd attacked had survived; but they had been so badly burned they would wear a 'body burn suit' for the rest of their life. That probably wasn't going to be all that long either, as once they got out they would be 'fair game' to those who had called for the 'hit'. No one liked a 'grass.' Paul's tattoos told a story of their own and they were all over his body, head and face. Domingez didn't stare too long though, as it was the one thing that Paul Middleton would react badly to. Domingez couldn't quite understand why someone would allow ink drawings to be placed in such uncovered places and then be sensitive about people looking at them. "Were you with the Brother's Arms?" asked Domingez, motioning with his hand to the tattoos. He sipped the tea and waited.

Both men exchanged a glance as noise erupted from the other wing. There was no way to see what was going on, but the sounds gave away there was a fight happening.

"I'm going to find a way to get some 'kit' in here" said Domingez, breaking the silence between them.

"Oh yea?" replied Middleton.

"Oh yea" repeated Domingez in a reassuring fashion.

The silence descended again for a full minute, then "I'm going to get Education to bring me things."

The silence returned until Middleton said, "How you going to make that happen?" Domingez was quiet for a long time and then got up and went outside to the covered exercise area. The two men worked out using an old noisy bike machine and grunting loudly as they pulled up on an exercise bar. The mood lightened as information passed between them and even laughter was heard from the area, by the officers monitoring them.

As the two returned to the sitting area Domingez said, "I will have him softened up first then he will know that we are able to get to him. His bike will come and go. His life will be inconvenienced. He will beg to help me in the end." Before he returned to his cell to shower Domingez walked to the dark tinted glass of the control room and asked to see an officer. Five minutes later Snr. Officer White walked onto the wing. He was an imposing sight and had earned the nickname 'Great White' by swooping in very quickly and forcefully to end trouble with his own 'particular' remedy. He also had tattoos, one was of a shark on his forearm.

"I want to see Education" Domingez stated.

"Hmph" went Snr. Officer White, "What do you want to learn then?" Without waiting for a reply, he turned and said, "I'll ask for you, but don't hold your breath, it will take a couple of weeks to process that."

Domingez shrugged and walked back into his cell.

Chapter Seven

Three weeks later: David was finally ready to pick up Natalie from the hospital. He'd spent the first week of his leave putting up mobiles and hanging them from the ceiling of Nathan's bedroom. He put together the cot and made various other preparations to welcome Natalie and Nathan. He had officially registered Nathan's birth and name and would be glad to have them all living under the same roof soon.

David had shopped, and then made and put meals in the fridge and freezer; anything to make life easier for Natalie. He wanted her to have everything at her fingertips, and not feel like she had to run around, looking after him and Nathan.

He parked the car as near as he could to the front of the maternity unit and walked through the security doors. He'd taken to holding out his driver's licence and waving it at the sour faced receptionist. She waived him through with a look of 'daggers' and he wondered why she worked there if she hated it so much.

He reached the room Natalie and Nathan were in and saw that they had been discharged and were ready to go. He picked up Natalie's bag and went to get Nathan but was prevented from doing so by a nurse who insisted upon carrying him. Natalie was not allowed to walk by herself either, another nurse wheeled her in a chair until they reached the front doors. Whilst they waited, David went to get the car and clip the special cot straps into the anchors he had bolted in earlier. He drew up outside the unit and Natalie was wheeled out and Nathan was handed to David who secured him in the rear of the vehicle. Natalie got into the back as well. David thanked the nurses and presented them with a couple of boxes of chocolates, and then jumped back into the driver's seat and pulled out of the car park.

"Take me somewhere I can run and run" laughed Natalie. I've not been allowed to do anything on my own for a week.

"Well, you had very low blood pressure and ..." started David.

"Never mind that" said Natalie, "I'm just so glad to be out of there and back to normality."

They arrived home, excited and nervous. Neither of them had been in this situation before. Natalie's mum, who had booked time off, wouldn't be able to come and help for another week. She had thought that she would be early for the birth, but now she was trying to change her flights. Frank and Endana wouldn't be around for another three weeks.

"We'll be ok" said Natalie. "We're both off work and can cover for one another."

"Yes" agreed David. "Plenty of people used to have to just get on with it on their own, we'll be fine." He took a deep breath and pushed open the door to Nathan's room.

"Wow" said Natalie, "You've been busy!" She took in the well ordered room, with baby changing station set up with a wall dispenser for nappies and plastic sealed bags and waste bin's situated in a couple of places. "I bet he and I can have this place looking like a bomb-site in no time at all" she laughed.

They put a still sleeping baby in his carry-cot into the larger cot, and then crept out of the room.

"I'll leave the door ajar" said Natalie.

"No need" said David. "I discovered that when you built this house you got the 'wired for sound' package."

"Well, Frank insisted" said Natalie.

"So" continued David, "I've used the existing hardware to install listening posts in several rooms. All switch-able. There's also a remote if you go outside."

Natalie turned to her husband and planted a kiss on his lips.

"Oh, I've missed you this week" he said.

"I'll bet there's something else you've missed too, for a lot longer than a week?" she replied and kissed him again hard. "Well mister, I'm firing on all cylinders now, and without the weight, I can chase you easily."

David laughed, and said, "Well you won't have to run hard, I can tell you. I'm tired from setting our home up for your arrival."

Natalie giggled, she looked well and seemed to have all her energy back. "I'm going to join a gym and get my figure back too. Do you want a decent cup of tea?" she called from the kitchen.

"Love one!" said David. "About the gym... I hope you don't mind but I figured with the money I'll get for the bike soon, I might buy some exercise equipment."

"That's an interesting idea" said Natalie.

"Good" said David, "Come and have a look at it in the garage, where my bike used to be."

David had set up the garage, by reorganising some of the storage shelves and had a small but effective York Gym assembled. Next to it was a machine that could be set up as a cross trainer, stepper and runner.

"Wow" said Natalie. "That's awesome. Now I won't have to show off my tummy to anyone and it's right here so I can go whenever I want."

David smiled, "It is rather good isn't it? I've enjoyed using it this week." Natalie pretended to look around for something else and David asked, "What are you looking for?" Natalie grinned, and said, "Just wondering if there was a gun range as well?" She skipped out before David could reply and went to make the tea.

David followed her in to the kitchen, and took the cup that she was holding out to him. They sat for a moment and then heard the faint sound of crying, and both of them got up to investigate.

Whilst Natalie changed Nathan, and then fed him before putting him down again to sleep. David looked on.

"It will be a while I'm afraid, before he wants to play or talk to you" she said.

"It's all just amazing." he replied.

When Nathan was back in his cot, Natalie started to go through some of the clothes she had put away, when she got too big for them. She organised her wardrobe a bit, whilst David went outside to check the post.

There were three envelopes in the box; the first was a power bill. The second a cheque from Swann Insurance for the written off Harley, and the last was a traffic fine. "What?" exclaimed David loudly.

"What's wrong?" called Natalie from the bedroom.

"Oh nothing!" said David. "Well it is something" he confessed. "I got a ticket for going through a red light."

"That's not like you," said Natalie coming into the kitchen. "Let me see?"

Natalie examined the ticket and said, "This isn't you. You sit taller in the saddle." Now it was David's turn to look more closely.

"Yes, and the date, look at the date. This is when the bike was stolen and by the look of it, it's moments before the thief got killed."

They both sat in silence and then David got up and reached for his phone. "I'm going to call them now and get it quashed."

"Just fill in the back and send it off" said Natalie. But David had already dialled the number.

Natalie looked at the other letters and saw the cheque from Swann.

"Hello?" said David, "Yes, traffic fines please." The call was put through and David spoke to someone in 'Fines management'. "Yes. I know I can fill the back in" he said, "but the bike had been stolen when the offence occurred... No I don't know the name of the person who was riding it... No. It wasn't me riding it, and I can't identify who was riding it... Why? Because the Police haven't told me who was riding it." He looked at Natalie, and shook his head in disbelief. Then, "No, no, no; I told you the bike had been stolen. Yes. I have reported it... Yes I have paperwork from the Police... Yes. I will take this to a Police Station and let them have it... Thank you." He terminated the call.

"You know if you want to take this cheque and buy another bike..." began Natalie holding up the cheque David had placed on the breakfast bar. David smiled at her and walked over to her and sat beside her. "Yes thanks, I know. I was planning on selling it though and this is quite 'neat and tidy'" he said holding the cheque.

"If you change your mind though." Natalie tried again, "I know you'll miss it, and."

"Ok. I'll let you know" said David to finish the conversation.

"Do you mind if I just nip down to Canning Vale Police station and let them have this?" David said holding up the fine.

"Yes, go!" said Natalie smiling, "I know you don't like things left unresolved."

David went into the garage to get his bike and then laughed out loud at himself; before getting Natalie's keys and jumping into the car. He arrived at the Police station and parked in the small carpark and walked into the waiting room. Thankfully it was empty. He waited for a full two minutes after ringing the bell, and was contemplating ringing it again when a white haired, portly Policeman walked slowly up to the counter.

"G'day sir. How can we help you?" David started to explain that his bike had been stolen and the police officer reached for a report pad.

"No, er it's ok officer. I've already reported it" said David. The officer took a deep breath as if he were tired of this enquiry already, and looked at David.

"I don't expect we've found it yet sir!" he said rather drolly.

"Oh, er yes you have actually" said David, "But look um it's about this fine I got for an offence that took place while it was stolen."

He laid the traffic fine on the counter. The police officer looked at it seriously; and then at David.

"Photographic evidence of your offence is difficult to dispute sir." The police officer said and pushed the fine back towards David. David then produced the report he'd filed at Armadale Police Station and pushed it back across the desk to the police officer, who wasn't looking impressed.

"You see, the bike had been stolen, and the offence was committed by someone else" said David. The Policeman turned the fine over and said, "Fill in the back sir, and the fine will be sent to the offender." David looked at the Policeman.

"Perhaps you could look up the case and tell me the name of the offender?" asked David.

The police officer drew himself up to his full height, and took a deep breath, "No sir. I couldn't possibly give out such information, especially if it was information that was to be used in a forthcoming court of law."

David was becoming exasperated and took a breath himself.

"Calm down sir" said the police officer. David laughed.

"I fail to see anything funny" said the police officer.

David took another breath, and began in a friendly tone,

"No. I don't either" he smiled. "Look, I just want to sort this out." He pushed both the fine and the Stolen Property Form back to the policeman.

"I had my bike stolen. It was involved in this offence. The Police found the bike. I am not guilty of the offence. I can't name the offender. I want the fine quashed."

David thought that he'd been quite clear. The policeman however was nodding and looking at the two pieces of paper when he said, "Well sir; you reported the theft after this offence took place. Why was that sir?"

David said that he'd been at a party and not discovered the bike was missing until later. He'd reported it as soon as he was able. "Well sir, it could be construed that you had time to commit the offence and then return to the party. Perhaps you should just tick the option to go to court sir?"

David shook his head. "No. I want this quashed. I have presented the 'Report of Theft' form to you, and I'd be grateful if you would copy it, and then look up the case, and then add this to the information. I've not been sent it yet."

The policeman looked down at the pages before him, he looked at the computer beside him. His expression seemed to convey he was reaching a decision. "Why should I believe you sir? I mean, you did have time to commit an offence and then report the bike stolen later?"

David calmed himself, he stared very intently at the policeman and said in a monotone voice, "Yes, but I didn't have time to write off the bike and get killed seconds after the offence took place, then go back to report the bike stolen."

The police officer looked confused, and then started to call up the details on the computer screen. He read for a while, and then nodded.

"Where's your copy of the report to say the bike was found and the time of the accident it was involved in?" he asked.

In the same monotone voice David said, "On your screen and in the post, I imagine." The Policeman started to say, that he'd need that before he could process the fine; and then thought better of it and started to print it off the screen. He made a big flourish of lifting the report off the printer and stapling the pages to the fine.

"Ok sir. Leave it with me and I'll send it in for you" he said in a condescending tone. David stood in front of the desk quietly.

"Anything else I can do for you today?" the police officer asked.

After David had asked for and received: copies of all the paperwork and made a note of the date and time with the officer's number; he left the Police Station and drove home.

Natalie greeted him at the door with Nathan in her arms, she kissed David.

"This young man" she said, "has missed his Dad and has grizzled the whole time you've been out."

"Mmm" said David, "he's probably been feeling ripples in the 'force'" and mimicked 'Obi-Wan Kenobi' in Star Wars.

David told Natalie what had happened at the Police Station. "The stupid is strong in this one" he mimicked 'Obi-Wan Kenobi' again.

Then in his own voice, "Well, that's what I wanted to say." Natalie laughed, and then realised that Nathan had dropped back off to sleep.

"Your voice has quite an effect on him." She said. Then she went to put him down again.

David watched on as the two people he loved most walked back down the bedroom corridor.

Chapter Eight

Jack Pritard was reading the Monday morning prison briefings from the Prison Security departments around the state. He had picked up the Corymbia report and was studying the SHU details within it. There were the usual list of concerns and notes on the transcripts of recorded conversations in the 'public areas.' He read down to Garcia Domingez's request to see the Education Campus Manager. By all accounts there had been quite a scene when someone from Education had called to talk to Domingez. Domingez had to be restrained and the Education staff member had received some counselling after the interview, as she had been quite badly shaken up emotionally. Thankfully Domingez had not physically assaulted her, but she had been frightened by the interaction.

Jack picked up the phone, as he continued to read. He dialled the Superintendent of Corymbia and waited.

"Matt" he began, "I've got the latest Security report in front of me and I'm wondering if you can shed any further light on the incident with Domingez in the SHU?"

Matt outlined briefly what had happened and the fact that things had calmed since then. He finished by saying, "Funny thing is, that Domingez started as soon as the Education officer identified herself as being from Education. He really wanted to see David James and gave no time for anyone to explain that he was on leave. It was as if he wanted to escalate things, so only the Education Campus Manager would meet him." Jack thought for a moment, and said, "Matt. Please get me all the transcripts from conversations that Domingez has had with anyone in the SHU in the past month."

"Phew, er ok Jack, that's a fair bit of reading though" replied Matt, making a mental note to read them all first himself, when he saw them.

Matt called the Assistant Superintendent of Security, thinking how odd it was that he'd been in that job just a few months ago. He passed on Jack's request and asked that he be cc'd in as well and said that it was important and it needed to be done today.

A few hours later a thick wad of pages were placed on his desk by Michelle Janes along with a cup of tea. An hour after this the same wad of pages arrived on Jack's desk, having been couriered to him. As soon as it arrived, Jack put other things aside and began to read.

He'd read for a full hour and a half before he read the following typed transcript:

Domingez: "I'm going to find a way to get some 'kit' in here"
Middleton: "Oh yea?"
Domingez "Oh yea. I'm going to get Education to bring me things."
Middleton: "How you going to make that happen?"

Domingez and Middleton went outside to the covered exercise area, where nothing was recorded.
Domingez and Middleton returned to the sitting area.

Domingez: "I will have him softened up first, then he will know that we are able to get to him.*
His bike will come and go. His life will be inconvenienced. He will beg to help me in the end."

Before he returned to his cell to shower Domingez asked to see an officer.

Snr. Officer White spoke to Domingez and was told by him, "I want to see Education"
Snr. Officer White informed the prisoner that the request would take a couple of weeks to process.

Jack picked up the phone again and called Matt.

"Hi Jack" said Matt, when the call went through. How did you know it was me?" Jack demanded.

"Yours are the only calls that I'm allowing to get through to me" said Matt. "I've been reading through the SHU transcripts, where are you?"

Jack told Matt where he'd got to, and Matt said that he'd finished them, but explained that he'd got an hour head-start on Jack. He told Jack that there was nothing more of any interest after the point that Jack had got to.

"Well that at least saves me some time" said Jack, "Why wasn't this reported earlier?"

Matt explained that when he'd asked the SHU staff that same question, he'd been told that Domingez liked to 'build himself up' and make out he was still a 'big man.'

"They quite simply hadn't taken him seriously" reported Matt. "Thing is, if we reported everything, you'd need to double the size of your staff, and they would never go home!" he added.

Jack thanked Matt for his help and said he'd be in touch. He wanted to get a 'rarely allowed' permission order, to monitor Domingez' conversations in the prison.

Jack typed up the request for the warrant and submitted it electronically to the magistrate court for action. While he waited to hear if his request would be accepted, he called David.

"Sorry to bother you David." Jack began, "I wonder if I could ask you a couple of questions about your bike getting stolen?"

"Sure!" Said David "As a matter of fact, I've been dealing with some 'fallout' from that." David started telling Jack. Jack listened intently to David as he recounted his frustrations with the Police. He was expecting Jack to fall into some friendly banter with him and make some jokes about 'law enforcement' but Jack said simply, "David. We need to talk. I'll be in touch." Then the phone went dead. 'Weird!' thought David.

Jack was already dialling out again, when the fax started printing out what looked to be a warrant to record and monitor Domingez.

"Yes!" shouted Jack just as the phone was answered.

"It's not been that long" came the retort on the other end of the phone.

Jack apologised and asked to speak to Sergeant Becky Wilson. Becky came on a moment later, "Traffic fines. Sergeant Wilson, how may I help you?"

"Becky, it's Jack, have you time for a chat?" said Jack.

"Always, Jack" she replied; and the old friends began a brief 'catch-up.'

"Well it's not the army" said Becky in reply to Jack's enquiry about how she was enjoying her change of job.

"You know how I'd always come to you if I wanted to know what was going on in the 'Motor-Pool'" asked Jack.

Becky laughed, "Bit of a bigger pool these days, Jack."

"I know I can trust you..." said Jack and went on to tell her about the past few weeks starting with David's bike being stolen and finishing with some of the information he'd read about Dominguez.

"Wow. That was a long winded way of asking me to quash a ticket" Becky said, and laughed.

Jack explained that what he really wanted to know was if there might be any way that a criminally minded person could bribe someone in the Traffic Fines department, and cause someone else to get a fine rather than quash one! After considering this for a moment, Becky said, "No, not possible. Every time anyone logs on to the system it's recorded. The person using the system must record a reason, even if it's just to say it was a mistake. Hey I just looked up your friend's fine. The Police have done nothing about it. He'll get another ticket or a court date next... There! I've sorted it for you." Then she added. "And I've made a note about the case number and stuff so it's all above board!"

Jack thanked her telling her that he 'owed her,' and said he'd be inviting her over for one of Mary's home cooked meals soon. He put down the phone and then picked it up again.

"Hello David" Jack said, "Sorry to drop you suddenly on our last phone call. I need to chat with you and Natalie, are you going to be at home tomorrow?" David could see no reason he wouldn't be, so Jack said he would come over in the morning.

Jack was about to leave for the day, when the phone rang again. He stood wondering if he should answer it. It was already past leaving time....

Chapter Nine

Dr Wayne Smith FRCPA FAICD was the Police Clinical Pathologist at the mortuary where the post mortem of an unidentified motorcycle rider, had just been conducted. The body had been so badly damaged by the semi-articulated truck that had crushed the rider under the motorcycle, Dr Smith was awaiting results from a DNA database to try and confirm the rider's identity.

Dr Smith had just finished eating a 'wrap' that his wife had put in his lunch-box, and he was looking for a paper-towel to wipe his hands on. He thought how funny it was that he still wore plastic gloves and scrubbed up to work on dead people. There was no risk of infection to those who had 'passed on', however it was still vitally important in most cases that *he* not contaminate the body of evidence. He smiled at his own pun. He washed his hands at the small sink by his desk and picked up the phone which was ringing.

"Pathology!" He said. "Oh good – send it through." He put the phone down and walked to the door of the lab where he was met by his assistant who passed him a large envelope.

"It's just been couriered over" she said. "Good, now we'll find out whether he's been DNA tested, and if so, who he is. Er 'was'!" replied Dr Smith.

The report, if you could understand it, specified various information marked on scales; it told of heredity and race, along with details of features and finally it revealed that the person had been identified through a match with the criminal database. The name was given as Richard Chino aged thirty-five. Dr Smith picked up the phone again and dialled out to report the information to the Police Detective in charge of the investigation.

"Detective Allen please." Dr Smith said when he was put through. Detective Pauline Allen was in charge of many of the related 'bikie' deaths. She suspected that there was something more to any death involving a Harley Davidson. She listened to the Pathologist as he fed her the information he'd received and confirmed that his report would also follow the phone call.

"I just thought you'd want to know ASAP" he said, as he finished the call.

Pauline had been surprised when the bike involved in the incident, had been traced to someone without a criminal record, and when it had been reported stolen by a member of prison staff, something had jogged her memory. She recalled another case which involved a prison officer; that one had the look of a 'gangland killing'. It had also involved a person with a Harley Davidson motorcycle. 'What was his name?' She asked herself. 'Mike Davis or Davies, that was it. He'd killed himself, and his wife had been murdered. Yes they suspected 'Rickie the Chin' had been behind the killings, but hadn't been able to get past the bikie who actually committed the murders and was now incarcerated himself; still awaiting trial'.

"Well, well, well." She said out-loud to herself, "Karma strikes again." Then she went to the computer and pulled up the file on the 'Brothers Outlaw Motorcycle Gang.' 'Yes' she thought, 'there he is. Suspected of a long list of illegal activities.' She sat back and thought, 'Good riddance,' then she thought, 'I wonder...'

Pauline picked up the phone and dialled out. The call was answered, "Jack Pritard 'Prison Intelligence'. You've just caught me leaving so it better be good!"

Pauline introduced herself and asked Jack if he remembered her, "I was the lead detective in that incident at Corymbia

Clear Bright Light of Day 53

Prison; the Mike Davies death. There was an Education officer that got shot when the VSO 'topped himself'" she said.

Jack thought for a moment, "Yes. I remember you. Not sure we met, but you gave my office some information for our investigation."

There was a pause and Pauline went on.

"Well I thought you might want to know that we've identified the bikie who stole that very same Education officer's bike"

Jack was listening intently and his knuckles had gone white on the hand which held the phone. "Go on" he said slowly.

"Well, we suspected this bikie was in contact with one of your prisoners at the time and had coordinated the criminal action of the gang members, one of whom was shot and killed in a Police bike chase, if you recall."

Jack said that he did remember and that he was dealing with information that Pauline might also be interested in. He finished the call agreeing to meet Pauline and walked from his office down St. Georges Terrace to Perth Central Police Station.

After clearing the Police security and being allowed to keep his holstered firearm, he gained access to the fourth floor and Detective Pauline Allen's office.

"This is very interesting as there can only really be a couple of explanations, the way I figure it" said Jack.

"Either it's a straightforward theft, that Rickie committed and then he got unlucky and was killed, or... is it possible that someone thought it was David on the bike, and tried to kill or scare him?"

Pauline looked over the witness statements, photographs and evidence lists from the traffic incident. "I can't believe that the 'truckie' was involved in a premeditated killing." She said, "He's been in therapy since the accident. Also the evidence doesn't support it. The Red-Light Camera images show a clear drive through. It's almost as if the rider was trying to get a ticket; look he slows here to ensure the camera gets the photo of the plate. If he hadn't slowed, he'd be alive today! No. this looks deliberate... miscalculated, but deliberate."

Jack thought for a moment and said, "Do you think that the rider might have been trying to do a U - turn there?" Pauline looked again.

"Well I'll be..." Pauline exclaimed, "You may be right."

Jack explained his theory; that he thought that the bikie was probably going to return with the bike and leave David in a position where he couldn't argue the fine!

After the 'pooling of information' and a strategy session, as to what they would do next, Jack left and headed home. He wasn't sure what was for dinner, but he knew it would be cold, as would be his reception from Mary.

Chapter Ten

The Australian Defence Force Vessel - 'ADV Fourcray' and it's crew, under the command of Commander Mark Baker, were making final preparations to sail. Commander Baker had just turned fifty. He was fit, but now greying and considered himself a confirmed Batchelor. He'd always considered himself 'married to the sea', but the sea was more of a mistress than a wife; promising more than it could deliver. That didn't mean that he wasn't interested in the opposite sex; in his younger days he'd had his fair share of 'girls in port'. But that had changed over the years; he still had no desire to settle down though. He loved the responsibility of commanding boats and he felt it unfair on any woman to sit at home and wait for a man who had no intention of living on dry land for any length of time. In the 'old days' as he referred to them, he had partied with the best of them. Then he had met Lucy. She had been a chaste 'no nonsense' Christian girl who made him swear off the booze. He'd even gone to church with her and had found a reality in God, that he never appreciated before. She had wanted him to leave the Navy though, and so he'd lost her. But he remained sober and made a point of asking God for wisdom on a daily basis. He attended church, or at least sought out the chaplain from time to time, for some lively discussions. He was happy as he was.

ADV Fourcray was one of two Australian Border Force Cape Class Patrol Boats with a crew of eighteen able bodied sea-men and women. It had been introduced into service with the Royal Australian Navy to complement the Armidale Class Patrol Boat, that defends Australia's maritime security interests as part of Operation RESOLUTE.

The Communications officer, Lt. Commander Robbie Taylor had settled into his place on the bridge and was running equipment checks. He wanted to ensure everything was working properly with both the on board and ship to shore communications systems, before they sailed at first light. Robbie considered himself a 'career officer,' but unlike Commander Baker, Robbie was interested in a 'work – life balance' that included partying. He still had age and stamina on his side though.

ADV Fourcray had replaced ADV Cape Nelson, which had returned to Cairns. It had been easily integrated into service with the Navy as a result of the close working relationship between the Australian Border Force and the Australian Defence Force. During the light refit the crew had enjoyed taking time in Darwin during the Dry season. It was a relative paradise and the posting, for the maintenance of the Patrol Boat, pleased all the men and women of the crew.

HMAS Coonawarra was located two kilometres or about fifteen minutes' walk from the Darwin city-centre. Darwin was a popular tourist destination, boasting several nightclubs, many restaurants, street markets and a Casino. During the dry season, May - October, the famous Mindal Beach markets operated, showcasing food, arts and crafts from Australia and South East Asia. Surrounding Darwin were a number of world class tourist destinations such as the Kakadu and Litchfield National Parks, Katherine Gorge, Adelaide River and there were plenty of other destinations for those willing to travel to some of the most picturesque places in Australia.

Life in Darwin was unique and had much to offer this small Naval Crew. The many attractions of great beauty within easy driving distance, and the city itself offered a relaxed and friendly lifestyle. It was true, the humid climate was different from much of Australia for part of the year. 'The Wet' as it was known, was a season that was often hot, very humid and of course, wet. The remainder of the year was called 'The Dry' and it was no mistake that it was best described as 'six months of paradise.' The crew had certainly enjoyed taking time in Darwin during the dry season and they would be even happier to be moving down the coast of Western Australia as their next duty demanded of them.

Commander, Mark Baker was reflecting on the two months he had been stationed at HMAS Coonawarra. Darwin had always been a vitally important Navy port - a gateway to Australia's northern neighbours, and the centre from which the Navy conducted border integrity operations. Just a year previously he had participated in a major Royal Australian Navy (RAN) and multi-national exercise from Darwin. The operation involved around 100 visiting Australian and foreign warships. Currently, almost 600 Navy men and women were based in the Darwin area, most of whom worked at Coonawarra or Larrakeyah Barracks, where they focussed on supporting fleet operations.

The base's vertical-lift facility had been essential for enabling their patrol boat to be mechanically removed from the water for maintenance. The facility had the capability to dock vessels with a draught of up to three meters at any tide, and lift up to 750 tonnes at a rate of 420mm a minute. The service provided much more efficient maintenance for vessels in Northern Australia, thus allowing more time to be spent on coastal surveillance.

Darwin, during World War I, had been used as a coaling station by naval vessels, but it was not considered a naval base back then. While RAN activity continued from this time, the first official naval reserve depot at Darwin was established in January 1935 under the command of Lieutenant Commander HP Jarrett, R.A.N. At that time, Darwin was part of the Naval Reserve District of Queensland, but in 1937, the Naval District of the Northern Territory was separated from the Queensland District and the first District Naval Officer, Lieutenant Commander JH Walker, R.A.N. was appointed. At the outbreak of World War II, the naval depot in Darwin was named HMAS Penguin, and on 1 August 1940, for security reasons, it was formally commissioned as HMAS Melville.

Throughout World War II, Coonawarra Wireless Transmitting Station, which had initially begun operating in September 1939, provided an essential communications service in support of Allied operations in the South-West Pacific Regions. Many of the RAN's small ships, such as the Fairmile and Harbour Defence Motor Launches, also operated from Darwin and its security was maintained by a complex system of fixed harbour defences, which included an anti-submarine boom net. This was maintained throughout the war by naval boom working vessels. In the post-war period, as demands for inner city real estate increased, the area of land occupied by HMAS Melville diminished. Consequently, it was decided to decommission Melville, but retain the central function of the RAN in Darwin via the Coonawarra Wireless Transmitting Station. This merger occurred on 16 May 1970, but HMAS Melville was retained until December 1974 when Cyclone Tracy destroyed it.

Since commissioning, HMAS Coonawarra expanded rapidly. A new Receiving Station at Shoal Bay was opened in 1975, and a new Transmitting Station at Humpty Doo became fully operational in October 1982. HMAS Coonawarra relocated from its original site at Berrimah to Larrakeyah in

December 2003. The move, closer to the waterfront, better reflected the changing role of Coonawarra from one of a global communications hub, to fleet support. Today, Darwin's naval base was a model of the latest technology for the home porting of patrol boats such as the Fourcray. The wharf could accommodate six vessels, berthed three abreast. Services such as fuel, electrical power, compressed air, sewerage disposal, oily waste suction, and defueling were available at the berthing points. Everything necessary to keep patrolling vessels in full service.

Commander Baker turned as he heard the Patrol Boat's call sign, "VMCF 311, VMCF 311, VMCF 311, completion of radio testing. TS Humpty Doo ceasing tests. Out!" Fifty kilometres east-south-east the Transmission Station at Humpty Doo had completed their radio checks and Lieutenant Commander Robbie Taylor was putting his station into standby mode.

"I'm calling it a night – with your permission sir?"

"Of course Robbie" Commander Baker said, "See you oh five hundred for 'Clear Bright Light of Day.'"

'Clear Bright Light of Day' was the code name for the operation outlined in their orders for the coming weeks, to patrol the Western Coast of Australia.

'It will be a trip home for the 'old girl' to Fremantle,' thought Commander Baker as he handed over to the night security officer, who had just come on to the bridge. 'Austal Ships' had built her originally, and as a 'Cape Class Patrol Boat' she was just over fifty eight metres long, with a ten and a half meter beam and a draught of three metres. She could pull twenty-five knots if she needed to, but most of the time twelve was sufficient and more economical; her range was four thousand nautical miles at that speed. The two diesel

3516C caterpillar engines delivered nearly seven thousand horsepower, and combined with a bow thruster made the vessel very manoeuvrable. It was armed with two 12.7mm machine guns, and a Raphael Typhoon 25mm automated cannon, which had a rate of fire of 200 rounds per minute. The latter, was interfaced with Electro Optics Surveillance System which was controlled from the bridge. It's job wasn't to engage larger war ships though and the guns provided a good defence against smaller boats. If they had to deal with anything larger, they would call for air or sea support from larger vessels.

Commander Baker made his way below deck to his cabin to settle in for a good night's sleep. He would leave the port in the morning and begin his movement down the Western Australian coast to dock at Fremantle and refuel. All the while patrolling the waters some one hundred miles out. Keeping the integrity of the boarder. They would monitor shipping and board and search any vessel they suspected of smuggling.

The Royal Australian Navy was very experienced in boarding operations in a variety of conditions. These ranged from the usually benign boarding of vessels carrying asylum seekers to those who were illegal fishing vessels, which might be an opposed boarding. Commander Baker had in his early days in the navy, participated in more dangerous boardings; of vessels in the Arabian Gulf as part of Middle East operations extending back to 1991. Some of those incidents had resulted in loss of lives: pirate's lives. Australian waters were much safer of course. There had only been 52 incidents of piracy since 2010 in South East Asian seas, and of those only 1 in the Indian Ocean. There had been illegal immigrants in boats of course. Some of the people ferrying them were pirates, but they didn't factor those in the statistics. He felt conflicted about the 'boat people' as they were called. People who were so desperate to flee their countries, that they would undertake dangerous journeys and almost certain capture. The security risks of preventing terrorists gaining illegal entry to Australia balanced against the humanitarian moral responsibility to help those in genuine need. It was a difficult call to make.

Chapter Eleven

Garcia Domingez sat 'stewing' in his anger. 'They had sent a young girl to him! Did they not know who he was? And the girl was black, two of the things he hated most; women and coloured people. At least the Brothers Motorcycle gang respected him on that score.' He took a slow deep breath. They would now send the manager. They would have to. He deserved the respect. Anyway, he refused to see anyone else. They had told him the manager was on leave, but not said for how long. His thoughts moved on to what he would say to the manager, when he did come to see him. There were the original threats he'd shared with Middleton, but now these would be brought with the full frustration of being made to look like a fool in Middleton's eyes.

Middleton hadn't laughed at Domingez, he at least knew better than that; but he had let slip an expression of scorn, that he was sure Domingez had seen. He doubted that Domingez would take his anger out on him though as Middleton knew that Domingez needed him; as he had the contacts, he had weekly visitors with whom he could interact. He was able to touch, hold and kiss his girlfriend. Domingez had non-contact visits. Nothing more than conversations, hardly visits! But just in case, he had decided to keep a watchful eye on Domingez and have his defensive senses tuned to a possible attack from the drug lord.

The cell door clicked open with a loud 'clack', as the mechanism moved against the spring and Domingez stood and made his way out of the cell. No other door opened. That's how it had been since he shouted at the black female. They were punishing him with solitary conditioning, he knew. In reality, the SHU staff had just made what they considered to be an ordinary decision based on sound. 'Occupational Health and Safety Policy.' That was, to isolate what they considered a danger to everyone; at least for a few weeks, until Domingez showed he was more compliant.

Domingez silently made his way to the kitchen area and made himself some tea, and then took it to the classroom, where he retrieved two pieces of paper and some pencils. He walked outside to the exercise area, where he sat on one of the machines and slowly sipped his tea. He rested the paper on the seat and drew a scene of his home, from memory, he wrote a note on the other page. He then put the cup on the seat and walked in circles around the whole area, until he was called back to his cell. On his way back to the cell, he replaced his cup in the kitchen concealing as he did so the note inside the cup. He left the picture on the kitchen benchtop. Returning to his cell to be locked in again; he knew that Middleton would retrieve the note at some point during the day – whenever his two hours of exercise was, and that hopefully he in turn would be able to reply in the same way.

Middleton was not the next person to visit the kitchen. There were two other inmates of the SHU that took their turn to make themselves tea, and who saw the note in the cup and the picture by the sink. Both inmates knew the note wasn't for them, and so they ignored it. It just wasn't worth the upset to another prisoner, and certainly not worth being implicated in 'note passing' by the officers. For all they knew it was a test placed there by the officers. Both had pretended to choose several other cups after placing the one with the note in it back on the shelf.

Eventually Middleton's opportunity came and when he saw the picture by the side of the sink, he made a 'show' of looking into cups and choosing a clean one to make a cup of tea in.

During his choice he 'palmed' the note and took it with his tea to the classroom. There he selected a book to read and sat with the book in front of his face as if reading it. He unfolded the note behind the book, all the time feeling the conflicted emotions of fear, of discovery and contempt, for the stupidity of the guards. The note contained Domingez's usual self-promoting statements, as if forming an argument for his worthiness to be helped; but it finished with a contrite request for a favour. Domingez wanted Middleton to get a message to his 'Brothers' and wanted reassurance that pressure was indeed being brought to bear on David outside the prison.

Chapter Twelve

David and Natalie had not slept much during the night. Both had been up attending to Nathan at various times, and it did seem that Nathan was determined to wriggle and squirm through the late hours of the night.

"See, I told you, idn't I?" said Natalie. "A footie player if ever I saw one."

"Well, he's not playing for Australia" said David.

"What do you mean?" asked Natalie frowning.

"Wrong time zone" answered David, smiling.

David, Natalie and Nathan slept late, and after Nathan's first feed of the day and a change of diaper; he was happy to return to sleep. Natalie and David gave up on any more sleep, they showered and had just finished washing up breakfast dishes when the door-bell rang, so David went to answer it. He appeared a moment later with Jack with him, and as Natalie was greeting Jack, she saw a tall woman in her late thirties hanging back in the hallway behind him. She froze for a second, as she saw the gun under a short jacket on the lady's belt, then she saw the police insignia and ID. For a brief moment she had been reminded of the female assassin that had entered Gerry's house. She recovered quickly and said, "Who have you brought with you Jack?"

Jack introduced Detective Pauline Allen, and while Natalie went to make coffee for them all, they settled themselves on the lounges in the family area; making 'small talk' until Natalie could join them.

"You going to buy another bike?" Jack asked David.

"No. I'm not actually... I was going to sell it, and now I don't have to" David finished with a shrug. There was a pause and Jack said, "Tired of riding or is it uh... Natalie not keen, now you have 'responsibilities?'"

David chuckled. "Nah, Natalie's all good with me replacing it, but it comes down to priorities and time. In this season of our lives the bike fairs a lot lower on the list."

Jack nodded, "Good to hear. I'd be sorry if you'd have given up riding."

David looked quizzically at Jack, musing on his last comment, but before he could ask him what he meant by it Natalie sat down next to him and put a tray with a coffee pot, milk and cups on the table. "There we go" she said. Then with a sparkle in her eyes she stared briefly at Pauline and said, "Now 'what gives' Jack? And what do you want with my husband?"

Jack took a moment to recover from the directness of the question and laughed.

"There really is no fooling you is there Natalie?"

Natalie transferred her gaze onto Pauline, "Detective?" Pauline looked at Jack and nodded.

Jack took a deep breath and took the initiative to pour the coffee into the cups and looking at David, he started by saying, "We don't think the theft of your bike was a random act." He then went on to tell them about the connection that the thief had with Domingez. He took great care to explain his theory, backed by the evidence that he had sifted through from the SHU. Pauline Allan contributed at times, with her 'take' on the incident and the identification of the bikie's body. Jack told them that he had a friend in the Police Traffic Division and how she'd sorted the traffic fine.

Pauline then started to tell them of the plan they had come up with.

"We'll issue a statement in relation to the accident; to say that, 'a known outlaw motorcycle gang member; Richard Chino of the Brothers OMCG died on his own bike...'"

David was still looking puzzled, but Natalie could see where this was going.

"David doesn't have a bike anymore though, so how are you going to 'sell' the idea he can be manipulated?" David looked at her and tried to make the connection, and then it dawned on him. "Jack? Are you asking what I think you are?"

Jack looked embarrassed briefly and said, "Look, it's just a matter of you going in and interviewing Domingez. Be 'a bit scared' and agree to help him and we'll record the whole thing. It's really important that we find out what it is that Domingez wants to get into the prison." David's surprise was evident in his expression, but before he could say anything Natalie was speaking again, "Not a chance!" she exclaimed, her voice rising slightly. "Apart from the fact that David would stand up to Domingez – certainly to begin with – Domingez wouldn't believe he could get something so easily. David would have to take some 'grief' from the bikies and that would be dangerous!" She got up and said, "Hold that thought for a minute while I change a diaper." She disappeared down the bedroom corridor after the sounds of crying; leaving Jack looking nervous and Pauline stifling a smile.

"I like her" she said to David, "Your wife is quite a feisty gal, isn't she!"

Natalie appeared a short while later and continued, as if she'd never left. "So, how are you planning to protect David, both in and out of the prison, and what measures are you putting in place to prevent David from having to pay traffic fines? From what you said..." she glanced at Pauline without pausing for breath, "The police don't seem to be all that competent in dealing with the facts!" She noticed Pauline's smile had grown wider. "What are you finding so funny?" she challenged, staring at her.

She looked around at Jack and David who were also smiling and said, "Too much? I've just had a baby, I'm not sure what is normal and what's hormones at the moment."

David slipped his arm round her and said, "You're fine, I think the detective here was just about to offer you the job." He chuckled. "Look," he said to Jack, and glancing at Pauline he continued, "I understand your plan, and the endgame here, but Natalie's right it would be pretty dangerous."

"I understand your position" began Pauline, looking at Natalie. "But, I am concerned that if we are right; and the evidence certainly seems to suggest that we are... then things are going to be dangerous for you anyway!" She let her words hang in the air for a moment, and then said, "What we are proposing, are measures which will enable us to get at the truth, whilst providing you with the best protection."

She turned her gaze to David, "For a start, we can access operational funds and get you a replacement bike. That way anything that happens to it, won't be at a cost to you. Then we have a system set in place so none of the fines come to you. They would all come to Jack or me and we would then get in contact with you to tell you how to act accordingly. Then there would be the options of allowing you to carry a concealed firearm. We know you are trained and have excellent competency."

"How on earth do you know that?" said Natalie. "You don't get that kind of permission if you are not on an 'operational standing.'" Pauline finished; and then added. "We know a lot of things actually, you'd be surprised."

Clear Bright Light of Day

It was Jack's turn to speak now, "Natalie has worked in Prison Intelligence, so I doubt, much would surprise her, but I know what you mean. Look, we're actually on the same side here and we are trying to make this work for all of us. Can we be friends?"

There was a quiet moment in which everyone took a sip of their coffee, which had cooled considerably, then pretended to ignore the past thirty minutes and made appreciative noises.

"Ok" said Natalie. "David what do you think? It will be you in most danger." David thought for a moment and said, "So, a new bike, no traffic fines and a licence to 'carry,' what's not to like?" Natalie smiled. She knew how David would really be feeling. She could see behind his eyes, the slight tautness in his smile which somehow prevented the dimple from appearing.

"Ok cowboy" she said to him. Then without a trace of humour and staring intently at Jack she asked, "Who has operational superiority? Because they are going to have employ me in some capacity, and I work from home these days!"

Jack and Pauline stared at each other. Jack 'willed' the detective in his mind, not to rock the boat and start an argument about who would be in charge. "Let's see who's interested in paying for this, first shall we?" said Pauline. "Then we'll have a chat about who does what. As I see it though, we're helping Prison Intelligence get the information we need to spread a net and press convictions.

The four looked from one to the others and nodded their resolve.

"We'll start next week" said Jack. The others registered slight surprise.

"Domingez has just been 'told' that David is on leave. So next week we'll arrange for David to go back in and see Domingez. I have my warrant, and I will get the system set up in the SHU to record the conversations and if Domingez talks in his sleep we'll make sure we have that as well!

Chapter Thirteen

Early the following day David found himself sitting at the kitchen breakfast bar eating dry cereal from a bowl and rubbing the sleep from his eyes. He had been awake several times in the night and both Natalie and he had tried to resolve the pain that Nathan seemed to be in, whilst the poor child cried and cried. Eventually, with gripe water and prayer Nathan went back to sleep.

David had not disturbed Natalie when he got up. She was still sleeping, but his internal body clock had woken him at the usual time to rise, and he quietly put on his dressing gown and slippers and made his way to the kitchen. There he made himself a cup of tea and poured cereal into a bowl. He looked for milk, but there was only just enough for a couple of cups of tea, so he decided not to use it on his breakfast. He was sitting looking at the weather app on his phone when he received a long SMS from Jack. It was so long that it had been converted to a 'multi media message' and David thought it was ironic that technology had advanced to be able to do this, but the 'SMS acronym' for Short Message Service was still in use. David read Jack's message and woke fully, with excitement now coursing through his veins. Jack had outlined the measures that were to be installed in the SHU and had confirmed that the plan he and Pauline had submitted to the Police Commissioner had been accepted. The news that had really lifted his mood though, was that a courier was going to call at the house that morning with equipment and a credit card. David was instructed to buy a replacement bike, jacket and helmet.

David couldn't help himself and he whistled softly as he anticipated the conversation he would have with Helen at the

Harley Davidson dealership. It wasn't softly enough however and soon a tired looking Natalie carrying a crying baby wandered down the corridor and into the kitchen. Natalie smiled at David and passed Nathan to him, "I can't find the 'off switch'" she said and opened the fridge.

"Kettle just boiled, I would have made you a cuppa if I'd known you were awake" he replied. Natalie poured the last of the milk into her cup and came to sit by David. Nathan had gone to sleep in his arms.

"Keep him upright" she said as she sat down, "He's had his breakfast and we want him to keep it down."

David moved him slightly into a more upright position.

"You look pleased with yourself" she added.

David read Jacks text from the screen of his phone and Natalie brightened up as well.

"It will be nice to have a new bike" she said, smiling at him.

David continued eating dry cereal and holding Nathan whilst Natalie showered and dressed, then he put Nathan back in his cot, and showered himself. Natalie went out in her car to get milk and other provisions and when she returned she found David dressed and holding a package about the size of a large shoe box. "Courier just dropped it off" he said by way of explanation. Natalie put the things she'd bought away and asked if Nathan was still sleeping. David confirmed that he had changed him and put him down in his cot, and he hadn't heard from him since. Natalie sneaked quietly down the bedroom corridor and put her head round the door to Nathan's room. She returned smiling, "Good job mister!" she said as she walked into the kitchen. David had made two cups of tea using the milk that Natalie had bought, they sat side by side.

He had then opened and spread the contents of the package on the stone bench top.

"Either one" he said as she looked at the cups, and then picked one up and took a sip.

With cup in hand, Natalie looked at the assorted items; a registration plate, slightly scratched, but still attached to the Grifter Box; a credit card, with a note telling them what the pin number was and the necessity for receipts. There was another card; which looked like a Federal Police ID card with David's photograph displayed on it, but no Police emblem. What took up more space was a paragraph of writing that was too small for Natalie to read. The final item was a holster moulded for a Glock 22 pistol. It was padded and designed to fit inside the waistband of a pair of trousers and clip on the belt outside.

"That will take some getting used to" David said when he saw Natalie staring at it.

They both read the note accompanying the package, and David went as he was instructed, to the gun safe and removed his Glock 22 from it, along with two ammunition clips. He laid them on the bench top beside the other items. He was wondering how Natalie was feeling, and the reality of having to carry a weapon in normal life was beginning to sink in.

"Want me to load those?" asked Natalie, breaking the silence. David looked at her and was amazed at her cool expression.

"You are something else" he said and smiled at her.

"Gotta do my bit" she said and started pushing 9mm bullets into the magazine clips. "Fifteen in each clip" she said. "One in the pipe?" Natalie pushed a clip into the pistol and racked the slide. She then ejected the clip and placed one more round in the clip and pushed it back into the gun again.

"Be careful, we've not carried these loaded like this" she said, "Bit like that 'Simunition training day' we went on, eh?" she smiled, but it was a grim, determined look that was forcing the smile on her lips.

David took a breath and carefully picked up the Glock. He pointed it down and holding it firmly he pushed it into the holster, past the trigger guard which enclosed and protected the mechanism. He placed it on the bench top again. "There, much safer!" he said.

"Let's go buy you a bike" said Natalie, suddenly excited. Of course, it wasn't as simple as just leaving the house and driving to Harley Davidson. While David cleared up the items from the kitchen bench-top, Natalie got Nathan ready to travel and then they left the house. Natalie sat in the back of the car with Nathan's cot strapped in, and David drove to the dealership in Beckenham. The gun was safely tucked into David's jeans and the grips outside on the belt held it firm. David felt continually self-conscious and kept making sure his shirt fell over the belt line so the gun was fully concealed. He had placed his ID and carry permit in his back pocket, but everything felt bulky and he wondered if he'd have to buy new trousers.

Arriving at the Harley Davidson dealership, Natalie suggested that David go on ahead of her and Nathan. She took the car keys and after locking up, she carried the sleeping baby in his cot into the shop and past rows of gleaming new bikes. She found David sitting talking to Helen at one of the sales desks. She strolled up and put Nathan's cot on one end of the large desk. "Hello little feller" Helen said looking into the cot.

"Wow he's good... So quiet." Natalie exchanged a glance with David, knowing the effort they had made to give the appearance of calm.

"Like a duck on water" said Natalie. Helen stifled a laugh and made violent paddling motions with her hands to indicate she knew exactly what Natalie was saying.

"So, a new bike?" said Helen after the initial pleasantries were exchanged. "Are you trading the old one?"

David explained that the old one had been stolen, and then written off by the insurance company. Helen tried to persuade David to try a different model or style, but David was adamant that it had to be the same as the old one. Eventually Helen agreed and called up David's original order and checked it with him. "It will take a week or so for us to get a Grifter box from the U.S." she said. David reached into the box beside him and retrieved the box and the 'regio' plate.

"What?" exclaimed Helen, "Same plate and old Grifter?"

"Has to be," said David. "All the old registration details will just update for this bike when you take it in to be registered." Helen looked sceptical so David said, "Let's just say I have a friend in the Department of Transport."

He smiled and Helen said, "OK then!" After the bike and accessories had been entered on to the sales order, Helen asked if he'd need anything else.

"Helmet? Jacket?" "Yes" said David, "and gloves."

David chose a new helmet almost identical to the one he'd lost, the only difference being that this Shark EVO Line 3, didn't have a quick release clip like the one he'd bought on line from Aerostitch in Germany. He pulled a Sena SMH10 Bluetooth communicator off the shelf. This was more expensive than he could order online, but he needed it now and Harley would fit it to the helmet for him. Lastly David asked if he could see a range of jackets and gloves.

Helen was helping David at the back of the shop try on various jackets and David walked out showing them to Natalie who was still near Helen's desk with Nathan. Natalie was nodding her approval at some of the jackets and shaking her head at others. As David stretched his arms into one jacket that Helen was holding for him, his shirt rose up and revealed the top of the gun in his belt. There was an awkward moment between David and Helen and then she just turned and walked away. David cringed and thought he'd offended or scared her, but she was back almost immediately with a lovely looking jacket. It was a Men's FXRG Switchback Leather Jacket.

"It's not cheap" she said, "but if you want to be able to get that gun out without having to take the jacket off first, this is the one for you." David stared at her.

Helen smiled, "You aren't like some of our clientele," she said glancing at his belt again. "I imagine *you* have a permit for that! This one is $795, but for you, and because you are buying another new bike I will heavily discount it."

David looked quizzically at her and she explained.

"You can zip from top or bottom, so it means that you can get at your... belt line, if needed."

David smiled and thanked her. He put it on and walked out to show Natalie.

"I liked the one with the orange lettering best" she said, "That one looks expensive." David suggested that she not ask the price, and said he'd explain later why this was the jacket of choice.

Sitting at the desk again, Helen totalled the amounts and asked, "I guess the insurance gave you a cheque for a hefty deposit, will you need some finance as well?" "Thanks Helen. No. Just put it all on this card" said David passing over the credit card. A slight 'look' passed over Helen's expression, and then she ran the card through the reader and nodded.

"Pin please!"

David entered the pin, and Helen processed payment without further comment. Then after a minute, "Ready end of the week I reckon, I'll call you" she announced.

Helen walked them to the door of the dealership and shook David's hand firmly when they left.

"Want a baby-seat?" she shouted after them smiling.

David left the helmet to be fitted with the SENA communicator, but he took the jacket and gloves with him; placing them in the boot of the car out of sight.

"I'm starving" said Natalie as she got into the car.

"Let's get some cash out and get Nandos" David suggested as they drove back through Thornlie. They pulled into the car park of Westpac Bank in Thornlie and stopped by the ATM to get some cash out; as David was collecting the money from the machine he noticed a couple of Police officers walk out of the office of Chris Tallentyre MLA. The Labour politician for Thornlie. They looked at him and immediately deviated from the direction of their car, towards him.

He turned to face them, "Can I help you?" he asked.

"Keep your hands where I can see them" one said. David held his wallet and the money he'd withdrawn in plain sight,

"What's this about?" he asked.

"Please turn around and face the ATM. Place your hands on the wall" the other officer said. Neither sounded stressed, and neither officer had threatened him, so he turned back to the ATM and did as he'd been told. Natalie could see what was happening from where she was sitting and so got out of the car. The second Police officer turned towards her as she stepped out from behind the vehicle.

"I have reason to believe you are concealing a firearm" the first officer said clearly, whilst the second officer put his hand on his gun and removed the leather strap, that would prevent him from removing the gun from it's holster.

"Left back pocket!" shouted David, "Concealed carry permit!"

The Police officer removed David's ID and read the card twice, "You don't see many of these" he said, "Mind if I ask which branch you are with?"

David looked at him and replied, "You can ask, but I can't tell you, because I'm not sure myself."

The police officer nodded and said in somewhat of sarcastic tone, "Sure... sure." He then turned and said to his colleague,

"Come on, let's leave 'Secret Squirrel' to his business." Then as he got to his car, he turned back to David and said, "Sorry to have bothered you sir, I have an eye for these things after so long on the force. Hope you don't mind sir. Better safe than sorry, I'm sure you agree?"

David and Natalie continued their journey to Canning Vale and Nandos in silence. Getting to the restaurant Natalie found a table large enough to put Nathan's carry cot on whilst David ordered food.

"I'm going to have to get some bigger shirts I think" said David putting the food down. Nathan was awake and Natalie was suddenly worried.

"I wonder if eating this food will affect my milk? Nathan might not like Mexican flavoured milk!" David laughed and said he thought it would be ok, but there was only really one way of finding out.

After the meal, they headed home and David phoned Jack to let him know how their morning had gone. Jack was encouraged that they had acted so quickly and confirmed to David that his ID would get him past all but the 'top security' places in the state. He also told David to come straight over to see him as soon as he picked up the bike.

"We'll get a GPS tracker fitted to it and then there will be no doubt as to where it is, at any time." said Jack.

The next morning, much earlier than expected Helen called to say the bike was ready, "All parts in stock and we have a vested interest in keeping your business" she quipped. Soon after the call, Natalie dropped David outside the Harley Davidson dealership. She didn't stay as she knew that Helen would want to have photos taken of David receiving the new bike, and she knew David wasn't going to let that happen. She didn't want to be a part of that argument. David spoke to Helen and shared a little about the need to pretend this bike was the same as the old one.

"I sort of got that, at the Department of Transport." Helen said. "It was weird, they had all the paperwork all lined up. They registered it in your name but at a different address. I just thought 'they know what they're doing,' so I just let it happen and didn't argue. The girl there said the instructions on the account were very explicit. There was no money to pay either, how did you swing that?"

David laughed, "I could tell you but then I'd have to shoot you." Helen looked serious for a moment then broke into peals of laughter, "You could to!" she said.

David rode the bike into Perth, to Jack's office and phoned him from the street outside. The door to the building's car park then opened automatically and David rode down the ramp and parked in a designated bike place, the bike's engine rumbling even more loudly in the underground carpark. He didn't have to wait long, before Jack appeared with another man, who was wearing overalls. The man went to work at once, fixing the small GPS tracker to the bike out of sight. Jack passed David some insurance documents and said he'd be in touch soon. David used the time that the GPS was being fitted to call the Education Department at Corymbia and told them he was coming in on Monday, but probably wouldn't be staying for long. He wanted to make sure that Meredith was going to be there and asked Tracey to cancel Meredith's morning classes, so that he could spend some time with her.

David then took the free-way home and just enjoyed the acceleration of the new bike, and the engine noise of the Harley Breakout. There was a certain amount of care-freeness due to the knowledge that no speeding tickets would come his way if he did exceed the limit unintentionally!

Chapter Fourteen

For the next few days the bike stayed in the garage. It was a tight fit, with the gym equipment in there, but David found a way of positioning it so it could still be walked around. David found himself frequently wanting to polish it, or just look at it out of sheer enjoyment. Natalie fell into more of a routine where Nathan was concerned; or perhaps it was Nathan that fell into a more regular pattern of behaviour. David willingly took his share of the work with their new baby, especially at night and Natalie felt a renewed energy to chase him around the bedroom. Despite the concerns each had about the current possible danger from the Brothers OMCG, they also felt a peace and love for one another which they knew would carry them into this new chapter of their lives together.

On Saturday, David had come back into the kitchen from the garage for perhaps the fourth time since lunch. Natalie smiled at him in a knowing fashion and said, "For goodness sake David, just take that bike out for a run or something. I can see that you are itching to do so. We'll be alright. Really. Go! Enjoy!" She grinned at him and he smiled back at her.

David organised his bike gear and with his Glock safely positioned on his belt, he rode out towards the coast. He thought of grabbing a coffee in Fremantle, but instead turned south and followed the Hampton Road, then Cockburn road towards Rockingham. He wanted to ride out via the curves in Henderson, and perhaps stop and enjoy the view over Cockburn Sound to Garden Island. He slowed as he took the sweeping curve near the Coastal Motorcycle Club and was glad he did when he saw the speed camera in the back of a white van on the corner. He checked his speed but was also struck by the thought that he wouldn't get the ticket even if he had gone through the corner too fast. He continued until the road terminated at the junction with Rockingham Road, near the Alcoa Refinery. He turned south, and eventually the road became Patterson Road and then he decided to turn onto the Kwinana Beach Road which took him along the 'sea-front' to Rockingham. He had been aware for the past ten kilometres that two other motorcycles were following him at some distance. It wasn't uncommon for riders to take the route that he'd enjoyed though, so he wasn't concerned. He slowed to enjoy the view towards Rockingham and the causeway that the Navy used to get out to the base on the Island.

There was no sign of the other bikes now, and he thought that they must have turned off or stopped. David continued along the Esplanade and pulled into the carpark near 'Sunsets restaurant'. He had been feeling carefree and relaxed, but seeing the restaurant and parking the bike, he now wished Natalie were with him. The car park had been full, so David parked as many bikers did, on the pavement area on the other side of the traffic bollards. He turned off his SENA communicator and carefully placed the helmet and his gloves on the bike gear leaver and walked into the restaurant. He ordered a 'double shot' long black coffee, with a dash of milk on the side; and whilst drinking it he looked out to sea. He saw people fishing from the boat pier and pondered on how blessed he was to live in such a beautiful place. Forty minutes and two coffees later he walked back out to his bike, only to find that two other motorcycles had parked either side of him, blocking him in. He couldn't stand the bike upright without hitting the right-hand bike and he couldn't stand on the left side, due to the other bike which had parked too close. He had just decided to try and move the bike on the right when two leather clad older men walked towards him. David waited to see what they would do. The men stared silently and intentionally at him, but both paused and sat on the concrete bollards in front of their bikes. David addressed them and said, "Hi guys, nice day for it." The men stared at him in silence. David noticed the patches on their jackets. One had a 1% patch, which David understood meant that this bikie was advertising, that he considered himself to be a part of the 1% that made all bikies look bad.

"Nice bikes. Er could you move one please?" he asked. The men continued to sit and stare in silence.

"Want me to move one for you?" David asked tentatively. The men stood at David's suggestion and continued to stare, until David lost patience and went to move the bike on the right. As he started to lift the bike off its stand, the Brothers bikies unzipped their jackets.

"You want to die?" Asked one of the men. David looked over at them.

"You touch a man's bike... means you might want to die!" the other leather clad bikie suggested.

David let the bike back down on to its stand and turned towards the men. He unzipped his jacket as he did so and said, "Look I don't want any trouble I just want to get my bike out. The bikie who had spoken first gently lifted his jacket to reveal the grip of a pistol sticking out of his jeans. He didn't touch the gun but it was a clear threat.

"Look mate" said David lifting the right side of his jacket - the side he wasn't wearing his Glock – and then holding his arms out, palms open.

"I don't want any trouble. He stepped back calming himself and concentrated on his breathing. He knew that to draw and fire a gun was not like it was in the westerns; slowly and deliberately was better than fast and wild. There was also the general public to consider, and the angles that bullets could fly off in after hitting an object. David knew that well, having been hit himself by a bullet that ricocheted, a year or so earlier.

The bikies were walking towards him now, and he took several steps backward to maintain the distance between them. He decided he would not draw his gun unless they drew and fired at least one shot. His breathing was keeping him alert but calm. 'So many people go into shock', he thought 'if they are held up or threatened'. It was because their breathing worked against them, and they found themselves feeling faint due too little, or too much oxygen. "Calm down guys, I'm not going to touch your bikes." David noticed his voice came out at a higher pitch. He noted that it wasn't a bad thing to be a little stressed, this would send the right message to these bikies as well as give him adrenalin in his system, to help him with his fight or flight.

The bikies moved their bikes and started them. Then without putting on helmets they pulled away. David was aware of another man on his right talking to him, "You ok mate, what was that about?" David turned to see the waiter who had served him his coffee.

"I have no idea" said David who was now feeling shaken. And then he realised that he had every idea what it had been about. "Don't worry about it." he said to the waiter. "Just bullies blowing off steam."

The waiter went back into 'Sunsets' and David walked over to his bike. He lifted his helmet off the gear leaver and pulled out the new gloves he'd bought from Harley. As he pulled them out something fell out of the helmet. It was a small box about twice the size of a packet of cigarettes. David looked down at it lying on the floor. After what seemed like whole minutes passing he reached down and picked it up. It was a mobile phone box, inside of which was a small mobile phone, which pre-dated any smart phone. There was also a slim small charger and a note. The note warned David, by name, that he would suffer much harm if he didn't take the phone to Domingez in the SHU.

David put the box in his Swing Arm bag and then strapped it closed. He looked about him and thought better of making a phone call himself. He didn't want to ride home just yet, and he certainly didn't want to be followed. He hadn't noticed the Brothers bikies when he left home, so maybe they didn't know where he lived. He decided to call in on Jack, at his home in Fremantle.

David kept a paranoid watch, for anyone following him as he rode to Fremantle, he even doubled back on himself once to be sure. He saw no one and was still wondering how the bikies had caught up to him. He wondered if they had waited for him near Hampton Road in Fremantle. It was possible. He occasionally rode to Fremantle for coffee on Saturday. He wasn't sure though.

He arrived at Jack's and parked on the street outside. He then walked slowly up the path, still looking around, still hoping not to see any evidence that he'd been followed. He rang the door-bell and when Jack answered he looked surprised to see David standing on his doorstep.

"Hey David, why didn't you call ahead? Is Natalie with you? No... what am I thinking you'd be in the car... What's up?"

Jack invited David in, and after David explained briefly what had happened, Jack folded his arms and stroked his chin thoughtfully. "Well..." he began, "It is good that they have made contact and have given you something. We'll have to think whether it's a good idea for the phone to get to Domingez. Let me have a look at it." Jack took the phone and slipped the battery out of it. "There is probably a way to short out the aerial. That would make it virtually useless." He went to get a small set of screwdrivers and when he came back, Mary followed him with two cups of tea.

"Hello David" she said, "I thought you could use one of these." She placed a cup in front of him on the table. "Have a seat" she invited. The other cup went in front of Jack who was already seated at the table with the tools and phone spread out before him. "Right, I'll leave you to it, whatever *it* is." she said and walked back to the kitchen.

Jack worked on the phone for ten minutes and then started putting it back together. It will read a signal and report poor strength, but I've disconnected the sender circuit, so it won't 'shake hands' with the cell tower, but the display is unaffected. David nodded, knowing that the battery would run down fast trying to make contact with the cell tower. "I will call the prison and arrange for you to 'walk it in'" said Jack.

David finished his tea and chatted with Jack for a short while, before calling Natalie to tell her he'd be home soon. Natalie sounded a bit stressed, but said she'd talk to David when he got home. David thanked Jack and rode home via the Leach Highway and then took the freeway, Roe and finally Ranford. He pulled into the garage and was about to wipe the bike down when Natalie appeared looking quite shaken. David was immediately concerned and left the bike to put his arm round her. "What's wrong?" he asked.

Natalie related what had happened after David had left, which involved a house-call from a couple of the Brothers OMCG.

She said, "Nathan was asleep and I heard this banging on the front door, and I knew something was wrong right away. So I went and told them to stop making so much noise. I then asked who it was but they wouldn't say. So I said I'd have to get the deadlock key."

"You didn't let them in did you?" asked David.

"No, its alright I actually went and got something else and then went around the side of the house. It was a couple of those Brothers bikies in full gear. I shouted to them over the gate and told them to leave. They said they'd come to talk to you about a job they had for you, and one tried to get over the gate."

"Are you alright?" said David, "They didn't hurt you, did they?" Natalie was looking a bit proud of herself.

"What happened?" asked David again.

"Well, I shouldn't be so pleased really, but when the guy got halfway over the gate I pushed my Glock into his groin and suggested that he stay very still. Poor guy actually wet himself before he ran away. I'm not sure that they will be back here again. Either way, I'm leaving my gun out of the safe for now." She saw David's face and said, "Yes. I know we'll have to be really careful, but these guys are serious."

David took Natalie back to the kitchen and called Jack to bring him up to date with the new developments. Jack agreed that Natalie should be able to protect herself and said that he would bring a holster over to the house, like the one David had been given.

"She can't carry it outside the house David." he told him in a serious tone, "But it will be safer if the trigger is completely covered when it's loaded."

David finished the call, and then told Natalie about his encounter, and calling in to see Jack. He was about to suggest that they stay at his old place; being that Frank wasn't using it for the next few weeks, when Natalie said, "Oh! And my mum is arriving tomorrow. She was able to change her flight and get some time off earlier than she first thought. This will be *interesting*!"

David liked Natalie's mum, Kate. She was warm and caring and keen to make things easier for Natalie as she started looking after Nathan.

"That's good" he said. "Lets not scare her though."

The rest of the weekend went quite quickly. It was odd to be spending the time at church in the 'Parents Room', where parents and very small children could hear the message that Pastor Tony delivered, through speakers, and even see the stage through soundproof glass. The babies couldn't be heard in the auditorium and thus disrupt the speaking part of the service. David and Natalie made a point of staying in the auditorium for the 'praise and worship' part of the service and Nathan slept through even the loudest of songs. David was unusually self-conscious with the gun secreted in his belt line. He didn't raise his hands in the worship and made sure the shirt he wore hung low over where the weapon was carried.

After the service they bought lunch at the church cafe and sat chatting with friends. They picked Kate up at the airport in the afternoon and brought her back to their house. Glad to be distracted by family news and Kate 'cooing' over Nathan, who was quite taken with his grandmother, and stared up at her quietly whenever he was held. It was just sinking in for Kate, that she was a grandmother. Every-time she mentioned it a small frown followed by a smile crossed her face. David, who had noticed this said at one point, "You are too young to be a grandmother!" to which she replied, "You are only saying that because it's true!"

Chapter Fifteen

Monday morning came and David had to get up early to go to work. It was a bit of an effort as he'd been up once in the night, feeding Nathan with a bottle and then changing him. Kate had responded on the other occasion and Natalie had been able to sleep through soundly. David turned the alarm on his phone off and as he swung his legs out of bed, he felt Natalie reach for him. He was tempted just to get back in to bed and be late arriving at the prison. Natalie murmured sleepily that she would catch him later and said she'd be thinking of him during the day. He kissed her and then went into the bathroom to shower and dress.

Once dressed, David wandered into the kitchen. He boiled the kettle and made tea in a cup, and then put a couple of slices of bread into the toaster. He got out a plate, knife, butter and the marmalade, which he lined up on the breakfast bar neatly, and when he heard the toast 'pop up' he retrieved it and put it on the plate. He had just started buttering it when Kate walked in wearing her dressing gown.

"Morning David" she said in a quiet conspiratorial voice.

"Morning Kate" replied David, "I've just made some toast, you want to take these and I'll put some more in?"

Kate agreed to take one, and David got another plate out and then put another couple of pieces of bread into the toaster; he also reboiled the kettle and took another cup out of the cupboard.

"So. David..." began Kate. "Tell me what's going on please!"

David looked at his mother in law as he continued making her tea and could see by her expression that she would not be put off easily.

"Women's intuition?" he asked. Kate took a bite of toast and chewed with a calculating expression. David could see that she was deciding how she would ask her next questions, and meanwhile her waiting was intentionally tempting him to just fill in the silence by talking, and perhaps give away more information than he'd intend to.

David waited and so eventually she said, "Well... Natalie won't tell me what she's worried about... she checks on Nathan more often than any mother might, and she seems overly concerned about the house being secure..." David was about to respond to what he'd heard and put Kate's mind at ease by saying something about 'new mothers', when Kate finished her sentence, "...and you are carrying a gun everywhere you go. What's that about then?"

David and Kate stared at each other across the breakfast bar. Kate sitting on a high stool and David standing, leaning on the stone bench top.

"Oh, you noticed that, did you?" David said to buy time, and he took a large bite of toast, to keep his mouth busy while he thought of what to tell her. He wondered what he could say that wouldn't make her more worried. He finished his mouthful of toast and took a sip of tea and decided on, 'outright tactful honesty'.

"It's complicated Kate." he took a deep breath, "And it has to do with my work. We've received some credible threats and have been told that this is an appropriate response to them." Then he added, "I'm not altogether comfortable with it either, but I've agreed to it because I've been told it's necessary."

Kate took a sip of her tea and said, "Does Natalie have one as well?"

David briefly explained that they both owned guns and were members of the prison pistol club. They shot in competitions and Natalie had a gun in the safe. He added that she didn't carry her gun but that at present Kate should not be surprised if Natalie did not keep her gun in the safe. He also said that Jack would call later and drop of a holster for Natalie's pistol, to ensure better safety for it.

Kate seemed to accept the information, and after David had tidied up the breakfast things and put the cutlery in the dishwasher she wandered back towards her bedroom, wishing David a good day as she went. David quickly sent Natalie a SMS so she wouldn't be caught out by her mother, and told her what he'd said. He then went and put on his leather jacket, helmet and gloves; and rolled the large Harley Davidson out of the garage so that when he started it, it wouldn't echo so much.

David did not ride directly to the prison. He detoured to the bakery in Livingston shopping centre, knowing it opened early. He bought some doughnuts and sweet buns which he safely secured in his Swing Arm bag, along with the phone that Jack had disabled. He continued his journey south and after a cold but exhilarating ride, he pulled into the carpark of Corymbia Prison. He made his way through the car parking area to the small undercover bike park, and pushed his bike into one of the spaces, engaging first gear to lock the bike in place on its stand. He turned off the SENA communicator and balled his gloves into his helmet, but did not place it on the gear leaver, or put his USB stick and Swiss Army knife into his gloves, as he would have usually done. He carried the items and made his way to the gate house, under the observation of the cameras in the car park. He saw other Education staff arriving ahead of him and stopped and returned to the bike to get the cakes and the phone; returning moments later and walking into the gatehouse.

"Morning Weasel" he said to Snr. Officer Stoat, using the affectionate nickname he'd become known to his friends by.

"David!" Snr. Officer Stoat replied, nodding as he did so. "Step this way please" he added indicating the visitors side, where he saw officer Graham the TRG Snr. Officer standing. David walked to his right and walked through the metal detector that bleeped loudly. No one paid any attention though and officer Graham opened the big bullet-proof glass door and took him into the Security area of the Gate.

"I've not been in here before" said David.

"We thought that since you were not using the range today that you should store your weapon where the Police do, and that we should ensure that this phone you are bringing in, really is disabled." He looked at David, who said, "Of course!" and started to disrobe his jacket. David removed the holster and gun together with the spare clip and passed it to officer Graham who removed the clip from the pistol and then racked the slide to eject the chambered round.

"You want for us to release the pressure on the clips for you and unload it, whilst you're in today?" he asked. "Good idea" said David. Although the clip was usually stored empty, thus allowing the spring enclosed in it to expand, the gun had been kept ready for several days and David knew that this weakened the spring and eventually the last couple of bullets would not load as a result.

Officer Graham put the pistol to one side, promising to store it safely, and David asked if he could leave the Helmet, gloves and his personal items with him as well. Officer

Graham showed him space where he could leave them and passed the box with the mobile phone to another officer who switched it on and tried to make a call. Satisfied that the phone was disabled, he erased the phone log and put it all back together with the charger in the box. David thanked the officers in the TRG area and then left to make his way into the prison. As David left, Officer Graham made a phone call to Matt Roberts, the acting Superintendent.

"He's on his way Sir!"

David reached the Lobby and was requesting a radio, when Matt appeared on the Admin side of the secure area.

"Got a minute?" he called.

David smiled and walked through Admin, following Matt to the Superintendent's office.

"Bet you didn't think you'd be back so soon" Matt said, as he sat down in the big chair behind the desk.

David was just taking his seat opposite when Snr. Officer White from the SHU knocked once and walked in.

"Morning Whitey" said Matt, "Thanks for coming at short notice." Officer White waited to be invited to sit and when Matt pointed to the chair by David, he sat in it.

"What's this about?" asked Whitey directly.

Matt took his time giving some background to what they were doing, and several times Whitey glanced across at David to see his reaction.

"So, when David comes in later today to see Domingez and give him the phone, you all need to be aware of what is going on and record the entire event on the new cameras that were installed last week. Here is a copy of the warrant, for recording sound." He passed a photocopy across the table,

"So it's all above board, and we want to catch Domingez trying to use the phone, so don't take it off him unless it's an obvious 'bust'." Officer White took a breath and exhaled before saying, "You sure that phone won't work?"

After receiving assurances, the 'smuggled phone' would not operate properly, he agreed to pass David into the SHU with it, but said that he was not going to tell the other officers working there that the phone had come in. That way there would not be any doubt or suspicion if Domingez was caught with it and allowed to keep it.

"Let's keep it real" Whitey said as he left.

David continued into the prison and found his staff in the tea room catching up with one another after the weekend. Some were surprised to see him, but Tracey and Meredith had known he would be there. David made tea for himself and put the cakes on the table for later. Appreciative noises came from those seated round the table and David told them he was in for a short while, to tidy up some work for the prison management; and that he probably wouldn't stay all day, "So act as if I'm not really in." He said.

Meredith waited until all the staff had left to begin their work and then reached for a doughnut and fixed David with her big brown eyes.

"Glad to see you alive and well boss" she said and smiled a big white toothy grin. David smiled back.

"I hope you've ditched that bike for a nice sports car now" she added.

David shook his head, "Actually no. But it's a long story." He paused and looking back at her, and he asked, "Are you up to talking about your 'run-in' with Domingez?"

Meredith spent an hour talking to David, telling him about the unpleasant encounter with Domingez. David asked many questions about his manner and posture, trying to gauge the prisoner's tactics and intimidation. Eventually he let Meredith go, and she thanked him for the time she now had to prepare work for the afternoon. David said that he would probably not come back to Education after seeing Domingez and he wished her well and invited her to contact him any-time. He then discretely left the Education area, calling at the ODP observation bubble to remove his name from the board.

David walked passed the chaplaincy and opened the gate to the courtyard outside the SHU area, he stepped through and secured the gate again. He was now under close observation by cameras as he walked to the door to the SHU. He rang the bell outside and waited, and after about fifteen seconds the gate clicked and swung open. He walked into the small cubicle lobby and closed the outer door. He waited a further ten seconds and the camera above him swivelled about making sure he was alone. Ten seconds later the inner door clicked and swung open. He walked into a room which had a raised platform in the centre of it and a row of lockers on one side. He had been here many times before and knew the drill; he walked to a locker and removed his keys, belt and all identifying items; placing them in the locker. He locked the door and put the key in the pocket of his trousers that also contained the small phone and charger, which was now out of its case. He turned and walked to the small platform and stood up on it, as Sn. Officer White entered the room from the other side. Whitey took a metal detector 'wand' from the rack and turned it on. He ensured it was working by waving it next to the metal bracket on the rack and nodded when the loud whine was emitted. He then approached David and asked the standard question: "Are you carrying anything that has not been cleared by security?"

"No!" said David clearly, for the camera.

Whitey then proceeded to slowly move the wand around David's body; when he came to the phone the wand whined loudly and Whitey moved in to pat down that area of David.

"Please remove the key's in your pocket he said loudly." David removed the key and held it up for the camera.

"Key to locker two" Whitey commented for the officers observing. He then switched off the wand and replaced it in the rack. David stood down and was led into the control area and then into the Education room to await Domingez.

Domingez was lying on his bed, he had already been out for his hour of exercise and was not expecting to be allowed out again. He heard his door click open a moment prior to the announcement, "Domingez. Domingez to control. Domingez to control!"

Domingez pulled himself from the bed. He was not in any hurry to perform for his jailers. He moved slowly to the door and pulled it open and stepped outside the cell. He then saw David in the Education room through the glass wall and chose instead to walk towards the kitchen to get a cup of tea.

The officer announced again, "Domingez to control. Domingez. If you do not come to control now, you will forfeit your interview with Education." Domingez paused. He had waited weeks for this interview, he knew he couldn't afford to jeopardise it, despite not wanting to conform. He turned and lumbered towards 'Control.' Stopping by the 'blacked out glass' control room grille he heard the officer say, "You have a visitor from Education. Proceed immediately to the Education room."

David could see the 'power play' being acted out and silently prayed for grace. He waited, seated on one side of the table until Domingez walked through the door; whereupon he stood and greeted him and held out his hand to shake the inmate's. Domingez just looked at him. David held his hand out and said, "Look, I don't have time for this crap, do you want this phone or not?"

Domingez looked at David's hand, and saw the phone in it. He shook David's hand and took the phone, deftly pocketing it afterwards. His first words to David were not to greet him, "Where's the charger?" he demanded.

"You get that with the next, and *last* handshake" said David.

Domingez sat down and stared at David in what he hoped was an intimidating fashion. He used to scare people a lot, but these days he just didn't know anymore. He looked at David, "Did you like my people? The people who gave you my phone?" he asked quietly.

"Not particularly" said David, "But idiots and bullies are common enough." Domingez sat silently staring at David.

"Ok. If that's all" said David, "I'll not bother visiting again, here's the charger." he stood and held out his hand as if to shake Domingez's again. "Sit down David James, and don't disrespect me or your wife Natalie, and your son Nathan, will suffer for your insolence."

David felt his face redden and he didn't have to feign the fear that rose within him. He felt his blood pressure rise along with his temper.

"What did you say?" the words were out of his mouth before he thought about them. "Are you threatening me? This is over, I'm out of here."

Domingez just sat there staring at David, "I told you to sit down" he said. David remained standing. He wanted to keep some measure of control and felt that he was losing it to this prisoner, which was never a good thing.

"I will not sit down..." he started to say, when over the speakers came, "Is everything alright in there?"

David sat down quickly and waived a thumbs-up at the camera. Then to Domingez, "Don't threaten me..."

"Or what?" replied Domingez. "Now I own you" he added. "You will bring me something." he finished.

"I've already brought you something, so now leave me and my family alone."

Domingez just looked at David and said, "You have no idea how much danger you are in do you? Your Family can be just like Mike Davies' wife. We can get to you." Domingez stood up and held out his hand, "Thank you for meeting with me today, I can't wait to receive my *'Education resources'*" He announced loudly.

David wanted to slap his hand out of the way and walk out but found himself shaking the hand and passing the charger to Domingez.

In the locker room as David was putting on his belt and replacing items in his pockets, Snr. Officer White met him.

"All go ok?" he asked.

"I guess so" said David, "He is quite a character, isn't he?"

"Oh yes" said Whitey, "One of the nastier ones if you ask me."

David went from the SHU to the Superintendent's office and was able to meet with Matt for a moment and fill him in on his meeting with Domingez.

"So, there's more to come in?" Matt asked. "Do you know what things?" David said that he didn't know but reassured Matt that whatever it was it would be going through security first.

David walked back down the long concrete path to the gate, feeling shaken and frustrated as his inability to control the conversation with Domingez. He picked up his Glock but took the exit to the gun range and grabbed a box of hydro-shock rounds from the officer there. He loaded the two clips with them and put up a target. For the next ten minutes he practiced drawing the weapon and firing quickly and carefully. The results were not as good as if he had shot in a competition, but they were all on target. David felt the tension of the frustration and fear leave his body.

After borrowing a gun cleaning kit and reloading the clips with his rounds and then chambering a round in the pistol, he collected his remaining items and walked out of the prison. He pulled the helmet on before he got back to where he'd parked his bike, hoping to just jump on and ride off. However, even at a distance, he could see the bike was not where he'd parked it. He looked around to see if someone had moved it to inconvenience him. He couldn't see it anywhere close. He took a deep breath and let it out slowly. One side of him just wanted to go back into the prison and shoot Domingez. He knew he wasn't going to do that though. He took his helmet off and sat on the bench beside a table often used by the 'programmes staff' for packed lunches in the sunshine. He rested the helmet on the table and called Jack.

"Hi Jack, they have my bike" he said, and went on to explain about his conversation with Domingez in the SHU. Jack talked to him on the phone, whilst he did real time checks on the tracking software which recorded data from the device on the bike. He also talked with Sgt. Becky Wilson to find out if the bike had been involved in any traffic incidents.

"Here's the latest," said Jack. "Your bike is parked outside your house. I've just arranged for the police to send a unit there" he added quickly. "There has been a red-light photo recorded and a fine and points intercept made as well. They are trying to make life difficult and upset you David."

David thanked Jack and then terminated the call and called Natalie. Natalie answered immediately and asked him if he was ok.

"I heard the bike outside, but you didn't come in" she said. "I was worried and called you." David looked down at the phone and realised he'd missed a call. He assured Natalie that all was well and told her that the police were about to call to ensure she was ok. He went on to say that he'd tell her how the morning in the prison had gone later. He then sent an SMS to Meredith. He knew that she wouldn't get it until later when she left the prison and turned on her phone, as he had done. It read; *'Meredith, I hope you don't get sucked into this, but if you encounter any OMCG members, don't stop or engage them. Knock them down if you have to but get to police.'* He hoped that the message wouldn't cause her to 'freak out' but he felt it was important that she be on her guard.

His phone rang again, and he saw it was Jack. He swiped to answer and said, "Hi Jack, what's up?"

"I suddenly thought, how you getting home?" asked Jack.

"Er not sure" said David, "Taxi I guess."

"Good" said Jack, "I just called one for you, and then thought perhaps you had other plans." They shared a nervous laugh at Jack's efficiency, and David thanked him.

The taxi dropped David outside his home and he saw the bike standing by the garage door. He looked it over briefly and could see the override wiring that had enabled the thief to start the bike. He removed it feeling frustrated that it had been so easy for them to take it and thought that he would upgrade the immobiliser and alarm on the next one he owned.

He also thought about switching off the automatic opener on the garage, it would be inconvenient having to open the door manually, but then no one could hack the remote signal if it was off. He decided instead that he would lock the garage door into the house.

Chapter Sixteen

Garcia Domingez was feeling particularly pleased with himself, he picked up some paper and a pencil before walking back to his cell. He regarded the meeting he'd had with the Education Manager, as a success. 'The fool!' he thought, '*he* could not stand in my way. This plan was coming together nicely.' Middleton had served him well to, and he would have to be given a place in the escape. It was Middleton's contacts in the Brothers OMCG that were keeping pressure on the Education Manager. 'He was the key to bringing in the last part of what they needed to get out of the SHU. It could only work if he could get out of this building.' he mused. Even as he thought his thoughts, the elaborate plans and the equipment necessary were being brought together; and even now the plan was in motion. His girlfriend had seen to that, and she had advised him of what would be coming for him, should he be able to fulfil his part of the arrangements. 'It was down to him now,' he thought.

Domingez sat on the bed in his cell and pushed the phone and charger deep into the foam of the mattress from the wall side. He had made the compartment many months previously and watched when his cell was searched. They always pulled the sheet off and threw the mattress aside expecting anything under the mattress to fall out. He wished he had a better hiding place in the sparse room; but it was the only place that wasn't in plain sight. Unless someone took their time and examined that side carefully they wouldn't see the slit cut in the foam. He thought to himself that he would use the phone tonight, when they thought he was asleep.

He took the paper and pencil and resting them on a book, he started to draw another picture. This was a scene of a Galleon on the 'high seas'. He used the pressure of the pencil to create shadow in the waves. He drew the sails on the ship, deployed and one cannon could be seen at the front port side. He drew a sailor in the rigging with a spyglass. The sailor, with his hand to his mouth appeared to be shouting something and in the distance there was a faint line of land. Then, Domingez drew a small helicopter on the sail. Unless you were looking for it, it would have appeared as a wrinkle in the canvas, or at most a logo or design on the sail.

Domingez finished the drawing and put it aside. Taking up a fresh piece of paper, he then drew a beach scene. The scene depicted himself sitting in a chair, smoking a large cigar under an umbrella. The figure of himself that he drew, wore loose clothes and a hat. He drew a drink into his right hand and then he drew his left arm pointing. Next, he drew what he was pointing at: he drew in to the scene, scantily clad female figures, and finally three thick set men in suits, one of whom was dragging towards him, a topless girl, with improbably large breasts and small waist. He thought about drawing in the sun and a few birds, but he'd tired of the picture already. 'He would live it soon enough,' he thought.

David entered his house and shouted, "Hi. I'm home! Just going to pull the bike into the garage." He turned to open the door to the laundry, off which the garage could be accessed. As he did so, Natalie came from the family area and walked towards him. Reaching him she threw her arms around him and hugged him tightly. "The police were here," she said. "they checked the house and switched off the garage remote door for security. That's why the 'clicker' isn't working." David stored his garage 'remote operator switch' in the Harley tank bag. He hadn't thought of getting in through the garage when he'd been dropped by the taxi.

"I thought of doing that myself" he said. Natalie followed him into the garage and he opened the garage door manually. She continued to tell David about the police's visit and her mother's reaction to it all.

"She's gone for a lie-down" she finished.

David was wheeling the big bike into the garage when a strange car drew into the drive behind him, he put the bike back on it's stand instinctively and reached under his jacket as he turned.

"It's Jack!" said Natalie moving past David, "Hi Jack, it's good to see you. New car?" David relaxed and pushed the Harley-Davidson into its usual spot, and then turned to greet Jack, who was explaining that his car was in for a service, and this was the 'loan car'. Natalie had practically pulled him from the car and was leading him up the last part of the drive. David reached out and shook his hand.

"I come bearing gifts!" said Jack mysteriously. "Not for you I'm afraid," he added, looking at David. Natalie led them inside after David had manually secured the garage door, and then made his way to the kitchen. He found Jack passing a bag to Natalie and joined them as she reached into it.

"A holster for my Glock! Thanks Jack" she said. "Think of it as a safety-holder for the gun in the house," said David, and looked at Jack who had told him in no uncertain terms, that Natalie did not have a 'carry permit'.

"That's cool" said Natalie, "Thanks Jack." Jack looked uncomfortable for a moment and then said, "Er actually..." and he reached into his pocket and produced a Federal ID card, like the one David had.

"The powers that *be,* agree that after a couple of visits from these bikies, and the security profile of Garcia Dominguez, it is a good idea if Natalie is badged to. It just means, that if necessary there will be no confusion as to who is considered to be, 'in the right'."

It was at that point that Kate appeared.

"I heard voices" she said. Then seeing their guest, "Hello, I'm Kate; Natalie's mum." She held out her hand to Jack, who introduced himself. "Someone else with a gun!" remarked Kate. Jack looked surprised.

"Kate seems to have an eye for that kind of thing, perhaps you have a job for her somewhere in security?" David asked. It was the sort of light-hearted comment that was needed to break the tension, and they all laughed.

While David made tea for them, Natalie and her mum sat chatting with Jack. David brought the mugs of tea over and passed them out, swapping two over as an after-thought. Natalie frowned and he said, "Sugar in Jack's" as an explanation.

"Thanks David" said Jack.

The four of them took a moment to sip tea and enjoy the un-rushed silence which passed between them.

Then Kate said, "David, I've been chatting to Stan and I'd like to arrange to take Natalie and Nathan back home to our house. Just for a couple of weeks till Frank and his wife get here and this *matter* blows over. Would that be alright?"

David was caught by surprise, but found himself open to the suggestion, at least in principle. Natalie however reacted with a sharp intake of breath and exclaimed, "Mum, I've only just got out of hospital and started to enjoy having my own family around me. I'm not sure I want to leave David fending for himself, here." There was a silence which followed her outburst. Natalie looked to Jack and David for support. Jack looked uncomfortable and said nothing. David paused and then said, "I'll support whatever decision you make Natalie." Natalie looked at him, "You think it's a good idea?" she said, her voice rising.

"Look Natalie" Jack started, and then stopped as she shot him a glance that would have frozen alcohol. The silence descended again. This time no one enjoyed it.

It was broken by Kate saying, "At least think about it, dear."

Natalie got up, excusing herself and said that she was going to check on Nathan.

"Well that went as expected!" said Kate, causing Jack to have to stifle a laugh. David looked at her incredulously, "You expected her to react like that and still said it?"

Kate smiled and looked in mock innocence, "Yes!" she said, "Now when I suggest that I take Nathan for a week to give you guy's some time together, and you come and spend a few days with us the following week... she'll be far more open to that!"

"Maybe there is a job for you in my department after all" said Jack under his breath. David caught the meaning of Jack's words and laughed nervously.

Natalie came in again, looking pale and shocked.

"What?" said David suddenly noticing he expression.

"Nathan's ok" she said quietly, "but I found this on his cot." She held up a .38 calibre bullet. "There's also a box in there, I've not touched it though." David got up and walked over to where she stood. He put his arms round her and was suddenly aware of Jack passing him. He was carrying his pistol, low and in both hands. David moved Natalie to one side and pulled the Glock from his own concealed holster, "Jack?" he called after him.

"Just a precaution." He heard Jack say as he disappeared down the bedroom corridor.

Jack appeared after half a minute. "All clear! But the side window's open and the screen has been cut though" he said, as he placed a small box on the kitchen stone bench top. "I didn't wake the baby" he added, glancing at Natalie.

They all gathered around the box and Natalie said, "I think the message is fairly clear. Perhaps it is a good idea for us all to move out somewhere." Jack had taken his knife, and cut the tape that sealed the box closed. He gingerly lifted the lid, half expecting to find some kind of trap inside. There was just tissue paper. He lifted that carefully with the blade of his knife to reveal a compact pistol. "Diamondback DB380!" he said quietly.

"It's a .38 calibre. One of the smallest 'compacts.'"

Jack lifted the gun from the box and unloaded it. He placed the ammunition to one side and opened the pistol's breach and left it on his other side. It was as if he felt safer, removing the projectiles some distance from the weapon that operated them. There was a note inside under the pistol, it was addressed to Dominguez, it read; 'Saturday midday, be ready.'"

"Well..." Jack said, "I fully expect you to be getting some directions for that soon." He looked at David. David looked at Natalie and saw that Kate had her arm round Natalie's waist.

"Come on Natalie," she said, "I'll help you pack."

It was if electricity had passed through Natalie's body, she stiffened as she heard her mother speak.

"No mum!" She said firmly, "I thought I'd made myself clear just now." Then she added in a more measured tone, "I do however think that it would be a good idea for you to take Nathan to see dad, and we'll come and get him in a week or so." Her face twisted as she felt the mental anguish of the thought of giving up her son even for a few days. She looked imploringly at her mother; who should have been looking happier in the circumstances. Instead she was looking upset and angry. It was Jack who defused the situation, "Ok. Let's finish our tea and have a chat about what to do next. No sudden decisions or reactionary responses. We will 'out play' these 'Crims' at their own game." He left the contents of the box and walked back to his seat and picked up his tea. The others followed slowly. The sombre mood reflected in their faces.

The sound of a baby crying broke the silence and Natalie ran towards her son. David made to follow, but Jack caught his arm and said, "I closed the window, it's secure!" Natalie appeared with Nathan a moment later and asked Kate to get the changing mat and associated things from the bathroom.

"I feel more comfortable here," she said. "You don't mind, do you?"

Nathan was awake now and once changed he fed quietly, lying on Natalie's breast, as she reclined on a seat to one side. She was within earshot but removed from the immediate gathering and so some privacy was gained. She didn't contribute to the conversation but listened to the options being discussed, knowing that in any eventuality, she would have final say in any plan that was suggested.

Jack made a few phone calls and answered the door once, drawing his pistol when he did so. He came back with a letter.

"I signed for it. Courier said it was to be placed in your hands David. I showed my ID to the courier, and then my gun. He seemed happy to leave it with me then."

David slit the card envelope open and reached inside. There was a photograph of Nathan sleeping, with the .38 calibre bullet resting on him. On the reverse side of the photograph, words had been printed in blue pen. 'Do not open the package. Deliver to Domingez as late on Friday as you can.'

"What is it?" called Natalie.

"Just a note." said David looking hard at Jack, "Instructions about the package" he said slowly and deliberately. Jack slipped the photo back into the envelope and placed it in his jacket pocket.

"Ok, we know what they want us to do with it, and when." He added calmly, "No real surprises there."

Nathan dropped back off to sleep, after filling one, and needing another diaper. Jack said he needed to pick up his car and left telling them that he would organise any flights they needed, so that their names did not appear on any flight manifest. Natalie said that she and David would come to a decision about the immediate future and would let him know in due course. It was obvious from her tone and words, that Kate would not be part of the decision; so, Kate made herself scarce, saying she was going to take a shower before cooking them some tea. Nathan was placed safely in his cot which had been moved into the living area, and Natalie had poured herself a small glass of wine and was sitting against David, who was still drinking his tea which was now cold. They held each other close, partly for affection and partly for emotional security, and then they began a much needed 'airing of ideas.' Both of them knew that at the end of the day, it would be what Natalie felt comfortable with, that would be the plan they would put into action.

An hour later they were happily cuddled up together, when Kate returned and went directly into the kitchen to prepare the meal. Natalie got up and walked over to her mother. She hugged her, and said she was sorry for her outbursts. She said that she knew her mum was only concerned for them all. She shed a few tears as she spoke, and Kate, holding her daughter as only a mother can, shed a few tears as well.

"So, what have you decided?" she asked finally.

David got up and slowly approached them. They were still holding one another and seemed inseparable. He outlined the plan that they had decided upon and explained that despite all the help that Kate could give: that it had been easy to decide upon what she should do; Kate would have to go home. Natalie had resisted any suggestion of her leaving David, and had given in to David's suggestion, that Kate take Nathan, 'out of harm's way' as he had put it.

Kate who had been holding her breath as David spoke, let it out suddenly and with such a gasp, that David jumped, turned and pulled the Glock out of the holster, looking for a threat.

"Sorry, sorry, sorry!" cried Kate, as she pulled air into her lungs to recover. David replaced the pistol in its holster and poured himself a glass of water.

"Please don't do that again, I don't want to have to redecorate the room, or explain the noise to the neighbours and police" he said.

Natalie stepped in as David drank his water, and then went and got himself a beer from the fridge.

"I will stay with David for a week and then come and get Nathan." Then she added, "after a few days with you and dad. Does that work for you?"

Kate nodded enthusiastically, "Of course, whatever will be most helpful, but I do wish you would come to."

"I will" said Natalie, "In a week, when I can see that the 'end is in sight' for this stuff David is dealing with." Her tone was adamant and Kate did not argue.

David then called Jack, whilst Kate and Natalie helped each other with preparing the meal. He explained what they wanted to do and Jack agreed that the 'compromise' could be the best solution all round. An hour later Jack called him back to tell them that the flights had been organised for Kate and Nathan, and arrangements had been made for Federal Police to escort them. They would have to be ready to leave the house at 3am. David just agreed with everything and decided he would share the news over tea.

As the food was being served and was steaming on their plates; David reached for Natalie's hand and offered his other hand across the table to Kate, who took it. He 'gave thanks' for the food; for God's protection; and asked for grace for the coming days ahead. They all said a hearty 'Amen' to his prayer. He then took a deep breath and slowly and methodically shared the arrangements he had made with Jack. Natalie's eyes filled with tears as she realised that she would be parted from her son, but it was replaced by a grim firm expression of resolve which told David, she was determined to see Nathan and her mother safe, and her support for David was not something to be questioned.

Natalie spent the remaining part of the evening packing for Nathan, and David cleared up from the meal that they had enjoyed, and then he put the dishes in the dishwasher. He couldn't help thinking about the 'Last Supper' Jesus had enjoyed with his friends, before the ordeal that lay ahead.

Soon they were ready for bed. David set an alarm for 2.30am and said 'goodnight' to Kate, who went to her room for a few hours of sleep. It seemed to David, that he had just dropped off to sleep when the trill alarm on his phone woke him. He swung his legs out of bed and started pulling on clothes again. Natalie was already up and came out of the bathroom looking fresh and wide awake.

"Amazing" muttered David, as he wondered how she was able to look so good all the time. Natalie smiled and kissed him. She smelled of minty toothpaste and flowers. They met Kate in the kitchen who was packed and drinking tea.

"Locked and loaded. That is the expression isn't it?" she said. David blinked and let it pass. Natalie looked at her and then hugged her close and said, "I love you mum." Kate started to tear up, and then took a breath and shook her head slightly.

"It's just a week, right?"

"Just a week mum." Natalie confirmed.

The doorbell chimed and David went to answer it. He put his hand on the moulded hand-grip of his Glock and pulled open the door. He saw a man in plain clothes standing there. He was holding up a badge, with a Federal Police insignia on it.

"Detective Simpson" he announced. "Call me 'Simmo'". He glanced at the gun in David's belt and the ID that David had placed next to it. "Which branch?" he asked. "Don't know" replied David. "Ah one of those" 'Simmo' said as if that identified exactly who David was working for.

"Let's get your *people* out of here. Plane has just touched down and will wait for an hour. Plenty of time really..." He followed David into the house, and another man waited outside.

Natalie kissed and fussed over Nathan, and David gave the little chap a cuddle before handing him to Kate. It had been decided to take Nathan out of his cot and fill the cot with

Nathan's 'baby stuff'. That way if the house was being watched, they might miss the child and think his cot was just a bag. Kate wrapped the baby in her jacket and kissed Natalie and David.

"See you in a *week*" she said placing the emphasis on the time involved.

It was over before they knew it. Nathan and Kate, were in the car and gone. Natalie was left staring at the tail lights of the car as it drove down the street. They walked back inside, and then she buried her head in David's shoulder and sobbed uncontrollably. David pushed a few tears out of his eyes himself and walked her into the kitchen and made her a cup of tea.

"They will call us from Jandakot before they leave, and again when they arrive at Bankstown airport in Sydney." He paused, "And then again after a short helicopter ride to Lithgow."

Natalie stared at him, "Are you telling me my son gets to fly in a helicopter before I do?"

David laughed. "Sorry. Yes!"

Neither of them felt like going back to bed, so they cuddled on the settee; chatted briefly with Kate some twenty minutes later, and then both snoozed for a few hours before David's phone woke them at 7am. He passed the phone to Natalie and she had a brief chat with her mum again.

"She's going to call from home, not the airport." Natalie said as she terminated the phone call. David got up and set about making tea and put some bread in the toaster. Have something to eat he said, and then he went off to have a shower. When he returned Natalie said that she had just spoken to her dad, who had been delighted to see his grandson. There were a few more tears, and then David made himself some breakfast.

"Now, let's see if we can't make sure that this Domingez never sees the light of day again." said David. Natalie met his gaze and nodded once in agreement.

Chapter Seventeen

The Australian Defence Force Vessel - 'ADV Fourcray' and it's crew, under the command of Mark Baker, had been at sea for eight out of the ten day; two thousand, seven hundred nautical mile journey to Fremantle; or more specifically, the Garden Island Naval Base south of Fremantle. ADV Fourcray was performing well and most of the journey had been smooth sailing at twelve knots. The Cape class patrol boat was capable of more, but in these days of economy and fuel efficiency, twelve knots would allow them to reach the base with a quarter of a tank of fuel remaining. This reserve meant that any deviations from course, bad weather or need to engage another 'way-marker' could be accommodated easily.

Lt. Commander Robbie Taylor had remained in regular contact with the Darwin Naval base via the Receiving Station at Shoal Bay, who had relayed his signal on to Humpty Doo Transmitting Station. Weather was clear and there had been no incidents or sightings to report. 'Business as usual for the most part' he thought, as he sipped a cup of coffee sitting at the Comms post on the bridge of the patrol boat. Commander Baker had left him in charge of the vessel, whilst he rested in his cabin. Robbie had asked if the Commander was well, and had been told 'it was nothing', but it seemed to Robbie that it was something. The Commander had not looked well. Perhaps he felt it wasn't worth mentioning, Robbie wasn't going to pursue the matter. He was about to refresh his coffee when the radio receiver crackled to life.

"VMCF311, VMCF311, VMCF311, this is T.S. Humpty Doo. I say again this is T.S. Humpty Doo, how do you receive? Over" Robbie often thought it odd that call signs were repeated as a matter of policy, when signal strength was so strong. He supposed that being clear and repetitive, probably saved the wrong person replying, but he was tempted to think of it as a bit, 'overkill.'

He sat back and pressed the send button, and spoke into the mic, "T.S. Humpty Doo, T.S. Humpty Doo, T.S. Humpty Doo this is VMCF311, receiving you loud and clear. Go ahead." The secure voice and data communication was transferred over a very high-frequency (VHF), and Satcom and Sea Boat's situational awareness systems managed the information so it was washed clean of static.

There was a brief pause and then, "VMCF311, VMCF311, putting you through to 'T.S. Harold E Holt Station'." Robbie knew that Naval Communication Station 'Harold E. Holt' was located 6km north of Exmouth. The area had a history of military activity; even before the COMMSTA was established, and this was taught at the academy. The submarine tender "USS Pelias", was moored in Exmouth Gulf providing submarine support during World War II, however, because of bad weather, it was subsequently decided to relocate the facilities, further south. Other military equipment remained at Exmouth, including a direction-finding station, a landing strip, an RAAF radar station and a squadron of RAAF fighters. After 1945 however, only a small base maintenance unit remained. He wondered what they could want with the Fourcray. He didn't have to wait long as the next thing he heard was, "Commander Baker, this is Captain Stirling, over"

Robbie paused before answering and he called across the bridge, "Lieutenant!" The junior officer replied, "Sir." Robbie's finger hovered over the transmit button, "Fetch the Commander immediately," he pressed the button.

"Captain Stirling, good morning sir. This is Lt. Commander Taylor, of the 'Fourcray'. I have alerted Commander Baker to

Clear Bright Light of Day 117

your request, sir. He will be with us soon. Over." There was silence for a moment and then, "Lt. Commander Taylor I have new orders for you, please open your secure pouch and select verification number seven." Robbie knew this was serious now, as the Captain had not waited for his commanding officer to arrive on the bridge and had instructed him to open a higher number on the verification code index.

There were only twelve unopened plastic pouches, and it was common knowledge that number twelve was 'nuclear'. There were six pouches in a draw on the port side, and another six on the starboard side. He pulled the key from around his neck and opened a draw on the starboard side of the bridge. He located number seven on the left side of the draw and reached for it. He could feel his heart pumping, but his hand was steady. 'This was just verification' he thought. 'Anything more serious would involve two keys and the safe in the Commander's cabin.' The verification was needed to confirm that this person calling the Fourcray, was who he said he was. Without verification orders could not be changed even if the caller claimed he was an Admiral!

Commander Mark Baker strode onto the bridge with the Lieutenant following. He was looking less pale now and smiled as he walked towards Robbie.

"Sir. We've been asked to verify seven" Robbie said, and held the plastic envelope out to his commanding officer. Mark took the opaque brittle envelope and snapped it in half. The coloured plastic card fell from it and Mark caught it. He held it up and said, "Verify seven." Robbie pressed the 'mic send' button and spoke, "Captain Stirling. Sir. Verify Seven." There was no pause and they heard clearly, "Mike, Whiskey, Four, Four, India, Tango, Victor, Mike" a short pause and then, "Verify."

Commander Mark Baker nodded and passed the card to Robbie. 'MW44ITVM' was clearly printed on the card. Robbie keyed the 'mic send' button again, "Mike, Whiskey, Four, Four, India, Tango, Victor, Mike VERIFIED, sir."

There was a brief silence and then, "Fourcray, this is Captain Stirling. We have an unidentified large vessel west, south-west of your current reported position. Two hundred nautical miles. Do you receive? Over"

Commander Baker now reached over and pressed the 'mic send' button, "Captain Stirling, this is Commander Baker. We receive your transmission, what are your orders sir?"

There was a pause and then, "Commander Baker, this is Captain Stirling. You will proceed to intercept the vessel on bearing two-four-five. Make your speed twenty knots and you will arrive in ten hours. Further orders to follow. Understood? Over"

It wasn't uncommon for patrol boats to intercept other vessels, but it was odd to be ordered so far off the coast of Western Australia.

Commander Baker did not question this though, and replied, "Captain Stirling, this is Commander Baker. Understood. Making our speed and direction two-four-five at twenty knots. We await to hear from you with further orders. Sir. Over."

The reply was short and to the point, "Received Commander Baker. Captain Stirling, OUT."

"Make your bearing two-four-five. Speed to twenty knots." Commander Baker called to the navigation officer.

"Sir. Two-four-five at twenty." came the reply. The boat picked up speed and swung to the starboard causing those on board to feel the centripetal force pushing them to port as they swung around. The patrol boat was fitted with a motion control system for improved passenger comfort though, so the force that was felt was not dramatic. The system consisted of two roll fins and two trim flaps, allowing the vessels to operate in more rigid sea conditions, and travel longer distances more economically.

"Maintain speed and direction" Commander Baker said, "and notify me the moment we have that vessel on our radar."

He added more quietly to his Lt. Commander, "Then we'll have a go at identifying her." The boat's two Electronic Chart Display and Information Systems (ECDIS), along with two gyro compasses, two Differential Global Positioning Systems (DGPS), a secure marine Automatic Identification System (AIS-S), Electro-Optical Sensor System (EOSS), radars and Voyage Data Recorder (VDR) tracked and recorded the whole event, from first communication contact, to the new course, which had just been plotted.

It would be some time before the Ship's radar system picked up the unidentified vessel, and Commander Mark Baker was hoping there would be some aerial reconnaissance to help him identify the type of vessel, well ahead of them picking up the ship on their radar. As highly advanced as it was, it would still only give them between ten and thirty miles warning. At least they would be able to get within 'identifying range' without being seen themselves.

Radar was the most valuable aid to navigation ever invented, and anyone who has had to rely upon it, knows this to be true. Certainly GPS, and the AIS systems along with the depth sounder have changed the face of navigating the seas for every mariner, from the largest Navy ships to the 'small boat' owner. The enduring magnetic compass is the fall-back for all, but radar is probably the most useful; as the device doesn't rely on satellites, other vessels broadcasting a radio frequency signal, or on-shore position enhancing beacons. It is this self-contained electronic autonomy that the depth sounder and radar have in common, but while the sounder can only tell you what's directly under you, radar alone can show you what surrounds you for miles.

The Fourcray's radar radiated a microwave signal that detected the energy that bounced back, rendering a view that was unaffected by darkness, fog or other elements that resulted in poor visibility. Many yachts carried radar as a first-rate collision avoidance tool that, unlike AIS, sees for itself what's in the vicinity. This meant that other vessels, with no AIS or radar equipment of their own, showed up boldly on the radar screen. Small sail boats, even inflatable dinghies could be detected, with the right equipment in the right conditions. The range selector allowed them to pick a useful radius of scan; a good rule of thumb for the navigation operator was, 'the lower the range, the greater the target detail displayed.' Filter controls such as 'sea clutter' and 'rain clutter' are quite straightforward and these lessened interferences caused by waves and weather systems, but some care was needed not to overdo the filter gain and cause weaker targets to disappear altogether.

Although the Fourcray's system was not 'weapons class', controlled by an 'attack computer', it was better than most systems installed on private boats. It was a digital system which allowed the officers aboard to choose how the data was displayed: with, heading-up, north-up or course-up alignments. At present the radar was set in north-up mode: the screen top remained aligned with true or magnetic north irrespective of the heading they had set upon. In heading-up mode; the radar aligned with the bow of the boat, regardless of the heading. But there was no need to track anything following Fourcray. Later when they neared the target vessel, the navigation officer would focus the radar in the 'course-up' configuration which would align the top of the radar screen with their pre-entered course route. The navigation officer currently had the radar range-ring settings to 'see' the maximum radius of its specific scan. Typically, these progressed from close-in ranges, starting at an eighth of a mile, to greater distances of up to twenty-four miles and even, thirty-six miles in perfect conditions.

Radar detects targets at these differing ranges with changes in the microwave or FM signal propagation. Many, even experienced sailors assumed that if a unit had a thirty-six mile maximum range setting, it would allow them to pick up all the targets out to that distance, but that's not quite the case. Intruding on radar's capability are several electromagnetic wave-propagation issues and one major geographic fact of life: the curvature of the Earth. In practice, the height of your radar antenna and the height of the target determine whether your radar will depict the object at all. Radar mounted on small craft, is not much better than the human eye when it comes to coping with a curving horizon. So, if your radar antenna is three meters above the water and you're trying to spot a big ship with a bridge height of thirty meters. A quick dipping-range calculation indicates that on a flat sea, the upper part of the ship's bridge might be seen by your radar at about twenty miles. Wave crests and troughs, the heel of your sail boat, pitching and yawing, plus radar wave attenuation and refraction reduce the range to perhaps ten miles which is still a good early warning. But the real reason for radar which has a thirty six-mile range setting, is to detect at night or in fog, a distant tall island, bold coast or towering headland.

Even to detect the skyscrapers of a coastal city, confirming your distance offshore.

The extra features found on the Fourcray's radar were more than window dressing. With the Electronic Bearing Line (EBL) and Variable Range Mark (VRM) they could pinpoint the location of a target in terms of its relative range and bearing, and even digitally transfer that target as an icon onto their Multi-Function Display, marine electronic maps. The radar would continue to track the target and update its position on the chart automatically. Guard zones could be set, so that an alarm operated as a target entered a specific zone. The unit also offered, dual range display on one screen, and it was linked to a dual-processor CPU, allowing it to work as if they had two independent radars running at one time. These features provided the operator with the ability to display two ranges at once. At sea, that combo could be set to between three and twelve miles, while a coastal cruiser might prefer half a mile to three miles.

Commander Baker left the bridge once more, and Robbie returned to his coffee making. He wondered if there were any RAAF reconnaissance planes in the air now, flying over the position they were heading towards, but in fact he couldn't have been further from the truth. The plane that had spotted the vessel but not been able to identify it, had been travelling in a search pattern looking for wreckage of a passenger flight; that had gone missing – presumed crashed, some months earlier. It had not deviated from it's search co-ordinates, but it had information about the shipping that should have been in the area as a matter of course for it's mission. This ship did not show on any military, commercial or private shipping manifest; so it was reported as a 'matter of interest' to the Border Patrol. They in turn took a satellite picture of the area and were alarmed to see, what they thought was an armed helicopter aboard the vessel. The Navy was contacted and ADV Fourcray was the closest boat to send.

Some two hundred miles away a 'Sea-Explorer 65m' was powering through the waves at it's top speed of fifteen knots, towards the coast of Western Australia. It was a huge luxurious yacht, which normally would have catered for twelve guests who wanted to tour, dive and fly around exotic places in the world. There was accommodation for twenty crew, but currently on the vessel there were only ten crew and no passengers. The main cargo was fuel for their long journey and they had a plethora of equipment to use it, including; a small submersible, a dive support boat, a rescue boat and a fully armed helicopter.

This 'Super-yacht support craft' had been developed by the Dutch super-yacht experts at Amels, and by their parent company Damen Shipyards. They were one of the most respected shipyards in the world, known for building military and industrial craft. They were the ultimate luxury because they provided the muscle, horsepower, and storage for an armada of toys; including in this case; a fully enclosed helicopter hangar, without requiring the sacrifice of any space or luxury. This 'Super-yacht support vessel' featured a significant payload, that made it easy to accommodate the sixty-foot tender, a submarine and two cars, that would otherwise be hard to fit on all but the largest super-yachts. The purpose built fully certified helideck; made it safer and easier on a support vessel for day and night operations, and with a fully enclosed hangar, so guests would not have to abandon their deck chairs when the helicopter came and went!

The helicopter in this instance was a highly capable and efficient rotor-craft, for armed scout missions. It's 'Airbus

Helicopters'; single-engine H125M, was the most capable armed scout helicopter in its two-metric-ton class; tailored for locating and attacking targets of opportunity – with excellent capabilities in high and hot environments. It was powered by Turbomeca's Arriel 2D engine, with a dual-channel Full Authority Digital Engine Control (FADEC) system. Also, the H125M had a small visual silhouette, reduced radar signature and the agility to perform combat flight – including nap-of-the-earth profiles; which was a low flight contour hugging ability. Its armament included a podded 12.7-mm machine gun, 20-mm cannon pod, 70-mm rockets and air-to-ground guided missiles. Side-mounted weaponry came in the shape of a 7.62-mm. machine gun and a sniper rifle was installed. It was owned by the Sinaloa Drug Cartel. Most of the time it provided hospitality to rich business men and women, who were either major customers of the cartel, or part of the distribution network. It had been fitted out for one purpose on this occasion.

That reason, was to free Garcia Domingez. It would require stealth, speed, and high impact arrival!

Technically, any person can buy anything. That is, if it is not on the International Trade in Arms Regulation (ITAR) Arms List. Even then it's possible by asking someone's permission. If it is an ITAR controlled item, one would need to get special disposition from the U.S. Government and or the government they are supporting, as there must be an 'End Users Certificate'. But these are only issued by authorised and recognised government agencies, such as Ministries of Defence and Interior. In order to use lethal equipment and or equipment that may interfere with the Air Defence, Air Space Control, GSM, and or radio frequencies, they have to have permission and coordination of the government in the territory in which they are going to operate as well. There are a whole host of other rules, but in the end, there is the legal way of doing it, which most contractors abide by, and then there are "other" procurement avenues.

The helicopter engines, albeit with the helicopter strapped down as it was, had been run to keep them operating well. It was now being lowered into it's hanger for safety until the next day, when it would be needed for a 'hot extraction' at a well-armed prison.

Back on ADV Fourcray, Commander Mark Baker had passed another kidney stone. With each one he had really hoped that it would be the last. They hadn't been a problem before this trip, and he had increased his water intake by what felt like gallons. They were small enough to pass, that at least was a 'mercy'. He felt that he would just have to bear the pain. What scared him more than the discomfort was loss of command, which was the main reason he'd not told the ship's doctor. He didn't want to be put on IV fluids or be threatened with having to take pain killers so strong it would impede his ability to make decisions. It was a losing battle though, and he picked up the phone and dialled the infirmary. The chief medical officer answered and Commander Baker said, "It's Mark. Doc. Can you come to my cabin please?" He replaced the phone and then called the bridge. Moments later Doc James and the Lt. Commander, Robbie Taylor, were standing outside his cabin. Robbie looked ominously at Dr James who shrugged and knocked on the door.

"Enter," came a strangled shout.

Both men walked in and found Mark Baker doubled up holding his abdomen.

"Quick, get him on the bed" said the Doc. Robbie moved to help the Commander and supported him towards the bed. But the Commander took steps towards the bathroom.

"Gotta pass another one out." he said.

"Better let me, sir" the Doc said, taking over and supporting the Commander whilst he tried to pass the stone.

"I'm betting Kidney stones, just by looking at you sir" said the Doc.

Robbie waited in the cabin and eventually the Commander and his Doctor came back in.

"Well, as you can see, I'm a bit incapacitated at the moment Robbie" Mark said. "I doubt, I'll be doing much more than pee bricks for the next few days." he turned to the Doc, "I'm feeling a little better, but I'm looking to you Doc for some stronger pain relief and an IV drip."

He turned back to Robbie, "Lt. Commander. You have the COM."

Robbie Taylor was the next ranking officer on board, he could command the Patrol boat, and had done so on many occasions, but he hated that he'd have to under these circumstances. It was one thing to cover leave, but to have the Commander there and ill was not ideal.

"Sir. Yes sir. I will assume command, but I don't accept that you are incapacitated to such a degree that I am no longer under your command sir!" The commander and the Doctor looked at him.

"Thank you, Robbie. Dismissed." "I will get my drugs bag" said the Doc and followed Robbie out. He caught up with him further down the corridor.

"Hold on there, sir. That was very *nice* of you in there, and I hope the Commander appreciates it, but he is not deemed fit to command whilst in this state. By the time I've drugged him up he won't be able to recognise his mother." Robbie was staring at the Doctor and had drawn himself up to his full height.

The doctor saw this and said, "Look sir. You will see after he's had some Pethidine what he can and can't do. I just need to know that if he is unfit and tries to resume duty that you will support me in this."

Robbie Taylor nodded slowly, "*If* he is unfit" he said.

"Ok" said the Doctor and hurried off to get his drugs bag.

Some eight and a half hours later Commander Baker was sleeping soundly; he was 'drugged up' and would stay that way until first light, whereupon the desired result would be him passing any more stones he was suffering.

It was dark outside and there was an eerie glow from the instruments on the bridge. Lt Commander Robbie Taylor was napping in his reclining chair on the bridge; he was now pulling a double shift, so he felt justified in sleeping in short naps.

Suddenly he woke to the Navigation Officer's voice, "I have a vessel bearing two-four-seven point five. It's a couple of degrees off the starboard side sir. Twenty miles. It comes and goes on the radar, sir. The problem is the distance sir."

Robbie was fully awake in a second. He had heard nothing from Captain Stirling during the past nine hours and now felt that he should report to him. He reached for the radio console in front of him and switched it to transmit.

"'T.S. Harold E Holt Station', 'T.S. Harold E Holt Station', 'T.S. Harold E Holt Station', this is VMCF311, this is VMCF311, are you receiving? Over"

There was a short pause then, "VMCF311, VMCF311, this is T.S. Harold E Holt Station, how may we direct your transmission?"

Robbie thought for a moment and said, "Harold E Holt Station, this is VMCF311, please connect me with Captain Stirling, I repeat, Captain Stirling. Over"

What seemed like a full five minutes of radio silence followed, and Robbie was about to call again, when the radio came alive, "VMCF311 Fourcray, this is Captain Stirling, are you receiving me? Over."

Robbie pressed the send button, "This is VMCF311 Fourcray, Captain Stirling. We receive you loud and clear. We have reached Way-point, minus twenty miles and have contact intermittently on radar. Awaiting orders. Over." The radio went silent for another minute then, "Fourcray, this is Captain Stirling. Stand-by"

Robbie waited a further twenty minutes and found himself becoming frustrated. Then as he reached for the transmit button to call again, the radio spoke again, "Fourcray, this is Captain Stirling. Are you receiving?"

He replied, "Captain Stirling, this is Fourcray. Receiving"

"Fourcray, this is Captain Stirling. What is your status? Over."

Robbie checked the instruments and read them off, "Captain Stirling, this is Fourcray. We are on an adjusted bearing of two-four-seven point five, at twenty knots and expect physical contact in seventy minutes sir. Over."

"Fourcray, this is Captain Stirling. Make your speed fifteen knots and change bearing to match unidentified vessel. Engage AIS-S and identify that boat."

"Captain Stirling, this is Fourcray. I can Engage AIS-S and attempt to ID the vessel, but this will lift our profile for them. Please confirm that you wish us to make ourselves known to the unidentified vessel. Over."

"Fourcray, this is Captain Stirling. It is preferable that you remain 'dark', however we must identify the vessel. It is confirmed to be carrying a small helicopter gun ship. I repeat it is confirmed to be carrying a small helicopter gun-ship."

Robbie sat silently and looked around the bridge, while he thought what to say. The navigation officer, and several others had heard the broadcast, and were staring at him expectantly. He pressed the transmit button and heard himself say, "Captain Stirling, this is Fourcray. We have altered our course and matched the speed of the unidentified vessel. I am placing the patrol boat on 'amber alert'. Please advise what are our rules of engagement. Over."

He reached over to another console and pressed a large orange button. Soft alarms sounded all over the ship, and he knew there would be sailors jumping out of bed, pulling on clothes and making ready the mounted guns on deck, as well as crews preparing the two high-capacity response tenders which were 7.3m Gemini sea boats. Each boat allowed for simultaneous launch to carry out operations, whether they were rescue or boarding missions.

"Fourcray, this is Captain Stirling. Be advised that you are not to allow that helicopter to take off. Rules of engagement allow for firing upon the helicopter only, but do not fire on the vessel unless you are fired upon, or you have reason to believe an international intention of war exists. Let's try and keep this simple shall we. Court Marshall's are tedious and stressful. Understood?"

Robbie pressed the transmit button, "Captain Stirling, this is Fourcray. Received and understood. I will contact you with further information which may identify the vessel. Fourcray Out."

Robbie could see others arriving on the bridge. A Lieutenant and several Junior or second lieutenants were finding places and observing equipment readouts, so that a commanding officer wouldn't miss anything. A second Lieutenant passed him a tactical belt made of nylon webbing with a holster attached, the 'Browning 9mm Hi-Power' pistol it contained had come from the armoury and was standard issue to bridge officers, and it was compulsory to be worn during alerts. With the thirteen round magazine it weighed a kilo, and had an effective range of fifty meters. Robbie adjusted the length of the belt and put it round his waist and pushed it lower onto his hips.

"Danny" he said to the Radar Officer.

"Sir" came the reply.

"Set up for 'course up' and..."

"Done, sir" the reply interrupted.

He let it go and said, "Nav's. Get me another three miles closer. Danny, engage AIS-S and attempt to ID the vessel.

"Sir?"

"Yes Danny" Robbie replied.

"It's over sixty meters and looks to be a Super-yacht of some kind. I'm guessing fourteen metres beam, and draught of four or five. The Dutch build some big fellers capable of carrying a helicopter. If it has one of those then it probably has boats on board to."

"Pull back Nav's, forget being closer." Robbie ordered the Navigation officer.

"Danny, shut down AIS-S. We've got to stay out of reach of that thing, it's bigger and better armed than us, I'm guessing. If we aren't seen then we have a chance of surprise."

Robbie ordered the lieutenant to take over his communication post, and then told another officer to report the information they had to Captain Stirling. Once that was done, he asked the new Comms officer to find the civilian radio wavelength that the target vessel would be tuned to. The officer reached for a reference card and then she tuned the transceiver to the correct UHF wavelength.

"I will monitor these bands, to be sure. We can transmit on an international frequency as well sir. They will hear us as their equipment will scan for it automatically." She put a single sided headset on and said, "I am also going to scan for low power transmissions, which are sometimes used aboard civilian vessels."

Robbie glanced at the radar array, then at the officers stationed on the bridge and said, "Ok, let's play cat and mouse."

Chapter Eighteen

It was not long after breakfast, and the dishes had been cleared away, that the door-bell chimed. Natalie had dressed in jeans and a loose white top, which fell over the concealed holster which held her Glock 22. She felt cumbersome with the weapon on her hip, her post-natal abdomen and swollen breasts added to her general feeling of annoyance. As she moved towards the door she pulled the pistol out and held it low. She stood to one side of the door and called sweetly,

"Who is it?" Jack was also standing to one side of the door outside.

"It's me. Jack. Please don't shoot me."

Natalie opened the door but did not holster the weapon until Jack was inside and she was sure that no one else was outside. She had concealed the gun from any watchful eyes on the street and tried to make the whole event look unhurried and casual. She realised that she had been holding her breath and let it out in a long sigh.

"You ok?" asked Jack. Natalie was briefly tempted to be sarcastic, but she bit her tongue and just gave Jack a look of annoyed resignation.

They made their way into the house and found David who was making coffee. Jack took a place at the breakfast bar and David poured the hot black Columbian brew into mugs and added milk. They took a moment to savour the smell before allowing themselves to drink in the flavour.

"So" said David finally.

"Well, I've been up most of the night trying to find any precedent for this situation. There is none, but the policy and procedures for this are well documented, and it's no surprise that the gun isn't getting to Domingez." He took another sip and made an appreciative smack of his lips.

"So, Domingez doesn't get the gun, and can't use the phone. Do you think that they will have any protocol in place for him to confirm that he's received the gun, and or that he is in place for an extraction?" Asked Natalie, her 'security mind' working overtime to stay one step ahead.

"Good question, Natalie" said Jack.

There was another moment of silence and Natalie said "We have to come up with a plan that will neatly address a number of variables and leave us in control of this situation. I may just have an idea, Jack..."

During the previous night, Domingez had woken and reached into the mattress, pushing past the foam into the cavity he had created. He retrieved the phone, and keeping it under the bed clothes he switched it on. It lit up and went through the sequence of searching for a signal and found the phone carrier, displaying the logo on the screen. He knew it would be unwise to speak to anyone so he called up the SMS function and started to type a message, confirming he had received the phone and was awaiting his next package. He pressed send, but the phone just seemed to freeze. He tried again. The same thing happened. He looked at the screen and could see that there was a signal strength displayed. He erased the message and tried again from the start. It didn't work. He was tempted to throw the phone across the room; to shout and swear; but he knew this would only give his purpose away, and he would lose the phone altogether. He dialled his girlfriend's phone number and pressed the green phone button to connect. Nothing happened. It was all showing it should work, but it was not working. He racked his brain but he could not think why. 'If there was a blocking signal' he thought, 'then would he read a phone signal on the phone?' he asked himself. 'Surely it would stop a signal coming in to the prison, not just going from the prison?' The truth though, was that he didn't know.

He switched off the phone and shoved it roughly back inside the mattress. He was feeling angry and frustrated, but he thought to himself that, 'All was not lost. So what? If he couldn't phone out inside the SHU, he would be able to call once he was outside the building. In any case the gun will be delivered by David and that was the real key. Once outside; at the right time, it was only a matter of waiting for the helicopter to fly in, and he would be gone.

He tried to go back to sleep, and dropped into a light slumber, dozing on and off for the rest of the night. At one point he found himself dreaming of being pulled up into the air on a rope ladder; up, up and out of the prison. He woke suddenly to a loud 'clack' and his door opening.

"Come on Domingez, you are first up today; get your tea and breakfast." came over his cell speaker. Domingez was tempted to shout some obscenity and turn over and pretend to go back to sleep. He didn't however, because he was hungry and he wanted to pass a note to Middleton.

Domingez pulled himself out of bed and sat on the toilet, he would get breakfast, but he would do it in his own time. He heard another cell door open and he finished up and walked out to the kitchen. He found himself pleased to see Middleton and said, "Good morning Paul."

Middleton looked up and nodded silently. He moved to allow Domingez to get a cup and bowl and fix himself some tea and pour cereal into the bowl. Middleton passed the milk, which was in a bladder, resting in a shaped plastic container. Domingez poured some into his tea and then on the cereal in the bowl.

Both men walked to the table and Middleton said, "Nice picture you drew. I especially liked the sail motif."

Domingez nodded smiling, he repeated, "You like the sail motif." and went on, "The sail motif is very good is it not?" He chuckled, but it came out more like a low grim growl.

"Do you have the time?" asked Middleton, who was clearly wearing a watch. Domingez caught his meaning and said, "The weekend will be nice, but I am waiting confirmation of the time." Middleton chewed thoughtfully and then took a sip of his tea.

"I have a visit today, my cousin is coming in. His 'brothers,'" he emphasised the word, "are interested in the education 'project' you are doing. They want to know if there is anything they can do to help?"

Domingez thought for a moment. The Education officer should bring me in some 'resources' soon, if there is a problem then it would be nice for them to provide a 'solution.'" The meaning was clear to Middleton and he nodded.

Domingez drank his tea and then placed his cardboard dish and plastic spoon in the waste bin; then he wandered outside to use the exercise equipment, but after half an hour, he anticipated being called back to his cell, and so he went to make himself another tea, to take with him. Middleton was doing the same, and Domingez said, "I will have you released as soon as I am." He turned and walked back to his cell, a full five minutes ahead of the call to return.

In the control room Senior Officer White listened to the cryptic exchange of words and picked up the phone.

Matt Roberts was just beginning his day. He'd arrived early and was sitting at his desk with a cup of coffee. This was his favourite moment of the day. Few had seen him arrive, the phone wouldn't ring for another thirty minutes, and if he closed the door then no one would know he was there for an hour. He anticipated getting some work done and a real 'jump on the day.' He sipped the hot coffee and was about to put it down when the phone rang. 'It begins!' he thought and breathed out heavily. He had really thought that he'd been covert enough today. He placed the mug on a coaster and picked up the phone.

"Superintendent" he said gruffly. Then, "On my way!"

Matt Roberts used the route to the SHU through the Justice courtroom and the back of the MPU. Keeping out of the way of staff meant he would not be distracted or delayed. He reached the SHU and walked briskly to Control, past officers who looked surprised and snapped to attention, greeting him with, "Sir!"

Snr. Officer White was waiting with the recording already set to replay the morning encounter. Several of the SHU security officers were looking a little puzzled but had guessed there was something more going on that they weren't privy to.

After viewing and listening to the interaction Matt said, "I agree. Something is happening. Can you call up and fast forward the night tape for Dominguez?" Some further tweaking allowed the officers to display the tape. "Fast forward at times eight speed and call me in an hour if you find anything." Matt then left to return to his office. He arrived at the same time as Michelle, who was putting her bag away and switching on her computer.

"Morning Michelle, please hold all my calls for a couple of hours and get one of the Assistant Superintendents to run debrief this morning. Send apologies from the SHU, they won't attend either." He disappeared into the office and picked up his phone. After several redirects, Matt finally caught up with Jack on his mobile phone. He related the conversations he had observed and heard, to Jack who said, "I think if your SHU officers find any evidence of Domingez using the mobile phone during the night, then we should 'ramp his cell' and confiscate it. Let's see if we can isolate him for a while – no visits either. Let's shake the tree and see what falls out."

Ninety minutes later when Matt was pleased to have been able to clear some of the paperwork on his desk, there was a knock on the door. Snr. Officer White came in with Michelle following him saying, "Sorry sir. I told him you were busy and not to be disturbed."

"I've been calling sir, but she won't put me through." said Whitey in an exasperated tone.

"Ok calm down. It's ok, Michelle, it's my fault, I should have been clearer."

Michelle retreated to her desk, and Matt said to the officer, "Ok Whitey, go ahead, what have you got for me?"

Upon hearing the report Matt, and Snr. Officer White returned to the SHU. They kept up the rouse about not knowing anything about the phone that David had smuggled into the SHU and asked the security officers to go through a section of CCTV footage which showed Domingez moving strangely in his bed. Matt tuned to the officer operating the display, "What do you see?" he asked.

"Sir! I see him trying to reach something under the mattress Sir" he replied. Matt looked at Snr. Officer White and raised his eyebrows expectantly. The senior officer caught the cue and said, "I think we should do an impromptu cell search." Then to his second in command, "Organise your men, and let me know what you find."

Two more prisoners were out of their cells and making tea when six officers; three with batons drawn two with pepper spray and one with a holstered Taser entered the communal area. Both prisoners put their cups of tea down quickly and put their hands on their heads. They were about to drop down onto their knees, when an officer said, "We're not here for you. Get to your cells. The men turned and started to go back to their cells, when Whitey called, "Take your tea with you, there's good lads." The men glanced at each other and picked up their cups and scuttled back into their cells.

"Secure those doors." Snr. Officer White called, and two officers pulled the heavy metal cell doors closed. He looked at the CCTV camera and raised a thumb as a signal.

Inside the cell, Domingez was thinking about reading a book he had just picked up. He was sitting on his bed when the speaker came to life.

"Domingez! Kneel by your bed with your hands behind your head. Do it now! Officers are opening the door. If you are not on your knees when they enter, you will be treated as a threat." Domingez knew what that meant and didn't want any trouble. Fear gripped his chest, but he thought that he'd been careful. Perhaps this was a routine exercise, and his name had been picked at random. He would find out either way in a moment. He folded the corner of the page again and closed the book, twisting as he did so, so his knees hit the floor by the bed. He heard the door open and managed to get his hands up behind his head as Snr. Officer White came in followed by four officers.

"To what, do I owe the pleasure of this visit..." began Domingez. He didn't finish however, as an officer pushed him forward so his head was in the bedclothes and his hands were roughly pulled down and cuffed behind his back. He made a noise that sounded like, "Omph." Then he was pulled back into a kneeling position. Two officers were either side of him now, lifting him to his feet. They escorted him out of the cell and stood him facing the wall outside. "You know the drill!" one of them said.

Whilst Dominguez stood outside the four officers in the cell started to pull the bedclothes off the bed and throw them in to the corner of the room. The mattress was pulled off the bench and then they moved onto the desk and personal items by the wash basin. Superintendent Matt Roberts and Snr. Officer White shared a puzzled glance. They knew that a mobile phone was in the cell somewhere. "Strip him for a cavity search" shouted Matt through the door. They heard Dominguez complain, "Is there really a need for that?" he shouted angrily.

The officers put on gloves and carried out the search but found nothing. Dominguez shouted and complained loudly throughout the whole procedure and threatened all manner of legal retribution for the treatment he was receiving.

"Nothing to report. Sir!" came the voice of one of the search officers from outside. The officers in the cell had stopped searching as well. One shrugged and looked at Snr. Officer White, who looked at Matt Roberts. "Do it again" Matt called to the officers in the cell. There was a wail from Dominguez outside, "Nooo!" Even Matt Roberts couldn't put Dominguez through that again and he called out, "Just the cell." The officers started searching again, and Matt walked outside to face Dominguez.

"Is there anything you want to tell me, Mr Dominguez?" Dominguez looked guilty, uncomfortable and dishevelled. He stared levelly at Matt Roberts and said, "Please don't think me rude, Superintendent. But you can, F-"

"Found it! Interrupted Snr. Officer White, from within the cell. Domingez closed his eyes and Matt Roberts turned to head back into the cell, reappearing moments later holding the phone and charger.

Domingez was quiet now and looking angry.

"So. Domingez." Matt said holding up the phone. "What have we here?" Domingez thought about being sarcastic and pointing out the obvious, but he held his tongue, not wanting to jeopardise his chance of freedom. "Charge him with possession of a controlled item." Matt said to Snr. Officer White.

He was walking away with the phone, when he heard Domingez say, "Don't you want to know how I got it?" Matt stopped and turned.

"Are you volunteering information Domingez?" Domingez thought for a moment; he weighed his options. If he gave up David, he would certainly end the man's career prospects, that seemed an attractive option to Domingez, 'it might be worth doing' he thought. 'However, David would not then be able to deliver the gun to him in an 'Educational Resources' package. Then again, maybe someone else could be pressured to do it? But there was no time.' "No, you can find out for yourself!" he said. Snr. Officer White was now up close and in Domingez' personal space.

"We know how you got it Dumbingez" he said making a pun out of the prisoner's name and insinuating he was dim-witted.

The awful truth began to dawn on Domingez. His mind went into denial, 'They couldn't know, could they?' he asked himself. His anger rose and he spat back, "You couldn't possibly know how I got it." Matt Roberts could see where this was going and tried to stop the Snr. Officer compromising the intelligence they had.

"Officer White!" Matt said. Whitey looked up, and a knowing glance passed between the two men. This was also observed by Domingez. Whitey had just enough time to nod to the Superintendent, before Domingez head-butted him, knocking him to the ground. Domingez followed this with a kick to his groin, and he started shouting and screaming. The two officers forced him to the ground away from the injured Snr. Officer, but Domingez appeared to be a man 'possessed' and he fought like a trapped animal. Suddenly a shout was heard which caused all who knew what it meant to withdraw immediately.

"Clear, Clear, Clear! Deploy, Deploy, Deploy!" The Taser sprang forth and delivered fifty thousand volts of electricity through two spiked prongs, which were now embedded in Domingez' leg. Matt Roberts watched the action unfold before his eyes. He couldn't help thinking that the static electricity voltage from a metal door knob was around twenty-five thousand volts. It was the amperage that did the damage! The Taser would be delivering less than five milliamps of power. Still, the effect on Domingez was dramatic. The man voided his bladder and bowels and shook uncontrollably on the floor.

"Desist" he shouted.

A 'Code Red' - medical alert, went out over the prison radio system immediately, and Domingez was treated by the responders, who also cleaned him up. He was then returned to his cell. An ambulance was called for Snr. Officer White who had suffered a broken nose and slight concussion. Matt made sure that this was not delayed at the gate, and a gate officer was able to accompany it to the back of the SHU.

Whitey was tender in other places, but remarkably, no permanent damage was found. He was reassured that, although there would be some bruising, he would recover quickly.

Matt Roberts, ordered all the SHU officers to isolate Domingez, and sternly warned them, "No contact whatsoever for him. No visitors. No legal visits. No prisoner contact. No Education. Nothing; and I want hourly reports on his condition" He then turned to the most senior officer and said, "I want to know when he wakes, what he says, what he does and I want you, to tell me." The officer nodded and Matt left shaking his head.

When Matt returned to his office with the intention of calling Jack, he found him sitting, waiting for him.

"I hope it's ok" said Michelle, "I know he doesn't have an appointment, but I figured it was part of what you're doing this morning." She was clearly flustered and Matt suggested that she make them some tea and get some herself. Whilst Michelle busied herself with getting the refreshments, Matt brought Jack up to speed with developments and gave him the mobile phone.

Jack turned the phone on and went through the logs. He made a few notes on a 'sticky pad' on Matt's desk. He then dissembled the phone and retrieved the sim card from it. Reaching into his bag, he produced an 'Asus Phone Pad' which he used to insert the sim card into. He played with settings and then said, "I showed them at the gate, that there was no sim card in it, so I was able to bring it in... Right let's see what we can find out." He called up an app to send messages and started to type. Matt got up and joined Jack on his side of the table, and it wasn't long before Michelle appeared with drinks. She smiled to see them pouring over the

Clear Bright Light of Day 143

tablet; and shook her head as she left, not understanding what they were doing, but nevertheless not being able to erase the picture of 'naughty boys plotting some mischief' out of her mind.

They were certainly talking like schoolchildren, almost egging each other on, to say something naughty, to complete the deception that it was Domingez who was contacting his girlfriend.

Jack sent three SMS messages before he got a response: *'Thanks for the phone'; 'I am in bed thinking about you';* and *'when I am getting out?'*

It was during the last text that a message came in from Domingez's girlfriend; professing her love for him and telling him to sit tight and all arrangements were in place. Jack and Matt looked at each other. They knew they would have to play it carefully so that they didn't expose the truth of what they were doing. Jack deleted the third text without sending it. "What shall we say?" asked Matt. Jack thought for a moment, thinking back through all the information they had, and said, "How are they going to get him out of the prison. It must be with a helicopter, or something huge to go through the gate. There's no way anyone could get over that embankment without a huge armoured tank, and there would be so much notice of one of those coming, there would be no surprise at all! If you knew someone was coming for you, you would want to know that you weren't going to get hurt in the process, wouldn't you?" He typed, *'when I get out of the SHU is there danger of me getting hurt in the extraction?'* They waited for what seemed several minutes, then the pad beeped; Jack read out loud, "That is a concern. They may have to come in fast and hot. I imagine they will fire on the gate and then hover over the SHU and drop a ladder. Don't come out until you see the ladder. Is there still two of you?"

Matt looked at Jack, "Two?"

"Maybe it's a trick or check or something, how do we answer?" asked Jack.

Matt thought for a moment and said, "We only know for sure that there is one – him. So, say 'No, just one.' That way if there were two, she'll think the plan has changed, and it was too difficult to get more out, or that he is crossing the other one. If it's a trick then hopefully there won't be a coded response." Jack typed, *'ONE'* in capitalised letters. They waited. The pad beeped again, and Jack read, 'The package contains more details including the time. Erase these messages and we only use the phone if there is a problem.'

Jack terminated the app. He removed the sim card and put it with the phone into an evidence bag.

"Now if you were flying a helicopter, where would you leave from and return to? So that you could ensure you got clean away." Jack asked out loud.

Jack left the prison declaring the items he was removing and they were noted in the Gate log book. He retrieved his gun and phone and then called Detective Pauline Allen. He asked her to investigate where a helicopter might fly in from and suggested that it would be armed with some means to damaging the gate area. He also asked what the Police would do to track one. Pauline said that she would get back to him, and then terminated the call.

Jack found his car and got into it. As he was leaving he was nearly hit, by someone on a motorcycle coming into the prison. The bikie swerved just in time, but Jack got a good look at the man's face. It was someone he recognised vaguely. 'Probably a bikie with a record. Visiting another inmate who was still incarcerated' he thought. He pulled onto the main road, but it wasn't until he was outside Natalie's house that he remembered visits were usually in the afternoon.

Jack rang the doorbell and stood behind the stone pillar. He knew Natalie was careful, 'but you couldn't be too careful, when someone was holding a gun, knowing they may have to use it and you're in the line of fire,' he thought. Natalie asked the caller to identify themselves and Jack did so. He walked in when the door opened and hugged Natalie who was looking a bit better than she had done in the morning.

"All good?" he asked as he made his way further into the house.

"Yes, all good" said Natalie.

"So, what's new Jack?" said David when he reached the living area. Jack shared what he'd been doing since he left them, and even the incident of nearly knocking a bikie off his bike, as he came into the prison carpark.

He finished by saying, "I thought visits were in the afternoon."

"Not for the SHU!" said Natalie suddenly. They paused wondering if it was a relevant piece of information.

"Well, Matt says that 'Domingez is in total isolation' at the present time and foreseeable future."

Jack explained that although no packages were going to be taken to Domingez, David would still have to give the appearance of going to the prison on Friday, as if he were passing something to Domingez as he'd been told to. David who was putting a couple of meat pies in to the oven, agreed that he would ride in the next day. "Want to stay for lunch?" he asked.

"Beer and a meat pie tempt you?" he said. Jack thanked him but said he had to get going.

It was as Jack was leaving again that his phone rang. He paused in the front doorway and then came back in to answer it. The number was withheld, so Jack said, "Hello," intentionally not identifying himself.

"Is this Jack Pritard?" the caller asked.

"Who is this?" Jack asked.

"My name is Captain Stirling and I'm an officer in the Royal Australian Navy. Am I speaking to Jack Pritard?"

Jack recovered from the surprise that the Navy were calling and said, "Yes. I'm Jack Pritard, but I was an Army Intelligence Officer. What does the Navy want with me?"

There was a pause, "Army Intelligence eh?" said Captain Stirling, "Well, our intelligence has us tracking a ship off the coast of Western Australia."

"I'm sorry, how did you get my number?" interrupted Jack, "and how can I be of help?" He was feeling confused.

Captain Stirling took a breath, he was used to people listening to him, not discussing matters. He hardly ever explained himself to anyone, but here he was having to make sense to this man.

"Mr Pritard..." He began. "The Western Australia Police commissioner has contacted me regarding a report that Detective Pauline Allen has made."

The wheels in Jacks head were now turning quickly, "Yes" he said.

"Detective Allen, is looking for a helicopter. I believe you know about this?" Stirling continued.

"Yes" Jack said.

"Well we have found one that we're not very happy about." replied Captain Stirling.

After Captain Stirling had briefed Jack on the whereabouts of the vessel carrying the helicopter and its armament. They agreed that this could well be the way Domingez's contacts had arranged for his release. When he got off the phone Jack came back inside and said, "I think I will have a pie and a beer after all. Any chips?"

David got some frozen oven-chips and spread them on an oven tray and placed them in to the oven along with another pie, twenty minutes later they sat down to a nice lunch with plenty of tomato sauce. Over the lunch Jack shared more about the vessel that the Navy had discovered and were tracking. The more they thought about it the more it seemed to make sense that this was the way Domingez was planning to escape.

"Once he's in international waters, the rules of engagement change" said Jack. To recapture him would take agreements at government levels and action by Interpol. Even if they 'invade' Australian waters, we would have to prove hostile intent in order to engage them. The armament on the helicopter isn't even enough unless it is used. It would be so much simpler to keep them away altogether.

They finished the lunch, and Jack said, "At least your part in this is coming to an end soon. You'll be able to get over and see your parents Natalie, and be reunited with your son, so much sooner than you thought."

Natalie's face lit up in a smile, it almost ached to smile, such had her face been set in serious expressions over the past week.

"So, when do I have to give the bike back?" Asked David.

Jack smiled and said, "When they ask for it of course, and you know how slowly the wheels of bureaucracy can move!" He laughed.

Chapter Nineteen

David was awake early the following day, but there was really no reason to get up immediately so he just lay in bed with his thoughts. By all accounts, Nathan seemed to be enjoying his holiday with his grandparents and Natalie was getting some well needed rest. They both missed the little chap, but it was also nice not to have to be up in the middle of the night; changing and feeding him. It had been an added bonus to be able to remind themselves what it was like, when it was just the two of them. They had cuddled on the settee, which had led to kissing. Then as layers started to come off, and their passion increased for each other, they moved to the bedroom where they were able to abandon all inhibitions and consummate their love tenderly and urgently. The stress, when released from them both, gave way to a sleep which was deep and fulfilling.

David reached for his phone to check the time, it was nearly six o'clock. He thought he might quietly get up and ready himself to visit the prison for what he hoped would be the last time. He started to move the bedclothes aside, but then felt Natalie's arm pin him to the bed. "Where do you think you're going mister?" she said sleepily. "If you think you can get away that easily, when we have the house to ourselves, you are greatly mistaken." Her hand moved lower, and David felt his resolve to get up, melt away as his passion for her returned. Soon any thoughts of sleepiness were swept aside in a tide of passionate caresses and embraces. They made love again, renewing their vows, to have and to hold one another, for the rest of their lives. Holding one another in their mutual afterglow; Natalie murmured, "This is nice." She held her naked body against his.

"Certainly is" David replied. It was nearly always at times like this that David wondered what he'd done to deserve such an amazing woman. "You are so gorgeous" he said.

"Even with my pot belly and big boobs?" Natalie replied.

"You are lovely" David whispered in her ear. He kissed her again and lay looking into her eyes.

He sighed. "I have to go into work for a few hours" he reminded her.

"Well..." she replied, "I shall be waiting!" She spread herself across the bed dramatically and then laughed at her own actions. David smiled at her and got up to make tea for her, before jumping into the shower.

Dressed and breakfasted David slipped the Glock into the concealed holster and pulled on his new leather jacket. He adjusted the zips for comfort and air flow and then put on his helmet, ensuring the SENA Bluetooth communicator was switched on. He pulled on gloves and after locking the door from house to the garage, he opened the garage door and pulled the bike out, making sure that anyone watching him, would see the empty box going into the 'Swing Arm bag'. They would not know it was empty of course. He closed the garage door looking around, but he saw no one. He sat astride the large Harley Davidson and flicked the gear lever to neutral, before pressing the starter button and hearing the large engine roar into life. He checked the street again for traffic and put the bike in gear and accelerated away.

The ride to the prison took a little longer than usual, due to the increased traffic of the later hour. When he did reach the prison, he saw a couple of motorcycles parked on the street outside. They were further up the road and there was no sign of their riders, all of which was unusual. There was not room to park on the country road, let alone leave a vehicle. He pulled into the car park with heightened awareness; looking for trouble as he headed for the covered bike parking area. It was then that he saw one leather clad rider, sitting on one of the benches near the 'out-care' building. Visits were not due for several hours so David thought it unlikely that this man was waiting to see an inmate. He parked his bike and decided not to leave any personal things with it. He took his helmet off and then retrieved the small box from the Swing Arm bag. He put it into his helmet, as if to conceal it behind his gloves and walked towards the gate. He purposely ignored the man watching him. 'All being well Weasel and his staff would have been briefed by Matt Roberts, from the information Jack had given him. He would then be able to take the box into the prison' he thought. He reached the gate and went through the first set of bulletproof doors and then through the next set and into the Gate security area.

He nodded to Snr. Gate Officer Stoat who nodded back and said, "David!"

"Morning Weasel" said David as he approached the lockers.

"I'm only going to be in for an hour or so, I'm going to leave all my stuff in a locker." He took his gloves and the box and laid them on a chair by the tall stack of lockers. There was no room for a helmet, so he placed this on top of the locker. He then put his jacket and gloves into the locker, along with his Swiss army knife, USB stick and the Glock, without taking it out of the holster. He locked the secure unit with the key provided and then walked back to the desk. He pulled the lid off the box, to show Weasel it contained nothing. Weasel nodded and David walked through the metal detector, without emptying his pockets. The machine bleeped and all the officers ignored it.

David keyed his code into the pad and selected his set of keys and a personal alarm from the electronically locked boxes, and proceeded up the path to the Admin block. He was somewhat later than usual and he knew that he would have only to wait a couple of hours before leaving again to complete the deception.

His first 'port of call' was to Superintendent Matt Roberts. He greeted Michelle outside the office and she got up out of her seat and hugged him. She asked after Natalie and Nathan and said that she had recently had lunch with Gerry McCubbin - a retired Superintendent, who had saved their lives by shooting dead an assassin who was trying to kill Natalie.

"How is Gerry?" asked David, "I haven't seen him for a while."

"He is doing so well" Michelle said, "He was full of news about the church he goes to. It's the one you go to I think. Anyway, it has really helped him." She paused and a knowing look passed between them. The church was very large with several services over the weekend. David thought he'd try and find out which service it was that Gerry attended. It would be nice to coincide him again. And then as if that part of the interaction had concluded; "The Superintendent is expecting you," she said, waving David towards the door. David knocked and went in.

Matt Roberts looked up and saw David come in and greeted him, "Hi David, how are you going?"

"Good, thanks Matt." replied David.

"Got the box?" asked Matt. David handed the empty box to Matt, and after he'd received it he threw it across the room as if it were a basketball. It landed in a waste basket on the other side of the room. Both friends smiled at the achievement.

"So, what are you going to do with yourself for a couple of hours?" asked Matt.

"Well," said David. "I'm not going anywhere near Education. Perhaps I'll sit and read online, if I can use a computer somewhere?"

Matt made arrangements for David to use one of the offices in the corridor; as an officer was on leave, and David settled himself comfortably and entertained himself. The time flew by and soon it was lunchtime. Matt passed the door to the office David was 'borrowing' and said,

"You still here?"

David laughed, "Yes, I better go."

Matt continued to lunch, whilst David packed up and locked the office. He made his way back to the Gate and replaced his keys and personal alarm in their secure locations. He then went out into the Gate security are, opened his locker and started to put on the concealed holster and retrieve his other personal items. He took a few strange looks from visitors who were arriving and being passed through the visitor's gate, but no one said anything. He pulled on his jacket and carried his helmet and gloves back to the bike. There was no sign of the bikie or the bikes on the street outside, so David turned onto the main road and headed home.

He was about to turn north towards Canning Vale, when he saw in his mirror, two large motorcycles following him. He couldn't determine at the distance between them and him, if it were the same two bikes he'd seen outside the prison but he wondered if he should see if they were following him, by taking a different route home.

David manoeuvred his bike and made the turn and accelerated. He checked his mirrors again and saw the bikes behind make the same turn and speed up, trying to close the gap. He saw Swamp Road on the right and thought to himself, 'If I take 'Swamp', 'Commercial' and then 'Anstey', I will still be heading in the right direction, but I'll know for sure if they are following me, and I will have more directional options when I get to Ranford.' He braked hard and pulled right without signalling. He twisted the throttle and accelerated up through the gears, now travelling ten kilometres per hour over the speed limit. He reached Forrestdale Lake and turned left towards Commercial Road. He looked in his mirror and caught a glimpse of the two bikies still behind him, as he continued around the lake. There was little doubt now that these bikes were following him. If he was being followed by a car, he would have been tempted to take the footpath to Boom Street, but these bikies could go anywhere that David could take his bike. He didn't know what they wanted with him, but he thought it would be best to just stay as far from them as possible. He accelerated hard again.

The bikies were closing on him. However, when he got to the roundabout where Armadale Road and Anstey Road met. He no longer wanted to be on isolated roads and so he turned right onto Armadale, thinking that he would head towards the Police Station at the end. He passed the Tonkin Highway intersection, with the lights in his favour and rode over the Ranford roundabout. The bikies were now less than thirty metres behind him as he accelerated along Armadale Road hoping to be able to reach the shopping centre and the Police Station behind it.

Unfortunately for David the two bikies had been given a job to do; and they intended to do it one way or another. They had been told that this 'Prison Officer' had served his purpose and was now a liability, to be 'tidied up' in much the same way any other loose end might be. In this case terminally. They had hoped to catch up with, and cause David to crash, making it look like an accident; but this Prison Officer seemed to know how to ride a bike, and despite their efforts to get close, he was staying ahead of them. All pretence was now gone and they accelerated dangerously towards David; the plan now was just to shoot him down in cold blood.

David reached the intersection with Railway Avenue; the light was against him, but he did not stop. Neither did the two bikes following him. He heard the squeal of brakes and the sound of a crash behind him and he looked in his mirror but the two bikes were still following. David turned right onto Orchard Avenue with the intention of reaching Jull Street, but he didn't make it.

The turn had slowed him, and now two bikies pulled along his left side and one tried to push him off his bike. David braked hard and the bikies pulled up ahead blocking his way. David quickly debated with himself what to do; and decided that he would be better off if he was able to get off the bike. He pulled hard right and up the ramp to the shopping centre and pulled into the first free parking bay on the right. He switched off the engine and put the bike on it's stand. As he swung his leg over, he pulled the zip of his jacket down, to give him access to his gun.

The bikies had accelerated after David up the ramp and saw him pull into a bay by the wall overlooking the street below. Both of them stopped short in the middle of the access road and got off their bikes. In unison they both unzipped their jackets and pulled out guns.

The pistols that David was staring at, looked like they were old Colt Army special .32 calibre revolvers, they were large and cumbersome and held just six bullets. He was trying to work out if they were there to scare him with the guns or if their intent was more serious. His question was answered for him as two bullets missed him by a fraction of an inch; one of them smashing the wing mirror of the car behind him. David crouched low and pulled the Glock from its holster. He could no longer see the bikies because of the car he had ducked behind; and he now worried that they knew where he was, but he was no longer sure where they were. Then suddenly he knew. They had not seen him draw his weapon and thinking him to be unarmed they confidently stepped into view. David fired the 9mm Glock at near point-blank range into the knee of the first bikie. The second bikie jumped back before David could get another shot off.

Suddenly pandemonium broke out and David was aware that people were running for cover and screaming in fear. There was no strategy behind their panic, many were running the wrong way, taking themselves closer to the danger. The bikie that David had hit, had collapsed as his joint had bent backwards like a 'stork' and the muscles were unable to hold his weight. He had dropped his gun and lay screaming on the floor, clutching his broken and bleeding limb. David looked around the front of the car for the other bikie hoping to see him running away. Instead a quick volley of bullets hit the front of the car. David was trying to count shots and work out when the bikie would have to reload. He suddenly had a memory of a Clint Eastwood movie he'd seen and the famous line that fictional detective, Harry Callaghan had said to a failed bank robber lying within reach of his gun, "I know what you're thinking. Has he fired five shots or six? Well in all the excitement, I've kinda lost count myself. So, the real question you have to ask yourself punk, is, 'Do you feel lucky?'" David didn't 'feel lucky' and was not about to look out again. He was trying to get an angle from under the car to locate the other bikie.

Suddenly there was a shout. A loud bang and all went quiet. David chanced a quick glance around the front of the car again and heard a shout.

"Drop your weapon and come out with your hands up!"

David had not heard anyone identify themselves as the Police, so he stayed where he was. He pulled off his helmet and put it on the ground.

He shouted back, "I am a Federal Agent. I am armed, and I will not drop my weapon. Identify yourself and drop your weapon."

There was a pause, then, "I am an Armaguard Bank Security Officer. I have shot one armed person here. I am holstering my weapon and would ask you to do the same. Come out and we can sort this out."

There were sounds of sirens getting closer and David stole another quick glance from behind the car. He saw a uniformed Armaguard standing at the back of a truck, that somehow in all the excitement, he had not seen when he pulled up the ramp. It was outside the Commonwealth Bank ATM. He shouted, "I'm coming out now. I have holstered my weapon. Where is your partner?"

"Behind me" came the answer.

The two men approached each other cautiously, neither wishing to spook the other into drawing a weapon. Both high on adrenalin and wanting to reassure themselves of the other's identity.

"I can see who you are," called David. Lifting his jacket to show the holstered pistol. "I am going to reach for my ID. He slowly pulled it off his belt and held it up for the officer to see. The officer nodded, and both relaxed a little.

David was still holding his ID when the first Police car hit the ramp. The two officers were out of the car before it had stopped behind the two bikes, and both drew their weapons.

"Calm down!" both David and the Armaguard said together.

"The situation is under control" the Armaguard added. The Police Officer looked at David's ID and said, "What the hell just happened here? And are you going to pull jurisdiction over me?"

David looked back at him and said, "No, you are welcome to it, mate."

The bikie that David had shot, had stopped screaming, he had fainted with the shock and blood loss. One of the police officers had recovered the gun that the bikie had dropped, and was now holding pressure on the wound, which David thought was also keeping the man in excruciating pain. Another officer was taking photographs for evidence, with a mobile phone. The first police officer asked for a statement, and the Armaguard said he would be happy to provide one as soon as a replacement unit for the bank arrived. He also stated that he was still on duty and would not give up his weapon. The police made a bit of fuss about this, but did not force him to do so, and David wasn't even asked for his gun.

When David made his statement he clearly laid out the facts. He said that the bikies had shot first and had not been attacking the 'Armaguard cash delivery'. They were solely trying to kill him. David said the bikie with no kneecap had been shot by him. The Armaguard had saved his life by shooting the other bikie. It was a clear case of self-defence. The officer made a note of their identification and then took some witness statements. Several ambulances had been called, and there were many shoppers who needed to be treated for shock. One of the police officers had been trying to do CPR on the bikie who had been shot by the Armaguard, but since he had died instantly from a large calibre bullet wound to his heart; there was not really much point, as the effort was just causing more blood loss.

David took a note of the Armaguard's details and he also noted the identity of the first Police Officer; he was Sgt. Williams, a traffic officer, who had been closest to respond to the report of shots being fired. David asked him to be in touch with Jack Pritard and Pauline Allen, who would be able to give details of the operation David was working on. The Police Officer thought he knew the name of Pauline Allen and relaxed a little more.

"Glad we're all on the same side!" he said and he moved his car out of the way.

David was allowed to leave, and after he had checked over his bike and equipment he rode away in the direction of home. He was unsure what, from all this he would share with Natalie, but he was certainly going to give a full brief to Jack. He quick dialled Jack on the SENA and spoke to him for the duration of the ride home, giving him a blow by blow detailed account. They agreed that telling Natalie a briefer version of the situation, with only the salient facts stripped of gore, would be best.

David pulled up on the drive and called Natalie on his phone, asking her to turn on the garage door opener. He could hear her moving around the garage, 'probably getting the steps' he thought. After a short while he tried the remote and the door opened and he parked the bike. He turned off the SENA communicator and removed his helmet which he stowed on the gear lever and walked towards the door between the garage and the house where Natalie was waiting for him. He hugged her and then flicked the switch on the wall to close the garage door. Natalie kissed him and hugged him again. She was dressed in her Lycra gym kit, but she smelled fresh and looked clean.

"I was just about to have a work out on the gym equipment that you installed in the garage" she said. "You need a shower, though" she said, smelling the sweat on his body, and then her eyes grew wide as she looked at her hands and the areas of his jacket she had touched.

"What's wrong?" She said, "You have blood splattered all over you!" David had not noticed, but it was true. He even found a bone-chip in his hair. He quickly reassured Natalie that none of the blood was his, and as he stripped off his soiled clothes, he related the highlights of his deadly encounter. Natalie walked with him to the shower but left him there and went to put his clothes in water to soak. She wiped his jacket with a soft damp cloth and then put the cloth to soak. She took the contents of his pockets and the holstered Glock and placed them on the bed and then she put out some fresh clean jeans along with a T-shirt, some socks and underpants. David was just getting out of the shower when Jack arrived, and Natalie let him in, after checking his identity whilst standing to one side of the door.

David dressed and enjoyed the feeling of being washed clean of the events of earlier. He thought it was a good thing that he was finished with prisons, at least for a good long while. He listened to faint conversation in the house and heard Natalie relating to Jack what he had told her moments earlier. He heard Jack agreeing with her and telling her that it was going to be over soon. He put his personal items in his pockets and walked down the corridor. 'Surely now, they could be left to enjoy some peace and quiet. Perhaps they should take a few weeks over East with Natalie's parents?' He decided he would broach the possibility with her later.

Chapter Twenty

The tension on the bridge of ADV Fourcray was palpable. Sweat had broken out on Robbie's forehead as he went through procedures and decisions he'd followed and made over the past few hours. He would have to write this up and would certainly be held accountable for the actions he took; which could make him a hero, or damn him for any mistakes he made. There were lives at stake, whenever weapons were identified or employed. He was responsible for the lives of his crew, and it was a responsibility that he felt keenly.

The day was breaking and the sun shone through the glass screens of the bridge as it hung low in the eastern sky. There was a five metre swell which had been expected, and was proving helpful to hide them from the larger boat's radar.

Commander Baker's condition remained the same. He would suffer acute pain, be treated with pethidine and then eventually pass a kidney stone. The pattern would repeat, and every few hours there would be both periods of calm and great discomfort. The doctor spent time with Commander Baker as he needed to be sedated and would then return to the infirmary, via a report to Robbie on the bridge.

By midday the Comms officer had identified the frequencies being used on board the target vessel. She had started recording the transmissions, which would have to be cleaned up through filters to be properly understood, but some of what was being said was understandable. They had also narrowed the identification of the vessel to a 'Sea-Explorer 65,' and the schematics of the boat were displayed for Robbie and the other officers on the bridge to view.

ADV Fourcray continued to 'shadow' the Sea-Explorer, noting that it was getting closer to the two-hundred mile limit of Australian waters. It appeared to be moving to a point which would be about two hundred nautical miles west of Fremantle, placing it very close to Australian waters. So far, they seemed to have stayed out of discovery of the Seaxplorer's radar. It was probably due to the way their radar was set up in the direction they were travelling. 'Surely they will do a total sweep before launching a helicopter,' thought Robbie. 'We might have difficulty staying out of sight then, but we might get a 'ping' warning.'

"Lieutenant. Contact Captain Stirling please." Robbie ordered. The young lieutenant made a note of her current monitoring frequency, and then turned the dial to the frequency that 'T.S. Harold E Holt Station' monitored on and made the call. "T.S. Harold E Holt Station. T.S. Harold E Holt Station. T.S. Harold E Holt Station. This is VMCF311, VMCF 311. Over."

After a short interaction with the receiving station, they were transferred to Captain Stirling. Stirling came on the line, without usual protocols and demanded, "Commander. Report!"

Robbie lifted the mic, "Captain Stirling, this is VMCF 311. Lt Commander Robbie Taylor in command. We have followed your orders and are currently monitoring transmissions and navigation of a Super-yacht class, Seaxplorer 65. Our commanding officer Commander Baker is indisposed at this present time. Over."

There was a brief silence followed by, "Listen Lt. Commander Taylor: We have good intel that this vessel is moving to within striking distance of the coast, to affect and aid the escape of a very high profile prisoner, currently serving time in Corymbia maximum security prison." The line went dead. Robbie had not heard Captain Stirling say 'over,' indicating he had finished his side of the conversation and so he did not respond.

He did however say to the weapon's officer, "Second Lieutenant, get me cartography of the WA coast, fifty miles inland and it's waters to our current position. Locate Corymbia prison on it and plot our position as well as the position of the target vessel. Then put it on screen."

"Lt Commander Taylor" continued Stirling, "I am ordering you to make contact with this vessel and make them aware that we have them on radar, and they are not welcome in our waters. Understood?"

"Captain Stirling, this is Lieutenant Commander Taylor. I receive and understand your order sir. I would like to inform you that this vessel is larger and better armed than ourselves. Over" There was a long silence, then; "Lt Commander Taylor, it is imperative that that helicopter does not leave it's base ship. You are authorised to get close enough to fire upon it. Captain Stirling, out!"

Robbie considered raising the alert level to 'Red', knowing that if they were close enough to shoot a helicopter, they would also be too close to avoid getting hit by the weapons on the Seaxplorer. He decided against going to 'Red' just yet.

"Navs." he called to the Navigation Officer.

"Sir?" came the response.

"Put us between the target ship and the coast. We may be come visible to them, but we'll be in a better position to shoot a helicopter heading west."

Robbie then turned to the Comms officer and said, "Make contact with the Seaxplorer and tell them we know exactly where they are and warn them not to enter Australian waters, or airspace." Then almost as an after thought, Robbie said, "Don't Identify our size or armament."

The Lieutenant adjusted her headset, and said "Sir." to Robbie. Then she dialled the wavelength back to the frequency she had been monitoring and said over the radio, "Unidentified Seaxplorer at grid reference 31 degrees, 46 minutes, and 44.7 seconds south... 112 degrees, 56 minutes and 22 seconds east. This is the Australian Navy. Do you receive? Over." There was no response. She changed frequency to the international shipping channel, and said again, "Unidentified Seaxplorer at grid reference 31 degrees, 46 minutes, and 44.7 seconds south... 112 degrees, 56 minutes and 22 seconds east. This is the Australian Navy. Do you receive? Over."

"They will have heard us sir," she said looking at Robbie. They waited, but heard nothing. It was at that point that Commander Baker limped onto the bridge.

"What's this I hear about us being ordered to contact this unidentified vessel in International waters?" He winced in pain and took a sharp intake of breath.

"Are you alright sir?" asked Robbie.

"Fine. Fine." said Commander Baker, waiving off Robbie's concern for his commanding officer.

"I am resuming command of the bridge" he announced, and winced again at his discomfort, "Report Lt. Commander!"

Robbie gave a brief report covering the past few hours, and about what Captain Stirling had ordered them to do. Finishing with telling him that he had put the Patrol Boat between the coast and the Seaxplorer.

The Lieutenant who was also looking at the current position display, was still trying to reach the Seaxplorer, "Unidentified Seaxplorer at grid reference 31 degrees, 50 minutes, and 20 seconds south... 112 degrees, 45 minutes and 20 seconds east.

This is the Australian Navy. Do you receive, over." There was still no response.

Commander Baker was getting paler by the moment.

"Sir, I really think you should lie down," said Robbie.

But the Commander did not agree, "My place is on my bridge" he said, "and no one is ordering me off my own bridge!" he added.

"Well I am!" said a voice at the door. All turned to see the ship's doctor walk onto the bridge. Commander Baker looked shocked that his position had been challenged and his face started to redden.

"Come on sir," said the doctor quietly to him taking his arm, "I did say this would take some time and that you should rest."

Commander Baker shook his arm free of the doctor's grip and made a protest. He was in obvious discomfort and was sweating with the effort to maintain composure.

"Sir, I will keep you fully informed. Please do as the doc says and 'get better.'" Said Robbie.

"I will not! Shouted Commander Baker. "My place is here!"

The doctor looked at Robbie and raised his eyebrows. He seemed to be looking for support, but Robbie didn't want to have to force his commanding officer off the bridge.

The doctor however was now committed and said, "Commander Baker, I will relieve you of your command on medical grounds. You are not fit for duty sir!" An expression of anger mixed with resignation and acknowledgement of the situation passed over the Commander's face; and Lt Commander Robbie Taylor stepped in, "Thankfully that will not be necessary, as the Commander knows that his recovery is of the utmost importance."

He stepped in closer to Commander Baker and said, Mark, I've got this and I will keep you furnished with all the details, but you do need to get better." Mark nodded and thanked Robbie. The doctor helped him limp away. When he had gone, Robbie addressed the bridge.

"Commander Baker is still in charge of this vessel. His devotion to duty has been noted by all of us here today." Then he added, "If I hear that anyone has spoken of this, in any other fashion, they will answer to me, understood?"

The silence was broken by a collective, "Sir. Yes sir!"

Robbie turned to the Comms officer, "Lieutenant, it's time to ramp it up a little." he said.

The Lieutenant keyed her mic and said, "Unidentified Seaxplorer at grid reference; 31 degrees, 55 minutes, and 50 seconds south... 112 degrees, 40 minutes and 14 seconds east. This is the Australian Navy. I say again. This is the Australian Navy. You are ordered not, I say again, not to enter Australian waters or airspace. If you do not comply with this order you will be engaged."

There was a short silence and then the radio came to life, with a clear transmission from close by. "Australian Navy, Australian Navy, this is Seaxplorer. We are a cruise ship on course to Albany carrying passengers who are on vacation to Western Australia. We are a registered vessel and intend to continue south until 28 degrees, 50 minutes south, when we will plot a course south-east into Australian waters toward 'Geograph bay.' Over"

The Lieutenant keyed her mic and said, "Seaxplorer, this is the Australian Navy. You are ordered not to attempt to enter Australian waters or airspace. We are aware of your position. If you enter Australian waters you will be engaged by the Australian Navy and you may be boarded."

The reply came after a few minutes silence, "Australian Navy, Australian Navy, this is Seaxplorer. We are a cruise ship on course to Albany carrying passengers who are on vacation to Western Australia. We have a member of our crew who is sick and needs to be evacuated. We intend to do this by helicopter. We will fly them into Fremantle hospital in the next twenty-four hours, when we have prepared our aircraft."

The lieutenant looked to Robbie for directions. Robbie moved closer to the Comms desk and picked up the mic, "Seaxplorer, this is Lieutenant Commander Taylor of the Australian Navy. You are ordered not to attempt to enter Australian waters or airspace. We are aware of your position. If you enter Australian waters you will be engaged by the Australian Navy and may be boarded. If you enter Australian airspace, I must warn you that we have orders to shoot you down."

Robbie turned to the navigation officer.

"I want you to stay between them and the coast; match their speed and set a course to intercept immediately if they enter Australian waters. We must have an option to fire on that helicopter if it takes off."

He reached over to the on-board ship communication system and spoke to the crew.

"Crew of the ADV Fourcray, this is Lt Commander Taylor. I am increasing our alert status to 'Red' and ordering gun crews to the fore and aft weapons. Team leaders report to the bridge for a briefing."

He pressed the amber switch up another click and the light changed to glow red.

Within five minutes all team leaders were standing in a small room on one side of the bridge. Robbie ordered the boat crews to ready themselves for boarding parties, full armament was ordered and the team leaders were left in no doubt that they might be called upon, to attack and board a well-armed boat with air support. The mood was one of sombre excitement. The men did not usually see this kind of action, and many felt that their training was wasted on arresting fishermen and looking for people smugglers.

The gunners had loaded the 12.7mm machine guns and were patched into the navigation officer and weapons officers systems along with the Raphael Typhoon 25mm automated cannon, which was interfaced with the Electro Optics Surveillance System and was controlled from the bridge to be able to locate and fire upon moving targets. The machine guns were not really designed to bring down helicopters, but they would do so if they could hit them.

The Comms officer continued to dialogue with the Seaxplorer who kept insisting that they should be allowed to enter Australian waters, and asked for the Navy to identify their vessel and location. The Navy ignored the request for information and repeated the warning that the Seaxplorer would be fired upon if it strayed into Australian waters. The stand-off was a stalemate, which would continue until one or other made a move, and committed both parties to the action that followed.

The day wore on and Robbie took a few hours off the bridge to sleep and he also dropped into Commander Baker's cabin. He was looking better, but the doctor had been firm with him.

"Doc says he will 'write me up' if I leave the cabin. Can you believe that Robbie?" he said in exasperation. "It will be the last time he sails with me, I can tell you!"

Robbie took a breath, "Well... sir. He's only doing his job. If it was me, would you want me taking shifts on the bridge? In charge of a vessel of this size, in that much pain?"

The Commander rolled his eyes.

"What's going on Robbie? I'm starved of information." Robbie looked at the Commander and said, "There's been no change really sir. We are maintaining speed and position and hoping it will be enough to intercept them if they come our way."

After making sure the Commander had everything he needed, Robbie returned to the bridge to find, indeed there had been no change. The day wore on and the officers handed over to their shift counterparts and went off duty to sleep, until they might be needed again. Robbie drank coffee, cup after cup. He had even asked the doctor to prescribe him a stimulant to help him through. The doc had not been keen, but when Robbie threatened to have the Commander relieve him, he gave Robbie what he'd asked for.

On board the Seaxplorer a small number of the crew were debating their situation. They had not identified where the Navy were, and some felt that the Naval boat was either too small to show on their radar, or too far away for it to matter. "Either way, we should have time to launch the helicopter" the man known as Esteban, said. He thought of himself as their leader, but he was not the 'Captain' of the boat. The boat was crewed by professional staff, who were being paid far more for this voyage than they would have made in a year of voyages.

"We must abide by what the Navy order us to do." the 'Captain' was saying, "They have the ability to board the vessel and arrest us all. They can even impound the boat." He was immediately hushed by those holding light machine guns.

"We can fly low," one said, "under the radar. They will not even know we have left the boat. The rest can defend the boat from any boarding craft they send."

"And what if they fire missiles at us?" asked the navigation officer, "We can't even see them on radar, we'd have no chance to react. We'd be sunk."

Esteban sighed, "They can't do that. International law allows them to posture but if they fire on a passenger ship, it will be an international incident. They are bound by Marine Law. We are safe."

He thought for a moment and said, "I like the idea of flying out very low, get me the pilot, where is he? He should be here!" One of the crew left the meeting chuckling, "He is throwing up over the side, with sea sickness. It's this swell. He'll be only too glad to get off this boat!"

The pilot was located and brought into the meeting and asked if he could take off in the current conditions. The man looked quite 'green'.

"I'd love to but we need less swell. I could take off and then the boat could come up under me and hit me hard or swat me sideways into the sea. The weather will be perfect at the planned time tomorrow morning."

Esteban considered the information and announced.

"Get a message to the lawyer. She will tell Domingez to be ready earlier than planned. We will send out the 'bird' when the swell is just low enough. Hopefully we will have him back here before lunchtime. Until then have the men, 'man the guns' and look out. We don't want to be surprised now, do we?"

The men had their orders, and the meeting broke. Many of them were undisciplined deck crew and 'manning the guns' meant just standing by them idly smoking. The Seaxplorer continued it's path, getting closer to the invisible line demarcating, Australian waters from international waters. The nervous staff were now ignoring Naval warnings which were coming in every hour. They did not reply to them, and hoped that Esteban was right, that they could launch the helicopter undetected.

Night fell and Robbie rubbed his eyes. He had had three hours sleep in the last twenty. He cat-napped in the 'Captain Chair' on the bridge and told the officers to wake him every hour or sooner if anything happened. Sometime in the early hours of the morning Robbie was woken with a jump.

"Sir!" Shouted the Navigation Officer. Robbie tried to get his bearings and rubbed sleep from his eyes.

"We are passing them, they have slowed." The Navigation Officer continued, "I've slowed further sir, trying to let them pass us again."

"All stop." ordered Robbie. "What time is it?"

The Navigation Officer started to argue and thought better of it and cut power to the engines. The big diesel 3516C Caterpillar units shut down and the boat continued to drift. Robbie looked at the screen they were still passing the super yacht.

"Reverse full!" shouted Robbie. The Navigation Officer, made the settings and the engines started up again in reverse.

"Pull back and drift" Robbie said. But the officer kept the engines in reverse.

"We can't drift and go back sir!"

"Good man" Robbie countered. "Keep reversing until we are level and five miles away. It looks like they have come to a stop. I think they are planning to get that helicopter off."

The boat manoeuvred slowly against the current and stopped effectively. Robbie looked at his watch, as no one had answered his question about the time. It was four in the morning. He looked for the Comms officer, a young male second lieutenant officer sat in the chair now.

"Get a message off to that boat, telling them that if they enter Australian airspace we will engage them with our weapons." 'We can maintain this ruse whilst it is dark.' He said to himself.

"Ping" The radar blipped.

"Swell's dropping, sir! I think they may have us on radar.

"Turn us starboard and face on to them" ordered Robbie. "Give them less to 'see' and hope the paint on this ship will do it's work at reducing reflective signals." The boat swung to the right and Robbie said, "Get us in to a position Northeast by east of their stern. Use the current to our advantage."

Commander Baker had prayed for sleep, and despite the sedatives he had slept fitfully, he was exhausted. He was so concerned about not being able to take up his responsibilities and felt keenly that he should be able to make the decisions in the coming few hours that would result in either engaging the 'enemy' or driving them off. He had not passed a stone for five hours, and he was hoping that this was another answer to prayer, which meant that he was through the worst of it. He was musing on a dream he'd just had. The strange thing was, he didn't usually dream, or at least if he did he didn't remember them. During his fitful sleep though, he had dreamt clearly that he was in prayer asking God for deliverance from his pain. He had called the doctor and the doctor had visited the cabin but he appeared in a fancy-dress costume, complete with eye patch and wooden leg. He woke feeling conflicted; the feeling was somewhere between concern for his mental health and feeling that there was an answer in this dream that was important. Then suddenly he knew what he must do. He reached for a book on his filing cabinet and turned the pages, until...

Commander Baker reached for the phone on his desk and made a call to the bridge, a second lieutenant answered and passed him to Robbie.

"Robbie, I need to see you. Now" he said.

"Sir, I'm a bit busy up here right at this moment" Robbie countered.

"Lieutenant Commander, I need to see you in my quarters, now!" Commander Baker said again. Robbie thought of disobeying, but the tone seemed urgent, so he handed control of the boat to the Navigation Officer who was ranked as a Lieutenant, and then he ran down to the Commander's Cabin.

He knocked on the door and entered without waiting for permission. Commander Baker was sat at his table looking at a heavy tome which Robbie recognised as the Navy regulations. "I think we may have been spotted on radar, sir." Robbie said.

"I have an idea Robbie." said Commander Baker.

Commander Baker turned the book, and said, "I've not slept much Robbie, but this is right isn't it? Robbie read the legal definition of Piracy:

United Nations Convention on the Law of the Sea 1982 Article 100. Duty to Co-operate in the Repression of Piracy. All States shall co-operate to the fullest possible extent in the repression of piracy on the high seas or in any other place outside the jurisdiction of any State.

Article 101 Definition of Piracy
-Piracy consists of any of the following acts:

(a) any illegal acts of violence or detention, or any act of depredation, committed for private ends by the crew or the passengers of a private ship or a private aircraft, and directed:
(i) on the high seas, against another ship or aircraft, or against persons or property on board such ship or aircraft;
(ii) against a ship, aircraft, persons or property in a place outside the jurisdiction of any State;
(b) any act of voluntary participation in the operation of a ship or of an aircraft with knowledge of facts making it a pirate ship or aircraft;
(c) any act of inciting or of intentionally facilitating an act described in subparagraph (a) or (b).

"How can we use this to our advantage?" asked Robbie. "How are they a pirate ship?"

"Well..." said Commander Baker, that's what I thought until I read down the 'Legal Perspectives' which show Australia's Response to Piracy. Article 103 says, '*Definition of a Pirate Ship or Aircraft: A ship or aircraft is considered a pirate ship or aircraft, if it is **intended** by the persons in dominant control to be used for the purpose of committing one of the acts referred to in article 101.* The same applies if the ship or aircraft has been used to commit any such act, so long as it remains under the control of the persons guilty of that act. If Captain Stirling is right and this ship intends to launch a helicopter gunship with the *intention* of breaking into a prison and aiding an illegal escape from prison, then I'm sure we can use this definition, and define the crew of that Seaxplorer as pirates. It therefore, becomes our duty to arrest them. Not wait for them to act. 'Article 105 says: *Seizure of a Pirate Ship or Aircraft On the high seas, or in any other place outside the jurisdiction of any State. Every State may seize a pirate ship or aircraft, or a ship or aircraft taken by piracy and under the control of pirates, and arrest the persons and seize the property on board. The courts of the State which carried out the seizure may decide upon the penalties to be imposed, and may also determine the action to be taken with regard to the ships, aircraft or property, subject to the rights of third parties acting in good faith'.*"

Robbie looked at his commanding officer. He realised that it might work.

"What about, Article 106 though? '*Liability for Seizure without Adequate Grounds. Where the seizure of a ship or aircraft on suspicion of piracy has been effected without adequate grounds, the State making the seizure shall be liable to the State the nationality of which is possessed by the ship or aircraft for any loss or damage caused by the seizure'.*" What if we are wrong, sir?"

Commander Baker pointed to the next article.

"That's the beauty of it." he said. "If by some amazing mistake we are wrong; we just give the ship back and make right any damage."

Robbie read on and said, "Well I guess we are the ones to do this; Article 107 says '*A seizure on account of piracy may be carried out only by warships or military aircraft, or other ships or aircraft clearly marked and identifiable as being on government service and authorised to that effect'.*

Robbie ran back up to the bridge, arriving a little out of breath. He grabbed the internal mic.

"ADV Fourcray. Hear this, hear this: All crews to battle stations, boarding parties to RHIBs." The alarms sounded all over the patrol boat and the teams assembled themselves according to the drills they had practiced many times. The two team leaders appeared on the bridge.

"What are your orders sir?" asked one. Robbie realised he had given the bridge no warning, and what he would say next would be news to all of them.

"Launch the RHIB's" Robbie ordered, "We are going to use the last hour of darkness to board, and arrest a boatload of pirates!" The team leaders turned on their heels and disappeared. The 7.2m Rigid Hull Inflatable Boats (RHIB) were capable of being rapidly deployed and recovered using the Vest Davit System, which enabled swift, silent and safe deployment and recovery of the RHIBs. Their crews would already be armed and in the boats, and the lift operator would be waiting for the order to deploy and lower the RHIBs into the water. The RHIB was 'over the horizon capable' and fitted with stand-alone communications and safety systems that enabled it to be a significant force multiplier, for the patrol boat. The increased boarding team capacity as well as a concurrent boarding capability, meant that the boarding teams would operate with greater effect and at greater range, with greater safety.

"Launch RHIBs" Robbie told the Comms officer. Who spoke into his mic. And then after listening, turned to Robbie and said, "RHIBs in the water and away sir."

"Monitor RHIBs on radar" ordered Robbie.

He said a prayer under his breath for the men under his command and then said, "Weapons. If you see a helicopter in the sky, put it in the water."

Then, "Get me Captain Stirling." He dictated a message for the Comms officer to pass on. Who then made a brief call, via the Harold E. Holt station and read the message to Captain Stirling.

"ADV Fourcray believes the launch of an aircraft from the Seaxplorer is imminent. We are engaging the Seaxplorer in international waters. We believe their intention meets the 1982 Article 100, definition of piracy. Fourcray out"

The navigation Officer looked at Robbie, "Lt Commander. Orders?" Robbie thought a moment, "Wait for the element of surprise. When the RHIBs 'send' that they are engaging the Seaxplorer we make a course for them at full speed." The next ten minutes of waiting was tense and quiet, apart from the sound of the sea and the engines thrumming through the patrol boat.

"RHIB1 to VMCF311" the radio said.

"RHIB1, go ahead" the Comms officer replied putting them on speaker.

"This is RHIB1, we have engaged the Seaxplorer"

Robbie pointed at the Navigation Officer, who changed the patrol boat's course.

The transmission continued from RHIB1, "We and RHIB2 are taking light machine-gunfire from the deck of the Seaxplorer."

"Return fire" ordered Robbie, "Board that vessel."

Reports continued to come over the radio and the bridge heard the transmissions between the RHIB teams as they progressed through the assault and boarding of the Seaxplorer.

ADV Fourcray arrived as the teams were cuffing the last of the 'Pirates'.

"We didn't even have to use our cannon" said the Weapons Officer, in somewhat of a disappointed tone.

"Comms. Send to Captain Stirling; 'Seaxplorer has been seized and the crew arrested. There were no Naval casualties. Two of the pirates were killed in exchange of gunfire and the remaining number surrendered. I am leaving a team aboard to bring the vessel to Fremantle Harbour. Please make the necessary reception for us'."

Robbie left the bridge and went to brief Commander Taylor.

Chapter Twenty-One

Three visitors were arriving early on Saturday morning. All of them were scheduled to visit the high-profile prisoners from the SHU. Two were women and one, a man dressed in leathers. Despite the fact that there were only a few of them, the prison security team knew that these prisoners, and their visitors would take as much work as a room full of normal visitors, and the inmates they had come to see. The visits would have to be conducted in the 'non-contact' visits hall, where screens of glass separated the parties and there would be an officer near each prisoner and each visitor, observing them carefully.

They reached the gate and were directed to pass through the metal detector one at a time. They were then allowed into the 'prison visitor's lobby' where they were stamped on the back of their hands with a clear sticky liquid, which dried to a light sheen. Each was then shown to the iris scanner, and a digital picture was taken of their eye. A scan of the ID they brought with them was taken next and the files stored together on the system. This was standard procedure for all visitors.

The prison had received a booking from Ms. Alexandra to see Garcia Dominguez. Ms. Alexandra always caused a stir when she arrived to see Dominguez. Her beauty alone made her a real distraction. She was also Dominguez's lawyer, so she had the brains to go with the looks. Dominguez was isolated at present, but the prison had not released a statement about that to his lawyer, and when she booked a visit, they allowed her to register in the usual fashion. There was no intention of letting her see Dominguez. In fact, she was walking into a trap of her own making.

Detective Pauline Allen was waiting in the corridor outside the visits room, which was a large open space filled with tables and chairs which were bolted to the floor. Cameras observed every angle. Normally this room was used by twenty inmates and up to thirty visitors. Officers would roam the room, and security personnel would monitor the cameras. Today Pauline Allen waited outside, dressed in a dark suit. At first glance she looked as if she might be a female prison officer.

Domingez's girlfriend was shown into the large room and she registered surprise, "Normally I see my *client* in private." she said in an accusatory tone.

"Don't worry." the prison officer said, "You will have all the privacy you require in here. No other inmates will be using this room." She nodded and looked around, noting the position of cameras. She chose a table and walked to it, sitting in one of the two chairs, on the 'visitor's side' of it. She waited.

The door to the corridor that Detective Pauline Allen was standing in, was then opened and she walked briskly through it, followed by the officer who had opened it. He stood to one side and locked the door again. Detective Allen walked towards the table at which Ms. Alexandra sat. She could see the expression on her face was one of annoyance, and then amusement. She sat opposite her in the 'inmate's chair'.

"I hadn't realised that Corymbia housed women to." Ms Alexandra said sarcastically. Pauline reached into her pocket and placed a small 'Dictaphone' tape recorder on the table and switched it on. Ms. Alexandra's eyes narrowed, "What is this?" she asked.

"I am Detective Pauline Allen of the Western Australia Police and I am interviewing Ms. Deborah Alexandra, at

Corymbia Prison." She spoke date and time into the recorder and then directed her next comment to Ms. Alexandra, "Would you confirm your identity for the record, and identify which prisoner that you represent legally, please?"

Ms. Alexandra was not sure what this was about, and the 'lawyer in her' bristled with indignation. She was not carrying anything she shouldn't have been carrying, so she couldn't resist the opportunity to make this cop look stupid.

"I can confirm that, I am Ms. Alexandra and I represent Garcia Domingez." then she added, "who I hope is waiting to see me. Because if he isn't then I will file a complaint and bring this matter before a judge." She looked pleased with herself.

"Thank you, Ms. Alexandra. Could you please confirm for the record your personal phone number?" Asked Detective Allen.

"Why should I do that?" fired back Ms. Alexandra. "I am under no obligation to give further personal details. Bring my client out here right now." She demanded.

"No problem!" said Detective Allen, "Officers at the gate are, at this moment looking at your phone to determine it's number." Then she reached into her pocket.

"For the record. I am showing Ms. Alexandra a mobile phone. Do you recognise this phone Ms. Alexandra?"

"Never seen it before in my life." Ms. Alexandra said, pretending to be bored and rolling her eyes. Insid her emotions were quickly sifting through information, options and what her rights were, but it felt as if time was slowing, and she felt nauseous.

Pauline Allen stared down Ms. Alexandra and waited. Ms. Alexandra stayed silent.

"This phone was confiscated from your client, and we have reason to believe that he contacted you on it." Pauline Allen said.

"You have no proof! Otherwise, I would have been arrested at the gate." said Ms. Alexandra. Detective Allen took a deep breath and replied, "No Ms. Alexandra. We decided to do that here!"

Ms. Alexandra looked confused, "On what charge?" she countered, standing up. "I'm not staying to hear this rubbish." and she went to walk towards the door.

The prison officer who had been standing quietly on the other side of the room moved quickly to intercept her.

"Touch me, and I'll sue you for assault," she said looking daggers at him. He faltered slightly, but continued to move into her way, looking to the detective for her approval. Pauline nodded and the officer swept her outstretched hand around behind her back and pushed her against the wall.

"Deborah Alexandra, I have a warrant to arrest you on suspicion of aiding and abetting an attempt to unlawfully free an inmate from lawful custody. You have a 'right to remain silent.' Anything you do say may be used against you. Your refusal to answer questions is not an indication that you are concealing guilt. Do you understand?"

Ms. Alexandra's other hand was now behind her back and a set of prison security cuffs was fitted snugly around her wrists. Ms. Alexandra kept her mouth tightly closed, in a firm straight line. Her eyes spoke for her though, and if they had been translated correctly and admitted into evidence, the charge might have been upgraded to attempted murder.

Deborah Alexandra was escorted to the gate, now protesting loudly and issuing threats of legal retribution. When she arrived at the gate, the prison cuffs were removed and a set of police custody cuffs were placed on her wrists. She was shown the items, which she herself had deposited, and they were sealed into an evidence bag.

"Did we get it?" asked Pauline as a large police officer pushed the lawyer out through the prison doors.

"Yes ma'am. Broke the code and have a message from someone about time changing for a pick up. There are also messages from the mobile sim card number that was originally in the phone you took in. The number is also stored in the contacts directory under the initials GD." Pauline grinned, "Got you!" she shouted.

A leather clad bikie sat waiting in the 'non-contacts' visit area; as Paul Middleton, dressed in an orange jumpsuit, which was zipped up the back and padlocked through two eyes in the material at the neck, to prevent him or anyone else from removing it. He was roughly pushed through the corridor and made to sit in the chair opposite a glass screen. The glass distorted the view slightly, but the holes in the glass made conversation easy.

"Brother!" the leather clad man said.

"Brother." replied Middleton,

"What news? Have you cleaned the stain off yet?" The bikie looked down and then crossed himself.

"Pauly, your brother's dead. I'm so sorry man, and Davey was shot through his knee, he'll probably lose the leg. He'll never walk properly or ride again, that's for sure."

It was if a dark cloud passed over Middleton. He struggled to stay in control of the storm that was brewing within him.

"How?" he hissed through gritted teeth.

"Armaguard killed him, thinking he was trying to rob the van."

Middleton was beside himself with grief and anger.

"What?!" 'This was all that David James' fault. If he'd only just lie down and die like the 'good boy' he was'.

The prison guard was moving closer, interested in the low voices. Middleton suddenly smiled, and said in a normal voice,

"How's your bike renovation going Mikey?" Mikey looked confused, then picking up on the misinformation, he replied,

"Really good mate, thanks." The effort that Middleton had made to smile, nearly brought him to tears. It was worth it though, as the officer stepped back.

"I gotta go, now Mikey." Said Middleton loudly, "But I'd pay big money to see that finished completely. Make it happen Mikey, make it a 'family affair'; take it to a professional. See it serviced properly." He spoke with his eyebrows raised staring into Mikey's eyes, and his 'brother bikie' knew full well what he was being asked to arrange; and it had nothing to do with a machine with two wheels.

No one had thought to monitor Middleton, he stood and as he was led back to the SHU he thought, 'he would have been leaving with Domingez soon; but it was all making sense now; Domingez cell had been 'ramped'; and he'd been placed in isolation; the 'filth' must have known the plan and stopped it. The education man, David James had found a way to spoil this, and now he wouldn't be getting out. Not only that, but Davey was crippled.' He tried to get his head around the fact that his little brother was dead.' He couldn't comprehend it, so he shut the pain out and pushed it down. 'That was the way to deal with it, and then be happy when he heard the James family was just as dead.'

Mikey stood and watched Pauly leave. Then retraced his steps back through the lobby and back to the gate. At the gate he had to identify himself once more with his driver's licence, he placed his hand under the ultra violet light and his stamp glowed visible, and his iris was scanned. He was then allowed to exit through the gate visitor's lobby into the gate area. He ignored all the officers and walked out to his bike in the car park. He would have to make some calls to arrange the 'hit', and he wasn't about to do that from his mobile phone. 'This was not getting back to him,' he thought.

He fired up his bike and listened to the 'short shot' pipes, bang and pop. It was too noisy to be legal but it sort of made the point, that he was exempt. He pulled the phone and pistol from the Swing Arm bag and shoved them into pockets. It was a risk, 'carrying' so near the prison, but again; he felt that it made a statement about being above whatever limitations the system tried to place on him. With the gun in his jacket he felt his confidence return to him, and he engaged first gear with a loud clunk and swung the bike upright. Soon he was on the road heading towards the free-way. He didn't take any of the free-way ramps though, and proceeded to the 'fuel servo' beyond the intersection. He topped off the tank with 98 Ron fuel and then paid for it.

"Got a pay phone?" he asked the cashier and was told that it was in the hall off which the toilets were located. He walked slowly to the services and dug into his pockets for change. He couldn't avoid it, but he didn't like to do this kind of thing.

Ten minutes and three calls later: he had arranged with someone known as the 'fixer', whose voice was so heavily disguised that he had no idea if they were male or female; to wipe out David and his wife and kid. He had checked in with the club house and confirmed that the personal details of David James and his family – including photographs had been passed to the email box of the mysterious 'fixer'. Finally he arranged payment from the club bank account to be transferred in two sums, one immediately and another equal amount in two weeks' time, unless otherwise instructed.

He left the fuel servo and rode south west to Kwinana where he found a tavern to spend a few hours and eventually get lunch. As he drank his beer, and looked at his phone, he realised he'd missed a call. He didn't recognise the number but called it back anyway. The heavily disguised voice told him who it was.

"The kid is with *her* parents. Is the contract extended to them; there will be further payment necessary if so?" Mikey was feeling uncomfortable about having arranged this. He certainly didn't want to have more blood on his hands.

"No, just who I said" he replied.

"I will subcontract the Sydney end; no further cost to you, is that acceptable?" Mikey heard, and he drank the rest of his beer.

"Whatever!" he said and terminated the call.

Chapter Twenty-Two

Jack insisted that David should remain for a few more days at least.

"Just to tidy up loose ends and make some statements to the Police." He said. David knew that it was important to get his testimony on record so he suggested that Natalie go ahead of him, and he would join her as soon as he could. Natalie booked her air ticket within the hour and then called her mother to tell her that she was coming out to see them.

David helped Natalie pack; not just for her, but items for Nathan to. Soon Natalie was ready and she and David were walking out of the front door, and about to get into the car.

"Oh, I'd better put this back in the safe." She said reaching for her Glock.

"No chance." said David, "You're taking that with you."

"How?" asked Natalie, "If I can't take a nail file and a pair of scissors on a plane, how do I get a gun aboard?" She laughed at the absurdity.

"What we will need is your gun case" said David. He ran back into the house and came back out moments later, carrying the small hard case.

They drove to the airport, with Natalie slowly realising that she was leaving David alone and travelling to the other side of the continent. She looked as 'conflicted' as she felt.

"You will come out as soon as you can, yes?" She asked, seeking assurances that David would be with her soon.

"Yes, as soon as I can. Give your parents my love and kiss Nathan lots for me, ok?" he replied.

They reached the airport and walked through the departure terminal looking for the 'Sydney-Bankstown check in desk'. On their way they saw two well-armed Federal Police officers, patrolling the area. David made a 'bee-line' for them, knowing that they would be called to supervise later anyway. They watched him approach and both swung their MP7 machine guns into a loose but ready stance. David waved the ID he was holding and said, "As you can see we are checking in a firearm. Can one of you come over and make sure we do it properly please?" The police officers looked at each other and then relaxed.

"I'll go" said one and followed David towards the queue.

"Not queuing, for carrying a firearm!" said the police officer and he interrupted the flow of passengers and waved to a member of ground-staff. He then led them up to a check in counter.

"I would have carried a gun more often if I knew it was a queue hopping hack" whispered Natalie. David smiled and shook his head.

At the counter, the police officer said, "Firearms" and the girl behind the counter seemed to assume a different posture altogether at the word. The officer stepped to one side, and the girl took a long breath and addressed Natalie.

"Please present your ID, and ticket to travel." Natalie did so and these were placed in front of her terminal, "Now I will need to see your authority to carry a firearm."

Natalie reached into her bag and produced the laminated card and passed it to the girl.

"Thank you" she said, and then passed it to the police officer who looked at it and then returned it to Natalie.

"Do you have a gun case?" asked the girl.

David stepped forward and put the case on the counter. "Now as discretely as possible, please unload the firearm and place it in the box with the ammunition. Then lock the box." Natalie removed the Glock from it's holster and dropped the clip from it. She placed the clip in the case and then racked the slide and deftly caught the chambered round. She placed this and the pistol in the case. The girl watched as Natalie locked it.

"Ok. All observed!" said the police officer, and he turned and walked away. Then he stopped and turned to David.

"You aren't travelling today are you sir?" he asked.

"No!" said David. The police officer turned and walked away.

"Thank you madam," said the girl. Then she murmured to herself as if reciting policy and trying to ensure she didn't miss a step in procedure. She placed notes on the system, and then said, "I must place this in your checked baggage is it locked?" Natalie unlocked her suitcase and the girl placed the gun case on top of Natalie's clothes. "Please lock the case" she instructed. Natalie locked the case and then the girl placed several stickers on the baggage and said, "You should be able to pick this up in the normal fashion in Sydney. Enjoy your flight!"

David walked to the departure security checkpoint but decided not to slow Natalie up by coming through to the gate, as that would involve him surrendering his Glock and going through a whole lot more red-tape. He kissed her hard and then again softly.

"I'll miss you" he said. Natalie put her arms around him and hugged him close.

"Don't be long" she said. Then she went through the checkpoint and disappeared into a crowd of people heading towards the gate.

David left the terminal building, paid for parking and then found the car and drove home again. The house seemed as dark and lonely as it was empty. He went and found his suitcase and started to pack it, more as a therapeutic exercise than a serious attempt to prepare for a trip. He thought, 'the sooner this is sorted, the sooner I can go on holiday with my family.' He put as many items as he could into the bag, whilst still leaving him with other essential 'every day' items he would use unpacked. He grabbed a piece of paper and made a list of the remaining things he wanted to pack. Although he was very organised he knew that, packing half now and half later would benefit from a list of things 'to pack' otherwise he'd forget something.

The exercise didn't take long, and so he ordered a pizza for tea and then cleaned his Glock and tried to distract himself by thinking of a movie to watch later.

Five hours later as David was finishing the remains of the pizza and a TV movie was coming to a close; Natalie was arriving at Bankstown airport in Sydney. She knew she would have to collect her bag before changing terminals; to then get the helicopter to Lithgow airport, where her dad said he'd pick her up. She felt excitement rise in her stomach. She hadn't ever flown in a helicopter, and with only a little apprehension she was looking forward to it. It was late and there had not been many people on the flight and she doubted anyone but her would be on the helicopter transfer to Lithgow. She waited patiently for the carousel to deliver her bag, and then she looked around to see if she was being observed by any officials. Her empty holster had caused some 'raised eyebrows' at the security checkpoint in Perth. Her Federal ID had got her through that, but she had no idea what the proper protocol should be here.

She switched on her phone and called David to let him know that she had arrived. He reminded her to take the Glock out of her 'checked baggage' and holster it. She had argued that she was about to get on another aircraft, but David pointed out that the helicopter would not be flying very high in relative terms, and it would not be pressurised, so it would be quite safe to carry the weapon holstered. He went on to point out, that until this matter was over she had agreed to be armed. She reluctantly looked around for somewhere to unpack and she found a large metal waste basket behind a pillar, where she was able to balance the suitcase on it, out of sight. She opened the case and without taking the hard case out, she unlocked that and removed the Glock. She pushed the clip into the grip and then worked the slide to 'chamber a round'. She then slid the clip out again and loaded the cartridge that she had expelled from the chamber at Perth airport. She holstered the pistol, just as a Federal Policewoman looked round the pillar, to see what she was doing. The policewoman immediately brought her MP7 up and pointed it at Natalie.

"Federal agent" said Natalie, her voice rising as she said it. She kept very still, and the MP7 remained level and pointing at her. The police woman had pressed a red button on the side of her radio with her free hand, and she stepped back so that her colleague could see her position.

"ID please... carefully!" The policewoman said. Her partner had arrived but seemed more relaxed and unconcerned.

"Mrs Natalie James?" he asked.

"That's me" said Natalie holding up her ID.

"No problem ma'am. Have a nice day!" He said and then leading his partner away, Natalie heard him say, "Got a call about her coming in on that flight. She's seconded to ASIS or something."

Natalie closed her bag and followed the direction the police officers were walking in. She could see the notices for the helicopter terminal ahead on the left so she started to veer to that side of the hall. She glanced back to see the police making a right turn, as they started to head towards the car hire and taxi ranks. Natalie kept on straight towards the signs.

It was then an odd thing happened. She saw her parents, Kate and Stan. They were standing near the signs for the heliport. She looked again, 'yes' she thought, 'it is them.'

She sped up her pace and called out, "Mum? Dad?" Her mum and dad looked towards her and smiled. Her mum held out her arms in welcome, and Natalie could see that Nathan was in her father's arms. He was cradling the little boy and smiling. 'They must have come here to meet me.' Natalie thought. Then suddenly she saw in her peripheral vision a rather unkempt man wearing a leather motorcycle jacket. He was wearing dirty jeans and a flannel shirt under his jacket. His boots were badly scuffed, his long hair hung low and limp as if it hadn't been washed in a while. He was holding his hand inside his jacket.

William Niblick, or 'Billy Nibbles', as he was known to his friends; because of his buck teeth; couldn't believe his luck. He'd been tasked and paid very well to meet Natalie as she tried to board the helicopter and he planned to take her hostage; with a view to getting her to tell him where her son was. He had passed two Federal Police officers and hoped they were far enough behind him not to be of concern. Now he was looking at the whole party right in front of him. The parents were not part of the deal, he knew that. 'But what the hell...' he thought he'd 'do them' for free. He'd also been warned that Natalie had been armed when she confronted the brothers OMCG in Perth, but he couldn't imagine that she would be able to bring a gun on a plane.

Billy's hand cleared his jacket and Natalie saw it held an Uzi machine pistol. In fact, it was a Norinco M320 machine pistol, with a huge silencer fitted to it's short barrel. Natalie didn't know it, but it was a cheaper Chinese 'knock off' of the Israeli Uzi type B; but nevertheless, she was under no false impression that it would be very dangerous at this close range. Although she had not thought about it, she was suddenly looking down the sight of the Glock in her hand, and she had dropped the suitcase she'd been carrying in her other hand. She recalled the training day a few months before the Africa trip; when she was ambushed and failed to subdue the attacker. She'd been 'painted' with simunition bullets then, and they had hurt. This was real life. Her family was in danger and this man wanted to kill her and those she loved.

Billy had decided to start with the small 'reception committee' of Natalie's parents and Nathan. Natalie heard the click and soft 'puff' 'puff' 'puff' as the bullets left the gun via the silencer. She watched as her father, Stan turned away trying to protect Nathan, and was hit once in his shoulder by a bullet, she saw his jacket fray as the bullet cut a hole in it. He fell almost immediately but it looked more like he was trying to control the fall and not to crush Nathan. He was trying to keep the baby under him and use his body as a shield, she realised. Kate screamed long and loud as a bullet sliced the air close to her face. She heard the sound of it, like a large bug with wings zipping past. Billy was moving fast towards them when Natalie fired her first shot. The sound was deafening in the concrete arrivals hall, and it echoed loudly. She couldn't believe she'd missed. She fired again, centring on the man with the gun. He seemed to jerk back slightly but ran on otherwise unaffected.

Billy knew he might encounter Federal Police and so he had taken the precaution of wearing a Kevlar bullet proof vest, with body armour inserts. He fired again, this time the bullets raked up the wall beyond his target. He cursed himself and determined to fire with both hands steadying the gun next time and aim to compensate for the way the silencer was affecting the trajectory of the bullets. He would be so close though in just moments that it wouldn't matter. Then suddenly he felt as if he'd been pushed forward by a series of rapid punches, and he tripped and fell headlong on the polished concrete floor, sliding the last few metres into Kate.

He got up and pulled her in front of him. The Federal Police woman whom Natalie had met earlier fired again, one of the bullets hitting Billy in his arm. It was a risky thing to do, but Natalie knew that the MP7 was recoilless, and a good marksman or woman, could hit exactly what they wanted easily, when the gun had a sight like hers did. Natalie suddenly heard the prison firearms instructor telling her during a weapons brief, "Even a child would be able to hit a clock across a room, with one of these."

The explosion of pain and sudden loss of blood caused Billy to howl and he fell to the floor where he flayed around for a moment, before gathering his strength and determination as he swung the machine pistol towards the policewoman and pressed the trigger. He emptied the remainder of the clip, and some of the bullets hit home, and she went down hard. Natalie was trying to get a bead on the man on the floor with the front sight of her Glock, when the policewoman groaned and got up, her own bullet proof vest having saved her from the shower of lead that had come her way. Natalie looked for the woman's partner and saw a horrific scene behind the policewoman. Her partner had been hit by the last two bullets which had stayed off their target as the machine pistol had bucked in Billy's hand. He had been hit in the head and was clearly dead. The policewoman was unaware of this and was approaching the man who was getting up off the floor again. He had dropped the empty gun and the policewoman had her gun up, aiming carefully at him.

Natalie listened as she heard instructions being given to the man, who was ignoring them and had now pulled her mother in front of him again. This time he was holding a smaller pistol against her mother's head.

"Put the gun down and lie face down on the ground" shouted the police woman.

"I'll kill her. Don't come any closer" screamed Billy. The police woman moved to get a better angle and shouted,

"Partner cover me... partner?" There was no answer, but she did not turn to look, such was the professional she was.

"I've got you" shouted Natalie, and the policewoman moved a step closer.

Billy pushed Kate between him and the policewoman and then pointed the pistol at the police woman. He fired once and tried to fire again, but he suddenly found that his hand wouldn't work. The policewoman, who had been hit again and knocked over was trying to get up off the floor, in obvious pain. Despite the ceramic armour-plated vest doing it's job of stopping the bullet passing through, it had only mitigated slightly the force of the blow which would show in big ugly bruises later.

Natalie realised that she had gone down on one knee and fired her Glock at the same time as Billy had fired at the officer. The angle that Billy had exposed had enabled Natalie's bullet to pass under Billy's right arm, above the Kevlar vest and the bullet exited behind his shoulder,

Clear Bright Light of Day

embedding itself in the vest from the wrong side. Billy's arm was inoperable and the compact semi-automatic pistol lay on the floor beside him.

Natalie kept her gun up and aimed at the man who held her mother with his other injured arm, then Kate did the most unexpected thing and twisted around and hit her attacker in the side of his head with her elbow. Billy sank to the concrete, unconscious.

The police woman looked to Natalie and said, "My partner!"

"I've got this." Natalie shouted. Natalie helped her mother up and ran to her father, who was still protecting Nathan.

"Dad, Dad are you alright?"

"Remarkably so!" said her dad, quite calmly. He seemed unaware that he'd been shot. Nathan was crying of course and Natalie hugged him tightly and kissed him over and over again. Eventually she passed him to her mother who took him, and then helped Stan over to some soft chairs near the heliport departure gate; where he bled on them, whilst they sat and tried to make sense of what had just happened.

The policewoman was back again and was cuffing the bikie on the floor.

"I've called for some ambulances," she said. Her face was screwed up in pain and Natalie went to support her, but she was shaken off.

"I'm ok, but my partner..." her voice trailed off.

"I know! I saw!" said Natalie.

"Are you hit?" asked the policewoman.

"I don't think so," said Natalie.

"Let me check you" said the officer and briefly patted Natalie down and inspected her for injuries.

"You are so lucky you're not dead, you had no vest or anything. Damn, you're a good shot though."

The Police and ambulances arrived and all thoughts about getting on a helicopter diminished from their minds. After Stan had been treated at the scene for what turned out to be no more than a flesh wound. The police made arrangements to accommodate them all in the 'airport hotel,' and placed them in 'protective custody'.

"Are you sure you are ok Dad?" Asked Natalie.

"The bullet practically bounced right off" he said.

"He's a tough old turkey; your father" Kate said.

However, Natalie knew that tomorrow, it would be another story altogether."

Stan was enjoying the attention of the pretty, young female paramedic who was treating him. He had been dosed up on pain killers and as soon as he got into his large, comfortable hotel bed, he went to sleep a 'happy man'.

It was the 'early hours of the morning', but with the time difference Natalie's call to Jack Pritard was relatively acceptable. She told him about the attack upon her family and asked Jack to arrange for police unit to be sent to their home to watch over David.

Miraculously, William Niblick had survived and was in intensive care, handcuffed to the bed, with a police guard. He had been operated upon to stop the bleeding and repair his lung and muscles in his arm pit. The police and forensic experts were still at the airport digging the bullets out of the walls and furniture, as well as the Kevlar vests. Niblick would be questioned later when he was stable enough.

Natalie then phoned David and relayed the events of the night to him. It was a long time before she was able to get to bed herself and David; although he stayed in his bed, hardly slept at all.

In the early morning David made his way to the garage and manoeuvred around his bike and Natalie's car to use the gym equipment he'd installed. He needed to work off some of this aggression he felt. He prayed as he exercised and the sweat poured off him, partly due to the effort and his heart rate, and partly due to the concern and fervour he put into his prayers for the family and God's protection.

At five thirty, about an hour after he'd begun his workout he heard a soft knock on the garage door. He jumped off the cross trainer in a bound and grabbed the Glock on his towel, which was resting on the roof of the car.

"What?" he shouted. "You ok in there? I can hear you moving around and out of breath." David put two and two together and figured it was a cop from the unit sent to watch the house. Natalie had said that Jack was going to arrange it.

"Yes, I'm fine... Look, I'll meet you at the front door." he said, not about to open the larger door and expose himself to a view from the street.

He walked through the garage towards the front of the house and opened the front door, his gun still in his hand. The cop who was slower, rounded the side of the house and saw him, "Whoa there! No need for that mate." David realised he was pointing the Glock at the cop.

"Sorry... And I'll be the judge of that!" he said.

After David had checked the policeman's ID, he said, "Come in. I'm going to take a shower but fix yourself some tea or coffee. The toilet is just there." He pointed to the relevant areas of the house as he made his invitation.

"I won't be long" he said, as he made his way back to the bedroom and en-suite. Once there he undressed and threw his sweaty gym kit into the wash basket and placed the Glock on the towel by the sink. He turned on the shower and stepped in to the water, which he'd set warmer than he was initially comfortable with. He let the soap and water wash away the aches and pains of the exercise and stress.

Fifteen minutes later, dressed and feeling much fresher, he stepped back into the kitchen to find both cops sitting at the breakfast bar eating toast and drinking coffee.

"Very kind of you sir, thank you... Hope you don't mind." said both cops together, through mouthfuls of food.

David chuckled, "No problem!" he said.

"I take it that you have a carry permit for that?" asked the second officer; as he eyed the gun holstered in David's belt. David had not properly met this man and so he smiled at him and said nothing.

The doorbell rang and David looked at his watch; six fifteen.

"Expecting anyone?" asked the second cop.

"Not yet" replied David. The officer shuffled off his chair and said, "I'll go."

He looked as if he were casually walking through the room, but he had removed the restraint strap on his holster and rested his hand on the butt of the pistol as he walked down the corridor.

Moments later he returned with Jack.

Chapter Twenty-Three

Natalie opened her eyes; it looked late, the sun was shining in through the curtains at the window, but when she looked at her watch it read, six in the morning. Then she remembered that she had not adjusted it for Sydney time so here it was nine in the morning. She leapt out of bed and looked around for her dressing gown. Pulling it out from under some clothes in her suitcase, she put it on and walked into the main part of the suite. There was a small kitchen where Kate sat, with a cup of freshly brewed coffee on the breakfast bar.

"Hi mum, where's Nathan?" Natalie had insisted that she had him in her room, but when she woke he wasn't there.

"Oh darling, he was crying in the night and you were 'out for the count' asleep. So we took him in with us. He's fed changed and asleep again." She smiled at Natalie.

"Amazing!" said Natalie. "How's dad?"

Kate's face fell. "He's in need of some medication. The hotel is arranging with the police to send a doctor." Natalie moved towards her parent's bedroom door.

"Can I see him?"

"Why don't you get a cup of tea, and take him one to?" suggested Kate.

Natalie made tea and poured two cups before Kate opened the door to reveal Stan sitting up in bed.

"Shshsh" he whispered, pointing at Nathan, who was wrapped up and sleeping in a small travel cot, that the hotel had provided.

"How are you dad?" asked Natalie.

"A bit stiff" he said, rolling his shoulder and then regretting it and wincing in pain. "A lot better than the feller you shot, I imagine."

Natalie sipped her tea and Kate helped Stan to drink his.

"What you did dad, to protect Nathan was truly heroic. Thank you."

Her eyes filled up and she blinked back tears. Her eyes slowly cleared, and she saw her father waive it off with his good arm, spilling his tea on the sheet.

"I did what any proud father would do."

She hugged him carefully and then heard a knock at the door.

"That will be the doctor" Kate said, and Natalie got up to answer it. The doctor and another person stood at the door, "Come in" said Natalie. "Where's the patient?" the doctor said. She was tall, thin and middle aged, with dyed brown hair and she was carrying a 'Gladstone bag.' She looked typically 'doctorish' in Natalie's mind. Natalie led her towards the bedroom and met Kate at the door and showed the doctor in.

"Who's with you?" Kate asked the doctor.

"I thought you would know, she just came up with me" said the doctor.

Natalie turned quickly sensing danger, but found the young lady standing with a note pad in her hand, a pen poised to write.

"What was it like to shoot an armed assailant, Ms James? And why was he attacking your parents? Our readers would like to know who you are working for, and why you carry a gun?"

Natalie's eyes narrowed, and she met the reporter's gaze squarely. She said, "How did you get up here? This area is off limits."

"Not my fault if they thought I was with a doctor." The reporter shrugged.

"You might need the doctor next, if you don't leave right now" Natalie threatened.

"Don't be like that" said the reporter, "We got off on the wrong foot. Is this incident related to any on-going investigation?"

Kate walked out of the bedroom with Nathan, and Natalie said, "This is my son, I don't know what you have been told, but I don't think it's appropriate for you to be in our room asking about who attacked us. I don't know the attackers name, and have never seen him before!"

The reporter looked confused, "But the CCTV footage shows you shooting him." She said. Natalie had taken firm hold of the reporter's arm and was leading her to the door.

"All I want is to ask a few questions for our readers" she wailed.

"I have 'no comment'" said Natalie, as she opened the door and pushed her into the corridor. The two police men standing either side of the door looked startled.

"A reporter!" said Natalie to one of them in a chiding fashion. She raised her eyebrows at him. "Deal with her!" she pressed.

"Oh. Yes of course" said the officer, taking hold of the reporter. Natalie closed the door, but not before she heard the persistent reporter say, "So, how long have you served New South Wales Police? And what is your duty here today?" The policeman hassled her along to the lift where he firmly pushed her in and selected 'ground floor' for her. As the door closed he said, "I see you again... I arrest you for harassment!" The reporter continued her reply even after the lift door had closed. The cop walked back to his place, as he spoke quickly into his lapel mic to alert other colleagues in the lobby what he had done.

Natalie locked the door behind her and was heading towards her bedroom when the doctor came out of her parent's room.

"Is he ok?" Natalie asked her.

"Yes, bit of infection and inflammation. All bullet wounds are 'dirty wounds'" she said. "How about you, are you ok?"

"Me?" asked Natalie. "Yes, I'm fine."

"Good" the doctor replied. "It's difficult to see from the TV news footage whether you got hurt, it mainly focuses on the police woman and her partner. But yours was definitely the shot that brought the 'terrorist' down."

"Is that how this is being reported?" asked Natalie. The doctor paused.

"No, no one is really sure what happened, but someone leaked the CCTV and the news-stands have all run with it." The doctor left, and Natalie who had been on her way to have a shower, turned on the TV instead. 'ABC News 24' was running the story. Showing the CCTV clip over and over again, with various 'experts' being asked what they thought was going on. Parts of the screen had been fuzzed over, and Natalie recognised that was where the body of the policeman had lain.

The commentary continued, "This brave policewoman, engages the 'terrorist' again and again, despite being shot several times. We go now to the newly appointed, New South Wales Police Commissioner Mike Fuller. 'Sir, you have been a police officer since your late teens, have you ever seen such a brazen'..." Natalie turned the TV off and heard her phone ringing. It was David.

She spoke to him briefly to assure him they were all fine, and she told him about the reporter she had ejected from their room. He said he'd seen the news reports and that Jack had come over early to warn him. She said she would ring him back later but would be taking a long shower first. She told him she loved him and he asked her to give Nathan a kiss and said he was missing her.

Natalie took a deep breath, collected her sponge bag from her suitcase and draped her dressing gown over a chair on the way to her bathroom. She turned on the shower and the extractor fan and pulled off the T shirt she had slept in. Looking at her body in the mirror, she noted that she still had a flabby tummy and an ugly scar from the 'C-section'. She wasn't sore anymore though, so she took that as a good sign, and then she stepped under the jets of hot water. She washed her hair, and then the rest of her, briefly wishing that David was here with her in the shower. Then whilst drying herself she looked at her reflection again, and determined to use some of that gym equipment to get her figure back. 'What's next?' she thought to herself.

She pulled clothes from her case and dressed in fresh jeans, and a loose T-shirt that covered the holster and gun in her waistband. She wore again the trainers that she had travelled in, because they were comfortable. Then she headed back to the kitchen to get some breakfast. However, when she went through the bedroom door she was met by two slim, aging men in suits. 'Obviously detectives,' she thought. 'I wonder how this is going to go?' she asked herself.

"Mrs Natalie James?" asked one of the men.

"That's me" said Natalie.

"Detective Inspector Harris." He extended his hand, and Natalie shook it. "This is Detective Sargent Ross." Ross waved a hand but did not move around the table or chair blocking his path. "I wonder if we could ask you a few questions about last night please?" Harris said.

"I'll make you some toast and another cup of tea." Said Kate.

They sat and Natalie made her statement between bites of toast and sips of tea; all of which was recorded on a small Dictaphone. Then DS Ross took something out of his pocket and laid it on the table.

"I wonder if you would be so kind as to swap this, for the one you have. That should be all we need to confirm ballistics."

Natalie looked at the new Glock 22 barrel lying on the table.

"Oh. Yes, of course." She said and wondered why they hadn't asked for the whole pistol, but this made far more sense. She stood up and the two detectives stood.

"It's ok, you don't have to get up." Natalie said, and they sat down again. Natalie removed her Glock and removed the bullets and stripped the pistol down to its main component parts. She passed the barrel to DI Harris, only because he was closest. She reassembled the weapon quickly with the new barrel, and then reloaded it. "These are not standard 'Hydro shock' rounds" said DI Harris when she dropped the clip and pushed in the round from the barrel.

"No" said Natalie.

She could see that the wheels were turning in his head... 'Government agent, using civilian rounds?' She really didn't want to get into that conversation.

"Mind if I see your permit?" he continued.

Natalie laid it on the table. He nodded and pushed it back to her.

"Can you tell me why you..." He began.

"No" said Natalie shortly.

"Okaay" he said as if resigned to not knowing. "Thank you for your time Mrs James."

Natalie showed the men out and as they left, she asked, "So what now?"

"What do you mean?" asked DI Harris.

"Well, how long are we to stay here? When can we go?"

DI Harris looked puzzled for a moment, then said, "We're done! So, you'll have to take that up with your boss."

Natalie then phoned David and had a long chat with him and Jack, who confirmed that the bill was being covered by the joint task force for the case they were working on. Jack also told Natalie, what he'd briefed David about. The Navy had intercepted a vessel, two hundred nautical miles, off Fremantle; and Domingez's 'girlfriend lawyer' had been arrested at Corymbia Prison. Natalie took it all in, and then asked to speak to David again.

"I think I just want to come home again," she told him.

"You can do that if you want." He assured her.

He paused and said, "Jack wants to know if you'd like to come back to Jandakot on a 'police flight?' You might have a crim in the plane, and it will take longer, but you would avoid all that security and immigration stuff."

Natalie thought and said. "Could my parents come to?"

There was a brief silence and then David said, "Jack says he's just going to organise a private charter for you all." David promised he'd call back with the details as soon as it was organised. Until then they were to stay at the hotel.

"The police guard will probably be withdrawn now that they have your statement." said David. "So, watch out for reporters."

They all agreed that it made most sense to stay and recuperate at the hotel until their flight was organised, and Natalie spoke to the main desk to warn them about reporters.

As it turned out, Jack couldn't organise a flight for two days, and the police were removed from guarding them almost immediately.

It was nice however, to rest up and have food delivered. The suite was large and comfortable, and the doctor made 'house calls'. Kate avoided the few reporters in the hotel lobby and did some shopping for Nathan and she even went back home to pack a bag for Stan and herself. The two days passed quickly, as Natalie caught up with her mum and dad. It was lovely for Kate and Stan to see their daughter and their new grandson; and as much as they loved David, it was a treat to have them to themselves.

David, had allowed Jack to usher the cops back to their car outside and make himself some breakfast and coffee. They spoke to Natalie and then Pauline Allen arrived, who wanted to tell the story of arresting Deborah Alexandra again. Detective Allen took David's statement which covered a 'blow by blow' account in sequence; from the day he had found his bike missing, to the present time. She made notes and asked questions to focus the action of each day and then she moved on to Jack, where she repeated the process. Pauline contributed to the statements herself at times quoting instances of collaboration, and facts concerning the joint task force.

Finally, she turned the recorder off. David looked at his watch and was surprised to see that over three hours had passed. "Come on David," said Jack. "Let's get some lunch... On me!" he added. Detective Allen declined excusing herself with, "Some of us have work to do. Enjoy your lunch boys!"

Chapter Twenty-Four

Monika Niven was not her real name, despite what was stated on the New Zealand passport she held, or on the credit cards that she held in that name. Her real name sounded very much like 'Monika' but was in fact spelled مونيكا. Her olive tan could have been of Maori origin, but her sharp features and almost black, almond eyes gave her away as having a heavy Middle Eastern origin. She had other nationalities in her gene pool, which softened the Arabic decent: with make-up and implants she had changed her features a bit and lightened her complexion a little.

Monika moved with a lithe ease through the gymnasium of the hotel where she was staying. She was attracting admiring looks from the women who were working out, and lustful ones from the men. She was dressed in a 'one-piece jumpsuit' crafted from a stretch knit. This sleeveless athletic garment featured a front zipper placket, a cross-weave strappy back, and sheer mesh panels at the end of each leg making the whole 'body hugging experience' a delight for the wearer and viewer alike. Although leaving little to the imagination, it technically covered most of her body. Monika's physique was clearly one built for strength rather than toned bulging muscles. She was toned, but still retained her feminine curves and slim build; her strength was far greater than the tone indicated. She had studied עֲגַם בָּרָק: Krav-Maga, which literally meant "contact-combat" and although it was a military self-defence system, developed for the Israel Defence Forces (IDF) and the Israeli security forces of Shin Bet and Mossad, she had studied it privately and practiced it for many years, attaining deadly proficiency. The art, consisted of a combination of techniques sourced from Boxing, Wrestling,

Aikido, Judo, and Karate along with realistic fight training. Krav-Maga was known for its focus on real-world situations and its extreme efficiency and brutal counter-attacks. Originally it had been derived from the street-fighting experience of Hungarian-Israeli martial artist Imi Lichtenfeld, who made use of his training as a boxer and wrestler as a means of defending the Jewish quarter against fascist groups in Bratislava, Czechoslovakia in the mid-to-late 1930s. By the late 1940s, following his migration to Israel, he was providing lessons on combat training to what was to become the IDF. From the outset, the original concept of Krav-Maga was to take the most simple and practical techniques of other fighting styles and to make them rapidly teachable to military conscripts. As a result, Krav-Maga built on its original base a philosophy emphasising aggression, with simultaneous defensive and offensive manoeuvrers. It would prove to be a skill that would be used for years by the Israeli Defence Forces' special forces units, as well as by regular infantry units. A version of it had even been adopted by Israeli law enforcement and counter intelligence organisations. Internationally there were several organisations teaching variations of Krav-Maga; the British SAS and the US Marine Corps to name two. The idea was to simultaneously attack and defend; attacking pre-emptively or counter-attacking as soon as possible. Developing physical aggression, not to be confused with emotional aggression or anger, that was the key. With the view that physical aggression was the most important component in a fight, continuing to strike the opponent until they were completely incapacitated made this a very unforgiving martial art. Any objects at hand that could be used to hit an opponent were used, and targeting the attacks to the body's most vulnerable points, such as: the eyes, throat, face, solar plexus, groin, ribs, knee, foot, fingers and liver, was a devastating means of overpowering your opponent; using simple and easily repeatable strikes. Maintaining awareness of her surroundings; while dealing with a threat enabled her to look for escape routes, further attackers, or objects that could be used to strike an opponent, had become instinctual to her. Recognising the importance of and expanding on instinctive response under stress, her training had covered the study and development of situational awareness. She was able to understand her surroundings, as well as the psychology of a street confrontation, identifying potential threats before an attack even occurred. Her discipline had taught her a mental toughness, using controlled scenarios to strengthen her mental fortitude in order to control her impulse and not to do something rash. Instead, she attacked only when it was necessary, and often with absolute deadly force.

She was feeling angry today though and countering it with exercise and discipline. She had called in help from a contact in Sydney. He had said he would deal with the work, but then he'd subcontracted the job to an 'incompetent'. She would have to follow up and do the work herself. It would be the last time that she used that contact, in fact she thought of adding him to the list of people she would kill. Instead, she decided that she would let him decide his fate: if an apology came with a return of the deposit she had given him, along with an offer to finish the job free, which she would reject, then he would live.

She breathed slowly and calmed herself as she used the bench press machine to lift one and a half times her body weight. She counted to five and controlled her movement to return the weight to rest. She repeated the exercise eight times and then stood and stretched. She repeated the whole exercise twice more before getting up to use the pull-down bar. This always presented her with a problem as her own weight was lighter than that of her ability, so she decided to use the weights at the other end of the gym and then use a pull-up bar, fixed to a large scaffold. She walked past several women one of whom smiled and winked at her; she raised her eyebrows and gave her a look of scorn, then she nearly collided with a large guy standing in her way. She stopped suddenly and assessed the situation; 'whatever this was it was full of testosterone,' she thought. She stepped to the side to manoeuvre around him. He stepped into her way. She stopped and looked up into his eyes, giving him a steely cold-eyed, hard stare.

"Excuse me" she said.

He smiled but did not move. He replied, "I haven't seen you work-out here before, what's your name?"

"I'm not interested" she said.

"Funny name that, can I call you '*not*' for short?"

He smiled and tried again, "Look, tell me your name... give me your number and we'll chat later."

Monika thought that she didn't want a scene, and she would be moving on soon anyway, so she smiled back and said, "Got a pen?" The guy moved to get his bag and the pen it contained. Meanwhile Monika moved to the strap weights and fixed fifteen kilos to each leg. The guy had returned but he seemed happy to watch for a while as she stretched and lifted her legs, to acquire balance. She then leapt up to the bar and started to do full pull-ups, first under arm then over, finally holding her-self half pulled up and lifting her legs so that her 'abs' muscles pronounced dramatically. The dismount was the hardest part as with the extra weight she didn't want to damage her ankles so she shimmied to the side and then let herself down slowly using a vertical bar, still extending her legs out in front of her until reaching the ground.

"Impressive" the guy holding the pen said, "Might have a go at that myself!" He immediately regretted saying it; as now it had been said, he hoped he wouldn't be called upon to try. Monika smiled and let it go.

She took the pen from him and asked, "Paper?" He produced a flyer which had a blank reverse side. She wrote upon it and passed it back to him.

"Thank you er. Margaret" he said, "I'll call you later!" He retreated a few metres and watched her remove the 'strap-on weights' and then walk back up to the other end of the room. The words from the song about a girl from Ipanema drifted through his mind, 'When she walked, it was like a samba. She certainly swung and swayed so that when she passed, he wanted to say, "ahhh!"' He looked at the paper again, the number she'd written was 993 918 3507. It didn't seem right. He entered it into his phone but the number wasn't recognised. He felt annoyed and walked to the other end of the gym to confront her. She was using the bench press again. He reached her and stood over her.

"This number you've given me doesn't work."

"Really?" she said, the sarcasm obvious in her voice.

"Look, I'm going to take you out tonight and I need your number ok!" he demanded. 'This is getting ugly,' she thought. Most men who bugged her just got the message and walked away. 'This lump of testosterone was going to have to learn a lesson.'

Monika brought her arms in and away from the chest press bars and then moved her feet back, and she stood up.

"Let me see?" she said. She took the phone and after a moment said, "I can see the problem, let me put the number in." She stepped forward and took the phone and started pressing the keys, 993 918 3507. "Bet you can't press the weight I'm working with" she challenged him nodding to the machine. "Hmph" he chuckled and sat on the seat. 'She had been doing reps of eight' he thought.

"No Problem." He said and flexed his arms and pushed back in to the padded seat. He pushed the bars forward and was immediately surprised by the weight. He grunted, "What are you working with?" It was then she stepped towards him holding the phone screen upside down displaying the number 993 918 3507 which now read LOSE BIG EGG. He felt her foot in his groin and dropped the weight with a crash.

"You have a choice" she offered, "and I suggest you take the option to stay and work-out when I leave, otherwise that message will come true for you. Do you understand?"

He nodded and winced in discomfort.

"Ok. I'm going now. Choose wisely." She moved a step away from him and he immediately went to get up quickly. Her foot was back in a second and she pressed him back down hard; he yelped and gasped.

"Last chance" she said.

"Ok, ok, ok" he begged. This time he watched her walk away and found himself sweating more now than when he'd used the 'step machine' earlier.

Monika took the lift and reached the fourth floor, then walked up a further three floors to the seventh. She swiped her card at the first door and went inside quickly. Dropping her personal items on the bed she quickly stripped off her clothes and walked into the en-suite bathroom. She turned on the shower and paused to look at her figure in the mirror. She flexed her muscles and admired her physique before stepping under the cascading hot jets of water.

After the shower she phoned for 'room-service' and a short while later a large 'brunch' was delivered to her room. She asked for the trolley to be left and enjoyed coffee, full English breakfast and bagels with cream cheese. She knew that her metabolism and exercise regimen would deal with the calories easily. Then she started to plan her deadly attack on David James and his family.

*Chapter Twenty-F*ive

Jack had arranged a charter plane, to bring Nathan, Natalie and her parents back to Jandakot. The plane was a Cessna Conquest II – C441; which sported wing mounted, twin turbo propellers and seating for eight passengers in single seats running the length of the fuselage. Natalie was told by the pilot when she was boarding that there was a toilet installed with a table for 'baby changing'. She thanked the pilot and asked if they would be the only ones flying today. "No, you are sharing with a Justice system transfer." She was told, "If you all go to the rear of the plane, we will board the 'crim' last and debark him first."

Despite it having propellers, the Cessna Conquest II was certified to fly at a similar height to a jet. Jack had decided in the end to share the charter, so that the costs as well as the flight time would be reduced. At 35,000ft the plane could cruise at 300kts which was 555km per hour, and this meant that they had access to the 'smooth air' above the weather in air-conditioned comfort. The plane was also being shared by a courier company, and so as they boarded a large cargo container was placed in the hold.

"Apparently, this type of craft can carry a thousand kilos of luggage" said Stan cheerfully, watching the loading taking place.

"Your father has been studying aircraft on the Internet recently" Kate said, and then added more quietly, "for some unfathomable reason!"

Overhearing his comment, the pilot said, "It also has an impressive short field capability making it the perfect machine for some of the smaller remote airfields we frequent. And we've added to the 1600 nautical mile range, with a modified tank so we can do nearly 2000 nautical miles. Mind you, it was a bit of a 'nightmare' getting that through aviation certification, but it does mean that we can go coast to coast." He made a signal to the hanger and a bus pulled forward.

When they were all seated comfortably and strapped in, the bus opened its doors and two police officers with one man in a green tracksuit stepped out. The man between them had his hands cuffed in front of him, but all seemed to be very up-beat and jovial. They climbed the short steps and greeted the party in the rear of the plane, "Morning all." The police officers seated the cuffed man in the seat opposite the door and then sat behind him and to one side. They continued to chat in a friendly fashion and Natalie thought that this must be an interstate prison transfer for release. In these cases, convicted prisoners who wanted to begin life in another place or whose families had moved away, could spend the last six months of their full sentences in another state's prison. This wouldn't apply to those on parole though, as they would have to stay within the state they had offended in; to report regularly throughout their parole period. Natalie had overseen several of these situations when she was working in the Corymbia prison security team, with prisoners heading out of Western Australia.

The plane taxied out onto the runway and having secured permission to take off, it accelerated quickly and lifted into the air. Being a small plane, every bump and lift was exaggerated as the plane continued to climb and bank steeply toward the west. After a short while the angle of incline lessened and although the plane continued to climb to its cruising altitude, it seemed to level off a bit. Natalie was still feeling a bit 'miffed' that she'd missed out on a helicopter ride, but she was glad to be alive with her family and to be able to be upset about the matter. They talked quietly for an hour and then Kate took out a book to read and Stan reclined his seat and closed his eyes. Natalie looked at him settle himself and drop into sleep. 'Her father had an uncanny ability to do that,' she thought; and wished that she was able to as well. Nathan was wriggling in her arms and she tried to feed him, but he didn't seem interested. He kept just looking up into Natalie's eyes, a smile playing on his lips.

A few hours into the flight the pilot told them that there were refreshments stowed in a container at the rear of the plane. Natalie passed Nathan, who had finally gone back to sleep, to her mum and investigated. She retrieved packets of sandwiches, crisps and fruit which she passed around. As she did so, she took 'cold drink requests,' and then went back to get small containers of carbonated drinks which she distributed.

Soon they could feel the plane dropping altitude and they saw clouds, which had been beneath them now come up to meet them, and then they flew through to see the ground five thousand metres below them. The decent continued to three thousand metres and then they cruised over the Great Eastern Highway until they reached Perth and turned south. The landing was smooth and when they taxied to the hanger they could see that there was a white prison transport waiting. The plane came to a standstill and the police officers opened the door and dropped the steps. One of the officers stood by outside and the other ushered the man in green towards the door.

"Thank you for flying 'incarceration airways,' we wish you a speedy journey to your new cell," the crim said to no one in particular as he departed. The second police officer who followed him out turned and said, "Real joker we have here!"

He smiled, "Have a nice day."

Natalie waited until the officers handed off their 'charge' to the security detail and placed him in the van. Then she got up to get off herself. Stan and Kate followed bringing Nathan and the two police officers now seemed a little lost for something to do. Natalie caught up with them on the way to the terminal building.

"Are you going back east today?" She asked.

"No. Tomorrow morning," said one.

"Recommend something to do in Perth?" He asked.

Natalie laughed. "Freo's nice," she suggested.

"I heard that." the other officer said.

Natalie watched the officers as they made their way out of the airport and head towards a taxi. David was not far away with Natalie's car, and he helped load the luggage into the boot, before securing Nathan in his cot. Stan took the front passenger seat and Natalie and Kate sat in the back with Nathan. It was just a short trip home and there was an audible sigh of relief from Natalie as she walked into her home. Stan and Kate took their bags to the guest bedroom and Natalie put Nathan – who was asleep, into his cot, which was still in her bedroom.

David carried her bag for her and after he had put it to one side for unpacking later, he put his arms around Natalie and just hugged her for what seemed like the longest time. He thanked God for bringing her safely back to him and then they walked back to the kitchen. Natalie boiled some water and made a large pot of tea, and David sent a quick SMS to Jack to let him know that they were back.

After David had lunch with Jack a few days previously, he had done some shopping to replenish supplies at home, and then bought some extra items. It was still a week or so until

Frank and Endana were to arrive, but David had made time to visit his old house and make up the bed for them. He had even switched on the fridge and placed some long-life milk and some frozen items in it. He had also put some dried and canned foods in the pantry cupboard. During his visit, Mrs Dee had wandered around and knocked on the front door to see who was there. 'You didn't need a monitored security system, when you had a Mrs Dee' David thought. David had not been surprised to see her, but she seemed surprised to see him and she had quizzed him as to whether he was returning to live in the small house. He had assured her that he and Natalie were still enjoying living in Canning Vale, but he mentioned to her that Frank and his new Kenyan wife would be coming back soon. Mrs Dee was most concerned about how she should relate to 'Franks foreign wife' as she called her, and David had told her not to worry about it, as he'd thought that if she tried to accommodate them in any way, she would probably inadvertently make things worse rather than better. She eventually wandered off muttering something about having to keep their cat inside when they arrived. David had a good laugh after she had gone back next door. He imagined what she might say to her long-suffering husband about the diet of Kenyans and the need to protect their cat and the vegetable patch.

Stan and Kate joined them in the kitchen and they all enjoyed a cup of tea whilst talking excitedly about the forthcoming visit of Frank and Endana. David told them that he'd prepared the house for them and about Mrs Dee.

"That woman" said Natalie shaking her head, "you could write a book or do a whole stand up comedy routine about her."

She laughed, and they shared more stories about Mrs Dee and her husband.

That evening they ordered Indian food from the Kudai King at Spencer Village in Thornlie. It was a short drive away, but David said it would be worth it and he returned with what they all agreed was some of the best Indian cuisine they had ever tasted. Natalie and Kate enjoyed a glass each of unoaked Chardonnay, and Stan and David drank Schmohz 120 Pale Ale. Stan was completely unaware that the brew he supped was alcohol free, as the Schmohz 120 was one of very few highly hopped non-alcohol beers; and as India Pale Ale is all about the flavour, David didn't bother telling Stan, and let the beer speak for itself. It was easy to be fooled by the eight different speciality malts and big West Coast hops like Centennial, Amarillo, Columbus, Cascade and Simcoe. David bought it because it had a solid 45 IBUs, but only 0.5 percent ABV.

At the end of the evening as they were going to bed it really felt like normality was returning; a few hours of happy chatter and good food had done wonders for their spirits, lifting them emotionally as well. Natalie decided that she would return her Glock to the gun safe in the morning.

Chapter Twenty-Six

Monika was eating breakfast at a cafe, overlooking the Swan River. She had chosen this particular cafe, as it advertised a free Internet connection via Wi-Fi. She had her coffee in front of her, her plate to her left and her laptop to her right. She had finished eating the Eggs Benedict with chicken and bacon and was sifting through messages which had been arriving in her 'In-box' for the past half an hour. She tapped several keys and changed the keyboard, then typed a reply to the message which had appeared on her laptop most recently. 'Я не могу. У меня есть работа, чтобы закончить в Австралии. Я отправлю сообщение на веб-сайте, когда я буду доступен'

"When will these people understand" she spoke out loud to herself. "I can't take another job until the current one is complete." 'I will post a message on the website when I'm available' she typed.

Russian was just one of the languages Monika spoke. The others included Arabic and then most of the European languages except Finnish, that didn't seem to conform to the rules of language in the region. Even the surrounding countries of Sweden, Norway and Denmark had puzzled over the language, which was not even like Russian. The closest relative was Hungarian, but only if you went back far enough to the original language. Her fluency differed with each language, but in many countries, she could pass for a native. It was a useful skill to be able to read and write the Cyrillic alphabet. She had grown up speaking many of the languages as she was dragged around the world by her parents, one of whom worked for the World Food Programme. When they had been killed in a traffic accident in France she had been told she would be placed in an orphanage for two years until she was old enough to fend for herself. That was unacceptable to her, she could already fend for herself and so she had taken everything of value and run away. At the tender age of sixteen she had found a 'benefactor' in Germany who put her skills to work listening in to conversations and reporting back. She didn't know it then, but her benefactor had been recruited by the Bundesnachrichtendienst, the Federal German Intelligence agency. In the course of her work a year later, she had out of necessity, killed a man who had realised she understood him, and then tried to rape her. She felt nothing afterwards and this had intrigued her guardian even more. Her work went from listening and the occasional translation to participating in kidnapping and later the murder of national enemies of the state. She was an almost perfect sociopath, so when she faked her own death - with the body of a girl she had 'picked up' in a nightclub and then disappeared, it was merely a means to an end. Now with new papers, several bank accounts and any identity she chose, she was a woman of wealth and skill and her expertise was so sought after she picked and chose the work. She would not have normally worked for a motorcycle gang, but The Brother's had connections and they went back to her benefactor. He had 'rescued her' and she had not forgotten. He had never abused her and if anything, he had shown unconditional acceptance of her. He was the only one from the old days that knew she wasn't dead. He was no longer in the service of the Bundesnachrichtendienst either, and so when *he* called she answered.

Monika had taken her time putting together the plan to neutralise the 'James family'. She studied their movements for several weeks, she knew where they shopped, worshipped and who their friends were. She knew they were armed on some occasions as well. She changed disguises often and appeared as an older lady shopping, a progressive gay lib supporter with purple hair and rainbow badge, and even a metro-sexual male in a suit, complete with a make-up shaving shadow. She had learned early that to avoid detection she had to blend in, and if she was to be remembered then it should be in a way that confused people. She had robbed a Post Office once, when in desperate need of money as a teenager. She had a tight T-shirt under which she wore no bra, a platinum blond wig and an elastoplast over her left eyebrow, despite there being no injury to cover. When the staff had been asked for a description of her, they only remembered the size of her breasts, her hair and the plaster. She walked out of the Post office and turned a corner, dumping the wig and plaster. She then stole a leather jacket off the back of a restaurant chair which she zipped up. She had walked past police and a security guard all of whom paid her no attention at all.

She really wanted to 'line up the ducks' with this job and get them all in one place. She had even thought about bombing the house itself, and that was certainly still an option. She could source the components of a bomb, but with so many 'counter terrorism units' in play it was never a good idea to draw attention to one's self unless it was unavoidable. She would often leave the making of a bomb to someone with the contacts and chemicals.

There were others living with the James family at the moment, and although this probably didn't matter she felt that it added to the challenge, and it was more professional to kill only those who were named in the contract. She pondered the wording of the contract, 'The baby was named in the contract. She had not killed a baby before. The youngest person she had killed was a teenager, who had been a part of a politician's family. She didn't know why she remembered that young girl out of so many she had terminated. Perhaps it was her innocence,' she thought. 'But no-one was really innocent, were they? It wouldn't matter in any case,' she thought.

She was armed with two knives: The first was a folding Quartermaster QSE-14tt Murtaugh Frame Lock Karambit, with a short, curved and vicious 6cm 'Texas Tea Black' stonewashed blade, and a titanium handle. The ambidextrous thumb stud, sculpted from one piece of titanium alloy doubled as an 'auto pocket-pull.' That meant that it both concealed well as a folding knife and with practice, she was able to deploy the blade automatically as she pulled it from her pocket, ready for immediate use. It was also one of the most comfortable ergonomic designs she had ever held. Its short but deadly sharp, silent killing edge was as fast as it was devastating. Her second knife was a Smith & Wesson 'Special Ops M-9 bayonet'. She wore it as a boot knife, and it was completely undetectable to security scanners as there was no metal parts; with its 20cm black 'Plain Saw-back' blade made from nylon, with a black thermoplastic handle and thermoplastic nylon Scabbard. Monika also carried a Sig Sauer 226 pistol. She favoured the 226 'Navy mark 25' despite the size, which looked large in her small hand. The short reset trigger which allowed single and double action, making it easier to get multiple shots off, had a lighter action than the Glock. It also had the 'Beaver-tail frame protection,' which made it very safe to use. She had added an AAC TI-RANT 9 silencer to the barrel which had a threaded end section and even allowed her to adjust the point of impact range on the silencer. With subsonic rounds this made it the quietest suppressed 9mm pistol ever made. The Navy version included internal coatings to protect the weapon from corrosion when in salt water. It was a beautiful, quiet, smooth killing machine. She also had a custom-made suitcase which allowed her to hide each component part of the broken down gun in a different metal section, making it look like a well-built piece of luggage rather than a hiding place. Unless you knew where to press and in what order; which was different for each compartment, you would never find the custom shaped titanium spaces. She could even carry over a hundred rounds of nine-millimetre ammunition, which she ensured varied in power and weight, so she could be as quite or as noisy as she wished. Her gun-cleaning materials were hidden in her make up bag; and she had been globe-trotting like this for years without discovery.

Monika had looked for an opportunity to present itself, with a viable escape route. Anyone could kill pretty much anyone else given the opportunity, but few people then got away with it. Even those that planned the 'perfect crime' usually made mistakes or encountered problems which they hadn't foreseen. Prisons were full of people who thought they had the perfect alibi or hadn't left any trace of themselves at the crime scene. Monika prided herself in her forensic attention to detail when planning. It was so much better than having an 'autopsy of sorrow' after the fact, which made it so much harder to disappear afterwards. She had watched, sketched, made meticulous notes and eventually put it all together.

She left the breakfast table leaving cash as a tip. The tip was not too much or too little, just enough to say 'thank you' but not be remembered. She walked slowly and deliberately back to her hotel room, keeping an eye out for others watching her. She thought, 'tomorrow I will check out of the hotel and affect the kill.'

She had booked a plane ticket whilst she was on-line, for a mid-afternoon international flight the following day, which meant that she had the whole morning to 'kill, clean and clear out.'

It was just a decision between hitting them at the house or in the Livingstone shopping centre car park. If it was to be at the house, she would dress as a sales woman and use a knife on the first person who answered the door, then work her way in with the silenced pistol. The upside to this plan was that she had everyone in one place and the house would provide some privacy. The downside, was Natalie's parents and any guests that happened to be there. The alternative was that she would wait in a parked car near the south entrance to the shopping centre. She had noted that over the past two weeks the James' did their shopping there on a Tuesday and Friday, the latter tended to be a faster visit to pick up milk and things for the weekend rather than a big shop. They always parked near the southern entrance though, and David was often the one that went in to the supermarket and Natalie tended to take the baby into the chemist. The advantage of this plan was that she could wear whatever she wanted, she wouldn't encounter the parents and she could watch and decide exactly how the action would go. The downside was it was public, and there was always the chance that someone she hadn't anticipated would show up in the scenario. She remembered a hit in Spain where a plain clothes policeman had pulled a gun on her, and she had to decide whether to shoot the policeman first and risk the contract getting away or complete the contract and possibly get pinned down or hit by the policeman's fire. The answer had been to slow right down and take very careful aim and she shot all parties once before finishing off the contract. She wasn't worried about bystanders, most of them ran in panic whenever incidents took place. This often helped with covering her escape!

Monika decided on visiting the house.

She laid out the clothes she would wear, and those she would change into afterwards. She then packed everything else away in the suitcase, leaving the pistol and knives on the bed. She placed the clothes and weapons in a bag and thought, 'If I'm quiet enough, I might even be able to take a shower and 'cleanse the scene.' She planned to clean the weapons and take those with her but ditch the clothes in a waste bin at Bentley hospital, for incineration. She figured the hospital was on her way to the airport, if she took Leach Highway. If she was unable to use the shower at the house, then she would try to use one at the hospital.

The remainder of the afternoon she spent in the hotel gym. There was no sign of the 'Leary man,' and when she finished her exercise she returned to her room to shower. Later she ordered some food from the hotel kitchen and whilst she waited for this to arrive, she phoned 'reception' and arranged to hire a small car for a week; to be delivered to the hotel at 6 am. She paid for everything with a pre-paid credit card, and then she went to bed, to ensure an early start in the morning.

Chapter Twenty-Seven

At 5.30 am Monika found herself packed and ready in the hotel foyer. She had paid her bill with the same credit card and told staff that she would leave after breakfast. She was dressed in a red blouse, over which she had on a tight black leather jacket. She wore black jeans and red calf length boots, inside one of which the larger of the two tactical knives was secreted. She had painted her false nails in the same colour red as her lipstick and hoped that this would sufficiently pass for a 'door to door cosmetics sales' look. The hotel had done as requested and by the time the paperwork for the car was signed, she glanced out to see a white Hyundai i30 being parked outside. She walked out and after identifying herself she placed her bags in the car. As the concierge handed over the keys she pretended to be excited about a trip to Kalbarri that she was going to take in the car, and promised not to take the car off-road, but to join a tour group to see the gorges. She locked the car with the remote and folded the key into its fob, placing it inside a small clutch bag, big enough to conceal the Sig 226 then she walked back into the hotel. Now that she was free of her luggage and checked out of the hotel, she could enjoy one last breakfast there before heading off to the James' house.

She arrived in the dining room and filled her plate, knowing that the next meal she would be served would either be at the airport or on a plane. She drank coffee and finished within forty minutes, only pausing to avail herself of the wash-rooms on the way out. Once in the car she pulled out into traffic and headed south on the Kwinana Free-way. Below the South Street ramp, she took the exit for the Roe Highway towards Canning Vale. She joined South Street further along and turned right onto Ranford. She was focusing on everything; the people in cars around her, looking for people she had seen recently, although she knew no-one here. She passed shops; an accounting firm called, 'someone, Quill, Kenny' and in her imagination she heard the voice of the 'South Park' character called Cartman saying "Oh my god, they've killed Kenny..." She smiled to herself. She liked the absurdities of the cartoon. Kenny was always getting killed in different and interesting ways in each episode.

She passed a large building on the right, which looked like a warehouse but identified itself as a church. She didn't know anyone who went to church and despite the amount of people she had sent to 'meet their maker,' she had no particular thoughts about an afterlife, religion or anything like that. She reached the intersection with Nicholson and noted the Livingstone Shops. The light was green, and she drove through being careful not to exceed the speed limit. The left turn was coming up soon, she signalled and took it slowly making her way into the housing estate that had been arranged around a large park with a lake. She turned this way and that and then pulled over some twenty-five metres short of the James' house. She switched off the engine and applied the hand brake.

Monika reached in to the back seat of the car, where she had a large make-up case. She was lifting it over when she saw the garage door start to rise. She put the case on the front passenger seat and watched as a motorcycle with two people on it exited the garage, followed by a car with two elderly people in the front seats. 'This is unexpected' thought Monika, 'this is just the sort of thing that undoes good planning.' She swore and started the car again. The bike had passed her and now the car was following. The garage door was falling back into place. Monika waited until the vehicles had turned the corner before dropping the clutch and doing a fast U-turn in the street. She accelerated after them, catching up with the vehicles on the other side of the lake. She then slowed down to pull back away from them as she didn't want to alert them to her presence. She had requested a car with a Sat-Nav system; and she called up a map of the area. She could now see that they were heading towards Warton Road. Sure enough up ahead the motorcycle was turning left. The car pulled up and then merged into traffic in the same direction.

Monika followed at a distance through Thornlie, and then onto the Kenwick link heading north. 'They were definitely going somewhere,' she thought. 'Perhaps a day out?' They had moved into the right lane and the light was green to the on ramp to the Roe Highway. She accelerated moving around the car in front which sounded its horn as she cut back in. The light was now red but she ignored it and drove through, across cars that had just started moving forward. More sounds of horns filled the air behind her as she accelerated down the ramp. She looked for the car and saw it briefly, up ahead about two hundred metres. There was no sign of the bike, that had accelerated off into the distance. She hoped the destinations were the same, as she overtook several cars to position her-self closer to the car she wanted to follow. The driver was an older male and the front passenger an older female. There was something strapped into the back seat, she could see the seat belt pulled forward at an odd angle.

Soon the car signalled left and joined Tonkin Highway. Then after a short distance they signalled again, this time taking a turn marked for airport business centres via 'Horrie Miller Drive.' 'This was a short cut to the airport terminals,' she thought as she studied the Sat-Nav. The car caught up with the motorcycle at the short-term car park and Monika followed them in to the carpark taking her turn to receive a ticket from the machine. The bike was parking in the international arrivals area. The car found a space to, and then after getting out, the older couple reached into the rear seat and took out a baby in a car-seat carrier. They then mounted the seat to a frame with wheels, which they had taken from the back of the car. Monika was confused, 'what would make everyone come to the airport, surely just one person would be sufficient. It would certainly be more practical.' She thought. 'This however, explained the multiple vehicles.'

Frank and Endana had travelled for hours on the flight and were arriving tired and hassled. It seemed that, at every opportunity, Endana had been pulled to one side and questioned or scanned, or asked for ID. Despite all the paperwork being correct, it was a slow process. Finally, they reached the baggage reclaim area and upon retrieving their bags they joined another long queue to negotiate customs. Frank had purposely put in a couple of cheap 'banana leaf' art pictures, and they joined the 'something to declare' line. This line was often much shorter and so surrendering something was a strategy that was worth the couple of dollars he'd spent. "I don't understand why we can't bring those pictures in" said Endana. "Frank tried to explain again, "Australia has very strict laws around the import of foreign materials. I expect we could bring these in." He said holding up the pictures. "But we'd have to pay a hundred dollars to have them sprayed with insect killer." "What! A hundred dollars..." Endana started and then dropped in to Swahili and spoke too fast for Frank to keep up. "Look" he interrupted. "We join the short queue, and then give them these and act disappointed" She looked at him and laughed, shaking her head. "What a funny country you have brought me to Frank Baker"

Outside the airport terminal, Monika watched David, Natalie's parents, and Natalie wheeling Nathan, as they went into the International Arrivals at Terminal 1. She sat and thought for a moment. She didn't know who they were meeting, but she could guess that they would return to the house at some point, and so she decided that she would return and wait for them there. It was a risk; she didn't know when they would be back or how many of them there would be, but she would wait and then surprise would be on her side. She got back into the car and drove to the exit. Placing her ticket in the machine. She had been less than ten minutes so the gate rose without her having to pay for parking, then she sped away, retracing the way she'd come.

Frank handed over the banana leaf paintings and when he was told that if he wanted to keep them, he'd have to wait a month and pay the fee; he said "No thanks, keep them." They proceeded into the arrivals hall and Frank saw his mother and father before he saw David and Natalie. The confusion and excitement mingled with questions, which with greetings and hugs were given and received. They made their way back out to the car with David explaining the arrangements to get them back home, due to the desire they all had to come and meet them. David put their tickets into the airport carpark machine and paid for the parking, and then gave Stan one of the tickets. They walked back to the car and loaded the bags in to the boot, and Nathan into his rear seat harness, with Endana insisting she be the one to sit next to the baby. Natalie said, "We'll race you back and put the kettle on." She pulled her helmet and gloves on and David started the Harley. The occupants of the car watched as the bike disappeared into the distance, and then they made their way to the exit of the car park and back to the highway towards home. It was particularly nice for Frank and Endana to have his parents to themselves, and a complete surprise to; as neither David or Natalie had shared any of what had transpired over the past month with them. Stan and Kate were careful not to say too much either at this time but said that they were visiting to help with Nathan and left it at that.

David, turning the corner and accelerated up the road towards home, overtook a parked white Hyundai i30 in the street. 'I do wish people would park on the drives of those they visit' he thought to himself. He pressed the garage remote in his pocket, through the leather jacket and the door started to rise. He paused outside and Natalie jumped off, looking exhilarated. She pulled off her helmet and stood it on the shelf by the door to the house. David parked the bike and put his helmet next to hers. They hung up their jackets opposite the shelves and then David took the keys to the door out of his pocket. "It's open!" said Natalie. David frowned. He couldn't remember locking it, but he was pretty sure that he would have. He said, "Let me check the place," and he stepped past Natalie. He glanced in the rooms as he reached them, but nothing seemed out of place or disturbed. He relaxed again and walked back to the kitchen. Natalie had followed him but remained in the kitchen where she had put water in the kettle and switched the power on. She was busily arranging mugs on the breakfast bar. She looked up and David shrugged as he joined her.

Monika had experimented with frequencies on a small transmitter outside the house for a while, before she was able to lift the garage door, once inside she had found Nathan's room and stepped into the closet to wait. Her plan was to kill the baby first and then move to the rest of the house. She had attached the silencer to the pistol and racked the slide but replaced the hammer on the firing pin so her first shot would either be a 'pull through - double action trigger press, or she would 'cock and fire.' She nursed the pistol in both hands and waited.

Stan had taken longer through the traffic, and he'd even taken a wrong turn in the housing estate. "All these roads look alike" he said, when Kate 'tutted' him. Frank suggested a helpful re-route and they arrived outside the house soon after.

"This is lovely" said Endana, "Such a nice place." She looked around at the park and the lake and she nodded her approval. Stan parked on the drive and they spilled out of the car, while Frank went to open the front door. Kate lifted Nathan out in his travel seat. The little boy was awake now and looking around. He looked up into 'Dana's face and smiled.

When they walked into the house 'Dana insisted that she take her bag, despite it being quite heavy. As she tried to close the front door it bounced off her bag, which had not fully cleared the door and the bag fell into the hall stand. There was only one ornament on the stand but it was a glass bowl, so when it slid off the table, it broke into many pieces. 'Dana was horrified. The crash brought Natalie running and she saw 'Dana trying to pull her bag in and pick up the bits of broken bowl at the same time. 'Dana started to apologise profusely, and Natalie tried to pass off the loss as insignificant to make her feel better, but she knew that the bowl had been a wedding present from David's dad and it meant a lot to him. It showed on her face, and 'Dana could see it. She continued apologising until Frank came, and then she burst into tears.

All the stress and hassle of the journey overflowed in the focus over the broken glass.

Frank took the bag and ushered 'Dana into the kitchen. Natalie was ahead of her and had just warned David what had happened, and he was struggling to make a choice to let it go. "I must clean the glass from the floor" 'Dana said and started looking for a brush and pan.

"It's ok" said David, "Let me."

"No, no I must..." 'Dana said again. She took the long-handled broom and the pan from David, and still crying she walked back to the front door.

It was at that moment Monika decided to strike. She had heard the upset and realising this was a perfect distraction, she decided to bring the action to the targets and use it to her advantage. She was in the corridor and started to run the last few steps into the kitchen; as she did so she turned her head slightly left and brought the gun up in both hands.

'Dana was so upset and angry with herself for making such a poor entrance into her host's home, that she nearly missed the 'warning' that dropped into her thoughts, coupled with an image of David and Goliath from the biblical account. She went hot and cold all at once. She knew in her spirit something was wrong, something in the atmosphere had changed. She had felt this way when the YWAM group that she had been a part of had entered an African village where a witch doctor held monopoly over the lives of those living there. This was worse she thought; she felt it was pure evil. Then she felt guilty and confused that she could think such a thing in her host's home.

Natalie was holding Nathan when Monika cleared the door to the kitchen and turned and fired at her. David was just reaching to take him from her and stepped into the trajectory of the bullet.

Dana looked back towards the kitchen and saw the last few paces Monika took. She saw the gun raised but it made no sense. "Oh Jesus!" she said as the first shot was fired. Then the adrenalin kicked in and it was as if she had seen a lion, and she knew what to do.

David was falling and Frank reached out to catch him. The bullet had literally bounced off the top of his shoulder. He had not seen what had hit him, he knew he was falling but he was also trying to work out what was happening. He'd heard a loud clack like an air gun followed by a hard thud. He swung round as he fell and saw Monika. She seemed to be falling as well.

'Dana kicked hard at the brush on the end of the long pole and heard it snap off. Then with many years of practice she hoisted the pole like a spear and sent it swiftly and firmly towards the woman with the gun. The shaft of the broom struck Monica in her right eye and sank deeper. Her head whipped back and she dropped to the floor.

'Dana ran forward to see the damage she had done. Her father had made them practice over and over; even though they would never be expected to do 'a man's business' and kill a lion, he had said that it was a useful skill to have. It had become a game in her childhood, and she could still remember beating the boys in the village, both in accuracy and power. She slid on the floor to stop by Monika and realised that she was not going to be able to remove the broomstick, which was embedded in her eye socket. David was now standing feeling his shoulder, his hand coming away covered in blood. Natalie was holding Nathan very tightly.

Kate was sitting on the settee in shock, and Stan had picked up a phone and was calling for the police and an ambulance.

Frank helped steady David and then moved around him to 'Dana, who was just realising what she had done. He lifted her up from the kneeling position she was in and held her tightly. He looked down at the assassin and kicked her gun away. 'Dana started to shake and cry again.

"Don't worry, no one is going to feel bad about you breaking the broom" he said.

"Not helping!" she wailed, and so he hugged her more tightly.

It seemed like ages until the police arrived with an ambulance close behind. David thought he'd met one of the police officers, and this was confirmed, when the officer asked him if he'd shot someone else. He knew then that this was one of the officers who had attended the 'bikie shooting' in Armadale. He gave a brief statement and told the officer that was all they would get for the time being.

"You can get a statement from everyone else tomorrow." He stepped into the path of the other officer walking towards 'Dana. The officer had tried to move him aside but David had already thrust his ID into the policeman's face; this was quickly followed by Natalie's ID. She had put her gun back in the safe, as had David; but both still kept the ID handy as it had solved a number of situations and was a great 'trump card' to play. The policeman, swore quietly and said, "It's a bloody den of spies." He stepped back to see Natalie holding Nathan in one hand.

"Bloody confusing den of spies at that!"

The officers cuffed the woman on the ground, and searched her thoroughly. She had no ID on her and some very interesting weapons. The silencer - illegal in Australia, was enough to arrest her for alone.

The paramedics cut down the broom handle, some ten centimetres from Monika's eye, or where her eye had been; they stabilised her and then took her away with one of the police officers at her side in the ambulance. The remaining paramedic saw to David's flesh wound and injected the wound with an antibiotic and local pain killer. She then gave him a couple of morphine tablets for good measure. Then when the policeman left she hitched a ride with him in his police car back to the hospital.

"Can you believe that?" said Natalie coming back from Nathan's bedroom. "He's only just gone to sleep as if nothing had happened." She hesitated and looked towards David.

"Are you ok? I think that bullet would have got both Nathan and me, if you hadn't stepped into the way."

"Well, I'm a bit sore, but ok." said David, "As for stepping in the way... I had no idea." Then he added, "I've been shot twice now, and both times it's been when I was in the same room as you!" He started to laugh. The pain killers had kicked in and he was getting a bit high. "I think I'd better sit down," he said, "I didn't mean to infer you are the reason for me getting shot."

He drifted off to sleep, mumbling about being shot through the heart by Cupid's arrow.

When he woke an hour later, things had settled somewhat. Natalie said that she would drive Frank and 'Dana to their place. Kate had perked up a bit and was on 'Nathan duty', as she liked to call it. She had even cleaned up some blood stains from the floor. Stan had gone to bed for a lie down as he was still in some discomfort with his wound.

"I won't be long" Natalie told David. He stood up and tested himself, he was steadier on his feet now.

He hugged 'Dana with one arm and then hugged Frank.

"Thanks 'Dana" he said and hugged her again.

As they were heading out to the car, David said, "I want you to get your gun Natalie."

"Way ahead of you" she said lifting her top to reveal the gun in her belt.

"Cup of tea David?" asked Kate as he went back into the house.

"Yes thanks" said David. He went to sit down at the breakfast bar, and it was then that he saw where the bullet had gone after it had hit him.

"Oh!" he exclaimed. Kate looked round.

"Yes" she said, "Pity isn't it." Another wedding present had been broken. "I can get you another one of those though" said Kate as she looked at the gift Stan and she had bought them. The mirrored clock face stared back at them with a neat hole drilled into it at 'six o'clock.

"Oh I don't know..." said David, "I could get used to looking at it like that."

David drank his tea and was joined by Stan as he finished.

"I've missed lunch and had an awful dream" he said in a voice that betrayed his frustration. He stared around the room and then muttered in tones of resignation at finding the reality,

"I'd hoped it was all a dream anyway. Anyone had lunch?"

Natalie returned ten minutes later, and threw her keys onto the hall stand, the ornamental bowl that usually held them was no longer there. The glass had been cleared up by 'Dana who had returned to the front door after the police left, and she had used the broken broom head and the pan to clear up the glass.

"Your father wants some lunch" said Kate, "he must be 'on the mend.'"

Natalie took out the things she had bought for lunch the day before.

"I'm glad you got a few things in for Frank and Endana" she said to David. He smiled back and saw the smile working around her mouth.

"What?" he asked.

The smile was fully fledged now, "They met Mrs. Dee" she said. "Frank must have warned her about the 'Dees' because she was splendid!"

"What?" said David. Natalie then launched into a recital of how 'Dana had engaged Mrs. Dee with great enthusiasm, telling her that she was so looking forward to meeting Mrs Dee's husband, and that if they decided to stay for any length of time in the area, they might make Mrs. Dee an offer for one of their pets. Mrs Dee had scurried away quickly.

Natalie was now laughing so hard, "She actually licked her lips as she said 'pets'" she gasped for breath.

Chapter Twenty-Eight

David and Stan sat together on the settee, after tea that evening, watching the news. Their dressings had been changed, but they were still clearly visible under their shirts, both winced occasionally and were moving carefully so as not to aggravate their wounds.

"The twins" Kate announced, when Natalie came back into the sitting room. She smiled and asked, "Anything I can get you boys?" They both looked sorry for themselves.

Frank and 'Dana were enjoying the privacy of 'their own place' and were up late due to the time difference. The TV was on a news channel and there was a reporter announcing that there had been a shooting in Canning Vale that afternoon, but only one person had been injured and the shooter had been subdued. There were no more details about the actual incident; but the reporter went on to say that the attacker was an unidentified woman who was in a stable condition in hospital.

Monika was lying in a hospital bed. She felt confused. Her head was swathed in bandages. She couldn't see through her right eye, but she didn't know why. She was cuffed to the bed and again, she didn't know why. She tried to think... nothing! She tried to speak, she was thirsty and she asked for some water. A nurse in the room came to the bed and stood there. Monika asked again for water, the nurse checked her vital signs and made no move to give her a drink. Monika raised her voice and demanded some water to drink. The door to the room opened and a uniformed policeman entered. She repeated the demand.

"Can't understand a word of what she's saying," the policeman said.

"Neither can I" said the nurse, "Some middle eastern gibberish by the sound of it." Monika understood what she had heard them say, and so she tried again this time using different words.

"Agua, water, voda, vand." She couldn't remember what words went with which language. The nurse lifted a bottle with a plastic straw to her lips. Monika sucked a short sip from it.

"Thank you" she said.

"What language is that?" asked the nurse.

The police officer stepped closer and spoke slowly, "Who are you? What is your name?" It was then with no small degree of horror that Monika realised that she didn't know who she was.

The police had recovered items from the hire car and they had a number of identities to choose from where the woman cuffed to the bed was concerned. All of them were false identities though, so they were no further ahead in identifying her. Her picture had been sent to Interpol, and the few reports that were returned just added to the fake identities.

Monika lay in bed, what concerned her most now was that she knew she could be out of the cuffs whenever she wanted. 'How did she know how to escape cuffs?' she thought. 'She even knew that there were different types of cuffs and the ways to escape from all of them.' Another concern she was feeling, was this underlying desire to kill everyone in the room. She knew the order in which they would die, and how she would do it. She felt sick at the thought. She tried to calm herself. 'Plenty of time to decide what to do' she thought, 'better recover first. Perhaps my memory will get better soon.' She drifted off to sleep.

The morning sun broke upon Western Australia, bringing with it a promise of a warm cloudless day. Frank and 'Dana were lying naked in bed together.

"My first morning in Australia" she said. "I'm not going to count yesterday, I'm starting again!"

Frank laughed, "Good idea" he said, "We will have to make some statements at some point today though, but I suggest we keep it really brief and to the point."

Natalie woke with the sun streaming through the blinds, David was still sedated having taken some more pain killers in the night. She got up and went to make them some tea. As she came into the family area of the house, she could see through the double doors out to the patio, where Stan and Kate were sitting in the sun together holding each other's hands, they had cups of something to drink in their other hand. She smiled to herself and made some tea, and then heard Nathan crying. Five minutes later, she had returned to bed and woken David and they sat with Nathan feeding at her breast and both her and David sitting in bed drinking tea. They prayed together that the day would be better than the last, and thanked God for His protection. David thought about the conversations he would have with Frank now that he was back in Australia and the plans they would form regarding the work to be done in East Africa. Once he was recovered it would be an exciting new chapter of their lives. He put his cup down and hugged his family.

Monika woke with the same nurse 'handing over' to another nurse in the room. The police were hovering by the door and a man dressed in hospital 'greens' was talking to them. When he saw that she was awake, he finished his conversation and stepped inside.

"I have some bad news for you Miss? Er..."

"I can't help you there" said Monika, "I can't remember a thing."

"Well at least you're speaking English," said the doctor.

"Am I" she replied. "What's the bad news? I think I can guess it has to do with my head and my eye."

The doctor explained the trauma and the loss of Monika's eye. He told her that they would continue treating her there, or in custody. When she asked why she was in custody, the doctor avoided the issue and said that he preferred to keep his consult purely medical.

As he left another man appeared at the door, this time in stark contrast to the doctor, he was dressed in a black suit with a white horizontal collar. He stepped into the room and looked kindly at her. She didn't know why, but she felt as if no one had looked at her like that.

"Hello" he said, "I'm Paul, I'm a chaplain here at 'Charlies.'"

"Charlies?" she asked.

"That's the name of the hospital. Well, 'Sir Charles Gairdner hospital' is the full name, but most just say Charlies" he continued. "Can I talk to you for a while?"

She nodded and suddenly found it difficult to talk. Her throat closed up and she coughed making her head hurt. A tear ran out of her left eye.

"I don't think I'm a very nice person" she heard herself say; although it sounded as if someone else had said it, as she didn't recognise the tone of her voice.

"None of us are I'm afraid" he replied, "but could I tell you about someone who came to help us and make us better people." He said.

She guessed who the priest was talking about, and one side of her rose in objection, but she heard herself say, "Yes please." The man reached out and held her hand. She couldn't remember that last time anyone held her hand, she couldn't remember anything really.

"Sometimes my dear, we have to lose sight of who we are, to see who He is. Only in the clear bright light of day so to speak, do we fully appreciate the person who is love and truth" he began.

Maximum Security Series

Book 1   "A Planned Death in Custody"

David is the Education manager of a maximum security facility in Western Australia. He has recently bought himself a Harley Davidson which brings him into contact with both good riders and those whose affiliations have darker undertones inside the prison.

His work with the hardened criminals at Corymbia contrasts with his desire to make a difference to their lives and complicates a romantic relationship he is pursuing with the Assistant Superintendent of Security.

A plot to kill an inmate is alleged, and Jack Pritard who is ex-military intelligence, working for Prison Security must go undercover to gather evidence. What he finds is much more dangerous than anticipated and Jack must rely on his experience from the army when it becomes apparent that he is known to a Colombian Cartel who are trying to kill him as revenge for taking down a major syndicate player. Few people know that 'inmate Jack Pritard' is an undercover officer, but David in Education is asked to be Jack's 'handler'. Jack becomes a 'confident' of one of the prisoners in protective custody and both exposes himself to discovery and discovers details of the murder plan.

The plot and procedures used in prisons along with dangers and ingenuity of officers as well as those compromising their positions for personal gain, is based around true events; describing how contraband such as mobile phones, sim cards, drugs and weapons are smuggled into the prison for use by inmates. The manipulation and power struggles result in a phone used to order an assassination being found and the assassin is foiled as he tries to carry out the kill. This fast-paced conclusion takes place both within the prison and spills out into the community.

Book 2   **"Hidden In Plain Sight"**

David is the Education manager in a maximum security prison in Western Australia. He rides a Harley Davidson - which brings him into contact with outlaw bikie gangs, both inside and outside the prison. In this book he is reminded about his vulnerability having been shot whilst helping to bring down a plot to murder an inmate and an intelligence officer. ("A planned death in custody").

The hardened criminals housed at Corymbia contrasts with David's desire to make a difference to their lives, and complicates his relationship with his new wife Natalie, who is the Assistant Superintendent of Security at the prison.

Drugs in great quantity are somehow being smuggled into the prisons in Western Australia. Natalie, working with Jack Pritard, an ex-military intelligence officer working for Prison Security; must go undercover to gather evidence. Natalie infiltrates Parviceps Prison posing as an inexperienced officer, and discovers things are not what they appear to be.

The plot and procedures used in prisons along with dangers and ingenuity of officers compromising their positions for personal gain; along with the people who grow and supply drugs to inmates in prison, is based around true events. The procedures to overcome such corruption result in a fast-paced conclusion that takes place both within the prison and outside.

The story follows how drugs are manufactured and who the gangs are, who protect, operate and exploit the lucrative opportunities to get the drugs into prisons. The struggle of those in security to expose the truth and find the drugs overflows into the community.

Natalie's very life is in danger as a hit is arranged to remove her. Contrasted is a glimpse into the human side of those who do great wrong.

Book 3   **"Capital Punishment"**

Natalie has worked in prison security, and the intelligence division, and has finally been promoted to Superintendent of the most secure prison in Western Australia. Her husband David – an unusual character who rides a Harley and might look more at home as an outlaw bikie - manages prisoner education; his insight and position is often used by security.

When Frank, Natalie's brother announces he is travelling to Rwanda and Democratic Republic of Congo (DRC) to do a favour for a friend and fulfil his desire to do some missionary work; Natalie and David have mixed feelings.

Frank's friend is interested in investing in a mineral mine; where security consultant Morgan Wesley has been employed in the Rumangabo region to defend the mine. Morgan is a South African, who lost contact with his parents, when they moved to Australia suddenly and mysteriously.

Frank finds experience of life in Africa, meeting beautiful Kenyan, Endana and voluntary work, life changing; especially when his excursion to DRC goes wrong and he becomes mixed up with Morgan just as rebel units attack the mine. Frank is arrested and imprisoned in Africa's worst prison, where political prisoners disappear and conditions are appalling.

Frank struggles to overcome his conflicted emotions, wanting to help whilst fearing the consequences of his own actions. Natalie and David must use their wits and connections, politically and with security, to see Frank released and safely into Rwanda. During the daring escape, they meet Morgan and discover through ASIO that his parents played a greater political part in African and American history than anyone knows.

They use security and education experience to free Frank and reunite him with Endana, they arrange for Morgan to find his parents, and they manage to get out of Africa with its entrenched military red tape.

Book 4   **"Clear Bright Light of Day"**

David and Natalie James have developed their romantic and spiritual relationship over the past few years as they have advanced through the ranks of prison staff. With contacts in ASIO and Prison Intelligence they have uncovered and contributed to the solving of several murders and drug operations and have even used their knowledge of prison security to free an innocent man from an African jail. Having returned from Africa and exposed a plot to kill the president of the United States of America, their lives are about to change forever. They are in the process of leaving Western Australia's most secure prison, where they both worked for many years, and Natalie's baby is almost due to be born. Natalie's brother Frank and his new wife 'Dana are returning to Australia and the future looks bright, with a new focus for work in Africa.

Natalie's parents are due to visit and help her at this crucial time but suddenly disaster strikes, and the police bring the news that David has been killed on his motorcycle. The circumstances surrounding the death result in the family fearing for their lives.

Garcia Dominguez; a high-profile drug lord, has found a way to escape the confines of the Special Handling Unit; the most secure unit within Corymbia prison. With the aid of the Brothers Arms outlaw motorcycle gang and his contacts in the Sinaloa Cartel, Dominguez puts pressure on David to help him. Meanwhile his contacts execute an elaborate plan to affect his escape by air.

Jack Pritard in Prison Intelligence must join forces with Detective Pauline Allen who is no stranger to the bikies and their murderous lifestyle. Between them they recruit Natalie and David to work undercover; and with the Australian Royal Navy working independently to begin with, when they send a patrol boat, to intercept a vessel in international waters. The Navy must overcome a larger vessel, a Commanding Officer who is gravely ill, avoid an international incident and realise that each holds parts of a mystery that together exposes the plan to free Dominguez.

When Domingez, realises that his plans are failing, he turns to another inmate who arranges a contract to kill the James' family. The assassin is meticulous but has not anticipated enough variables, not least, Franks new wife and fails to achieve the goal.

Book 5   **"Explosive Atmosphere"**

Political unrest prevents David and Frank with their families, from returning to East Africa and so David's wife Natalie returns to work for Prison Intelligence. Terrorists are planning to disrupt Western Australia's government buildings, including the prisons and associated administration. A plot is exposed which appears to implicate Natalie who is then arrested. Monika the assassin who tried to kill Natalie and her family has been imprisoned, and appears to have has lost her memory, but Jack Pritard, head of Prison Intelligence thinks she may be faking amnesia. But Monika has had a life changing encounter and she has discovered a 'terror link' within the prison.

Natalie and Jack are caught up in an incident when a terrorist tries to take hostages and Jack is shot and dies for a short time. Natalie saves his life but Jack is forever impressed by his 'near death experience.'

When the prison is attacked she saves the life of a security guard and her testimony is taken seriously. Dale Jeeves ASIO/ASIS is interested in whether she can help infiltrate the terror cell and so he sends Monika undercover. Monika discovers that the cell is planning to attack the seat of government in Perth but cannot stop the cell acting. Monika is implicated in the death of one of the terrorists and so Jack enlists the help of Natalie and David to take down the remaining members of the group as they attack Parliament House, Perth. In the ensuing drama can Monika save David.

The Author, Stephen Jones;

After working for an International NGO for a decade and a half, in Europe, Africa and Asia, the author worked in prisons in the UK and Australia; including the most secure prison in the southern hemisphere.

As an Education Coordinator for over twelve years, Stephen had access to prisoners, security protocol and a wide first-hand experience of procedures and tactics. On occasion he was included in operations within the prison, due to his position in Education giving him close contact with prisoners.

Stephen's ability to establish rapport and support staff and learners made him popular with those he worked with in every department within the prison.

This experience has enabled him to create characters and stories which are based on real situations.

Stephen lives with his wife in Mandurah, Western Australia. He has three children and two grand-children. He enjoys four wheel driving, motorcycling, fishing and writing.

He is an active member of a pentecostal church and travels to teach in missionary seminary on occasions.

Stephen is influenced by such authors as, Tom Clancy, David Baldacci, Mark Greany and Michael Connelly.

Stephen can be contacted through the following link:
https://www.facebook.com/prisonfiction/

Printed in Poland
by Amazon Fulfillment
Poland Sp. z o.o., Wrocław